OF ALLIANCE AND REBELLION

Micah Persell

AUTHOR OF *OF CONSUMING FIRE*, *OF ETERNAL LIFE*,
AND *OF THE KNOWLEDGE OF GOOD AND EVIL*

CRIMSON
ROMANCE

F+W Media, Inc.

Published by
Crimson Romance
an imprint of F+W Media, Inc.
10151 Carver Road, Suite 200
Blue Ash, OH 45242. U.S.A.
www.crimsonromance.com

ISBN 10: 1-4405-8887-2
ISBN 13: 978-1-4405-8887-7
eISBN 10: 1-4405-8888-0
eISBN 13: 978-1-4405-8888-4

It is a widely acknowledged fact in our house that heroes with beards are not represented as they should be in the romance genre. So—— Cameron, my love, this one's for you (and your epic beard).

Glossary of Terms

Compulsion: A phenomenon specific to angels. Once an angel plans out his or her mission, free will is not a possibility. At a certain point, the Compulsion will take over. The angel will complete the mission regardless of whether he or she wants to.

Daughters and Sons of Men: Humans.

Fall, The: A heavenly being who succumbs to his or her Temptation Falls: a phenomenon through which the heavenly being loses divine status and some or all of his or her powers.

Impulse Pair: Anyone who eats of the Tree of Eternal Life will experience the Impulse—a phenomenon in which the human pairs with his or her intended mate. The humans in an Impulse pair will experience intense longing to be with their Impulse mate, and the longer they abstain from each other, the more intense the side effects of the Impulse. Impulse pain will grow until it becomes debilitating. Impulse pain can only be cured and avoided by the Impulse pair's consummation.

Knowledge, The: The ability, provided by the Tree of the Knowledge of Good and Evil, to determine whether someone's intentions are *good* or *evil*.

Sons of God: Angels; not always "sons," which is an archaic reference used to encompass all of a species. Angels can also be female.

Temptation: Each heavenly being will at some point encounter his or her Temptation—the one thing that will tempt them to Fall. Temptations can take several forms, but the most common is a daughter (or son) of man.

Tree of Eternal Life: The tree in the Garden of Eden that bears fruit that turns living beings immortal.

Tree of the Knowledge of Good and Evil: The tree in the Garden of Eden that caused the Fall of mankind. The fruit of this tree counteracts some of the effects of the Tree of Eternal Life. The fruit gifts humans with the Knowledge.

Voice, The: A mysterious, disembodied entity that speaks directly to the minds of those who have eaten of the Tree of Eternal Life.

The Lord God made all kinds of trees grow out of the ground— trees that were pleasing to the eye and good for food. In the middle of the garden were the tree of life and the tree of the knowledge of good and evil.
Genesis 2:9-10

After he drove the man out, he placed on the east side of the Garden of Eden cherubim and a flaming sword flashing back and forth to guard the way to the tree of life.
Genesis 3:24

Now it came about, when men began to multiply on the face of the land, and daughters were born to them, that the sons of God saw that the daughters of men were beautiful; and they took wives for themselves...
Genesis 6:1-2

Chapter One

Somewhere in the deserts of Afghanistan

A moan rent the air, penetrating Max Wright's fitful sleep. The sound rooted its way into his brain, and he buried his head in the crook of his arm. When another moan followed the first, he made his way to wakefulness, prying open gritty eyes.

He blinked once, trying to make sense of the crumbling stone wall inches from his face. Max felt his forehead pucker as he came even more awake. He blinked several more times, but the view never changed, only grew clearer.

Moisture veined the ancient stones with white markings, and the cold night air of the desert penetrated the last of his grogginess. As always happened when Max remembered where he was and why he was here, his hand hovered over his face, fingers trembling, before he brushed them over the raised, ugly flesh that marred him. With the lightest of touches, his pointer finger traced the scar that began at his right temple. A weight settled in his gut as his fingers traveled the path of scar tissue down his ruined eyelid and across his nose to where it ended at the left corner of his jaw.

He licked dry lips. *It was not a dream.*

Another moan, almost a wail, wandered over to where Max lay. With a sigh, he planted one hand on the ratty cot mattress and shoved himself up.

Knowing what he would find when he turned around, he plowed fingers through his matted hair, raking the strands over his right eye. He fought the urge to shake the unruly mop even further over his face. Acting as though it bothered him as much as it did was a show of weakness he could not indulge around the other two prisoners.

Max sucked in a breath and held it until the sting gave him enough courage to face the rest of the cell. Through the dank light filtering in from the cell's only window, Max could see the dark form of Luke huddled over Oliver. Even through the barrier of his hair, Max's ruined right eye zeroed in on the two men with a mental snap that never failed to steal Max's focus. His sliced eye, which was good for practically nothing but this, spoke directly to his mind and informed him that both Luke and Oliver were *good*. It always informed him of this whenever he looked at them, just as it always informed them that their prison wardens—the few that were left—were *evil*.

Useless bits of information. Max gritted his teeth. He already knew his fellow soldiers were good men, and he certainly knew the fuckers who had kept them locked in this cell for nearly nine years were just about as evil as anyone could get.

Max swung his bare feet around and planted them on the stone floor, flinching as his toes encountered frigid rock that had lost the earth's heat soon after sunset. His sudden movement stole Luke's attention, whose gaze collided with Max's. Max again fought the urge to shake his hair over his face. He settled for turning his eye, the worst of his scarring, away, gazing at Luke with his good left eye. Even in the absence of light, Max could see the straining lines at the corners of Luke's mouth.

"Is he still conscious?" Max's sleep-ravaged voice seemed loud in the small cell, bouncing off of the rock that imprisoned them.

Luke's equally dirty nest of red hair brushed his shoulders as he nodded once.

Max hadn't missed the screams while he slept then. He clenched his fists when his hands wanted to tremble. It had been, what, four days since the last time Oliver had—done whatever it was he did every seven days? Max refused to think of it as dying, though that was probably the closest to the truth.

"When's the last time you slept?" Max asked Luke.

Luke sighed before turning his attention back to the twisting form of Oliver.

Max shoved to his feet and shuffled forward. "Come," he said while gesturing to the cot he'd just vacated. "My turn to keep watch."

Luke didn't seem to hear him. He still hovered over Oliver, reaching toward the man once then clenching his hand before allowing it to fall to his knee.

Max glanced at Luke's fingers as they flexed and felt a commiserating bitterness fill his mouth. Neither Max nor Luke could offer Oliver any real comfort. No pats on the shoulder. No holding his hand when the screams started. The lightest touch from either of them only increased Oliver's torture.

"Luke," Max said gently—or at least, as gently as Max could say anything. When Luke jumped like he'd been poked, Max guessed his attempt at *gentle* had far missed the mark. "You can't help him right now. Get some sleep. I'll watch him, I promise."

Luke's light brown eyes, so full of innocence that Max had to remind himself he and Luke were the same age, briefly closed before he got to his feet and walked over to the now-vacant cot, pausing in his stride to pat Max hard on the shoulder, a touch Max tolerated only because he knew it offered Luke comfort.

Max made his way on heavy legs to Oliver's side, feeling Luke's gaze on his back as he settled on the edge of Oliver's cot, making sure that he didn't brush him in the slightest. Luke's stare made the skin stretching over Max's scar burn, even though it was focused on his back, not his face. It wasn't until Luke's breathing evened out and deepened that Max took a breath.

With Luke asleep and relatively safe, Max's responsibilities narrowed down to Oliver. Max focused on Oliver's face—on the scrunched eyes, the thin, grimacing lips almost hidden from view by the unruly beard all three of them sported thanks to several years without access to a razor of any kind.

Those lips parted around a deep moan, and something clenched in Max's chest. "I know, buddy," he whispered to the man, feeling every inch of his uselessness in this situation. "I know."

Oliver's eyelids cracked open. The blue eyes that had charmed many a beautiful woman when they were in the army were now glassy and swimming with pain. "Hurts," he groaned through parched lips. "So bad."

Max cursed on an exhalation of air. "I know," he said again, rage and hopelessness coursing through him.

"The One." Oliver grunted as he tried to shift into a more comfortable position. "I need her."

He was asking for her again. Max's hands clenched on his thighs. That damned woman! Oliver had seen her once. *Once.* Nearly two years ago. He had been ruined ever since.

Quick calculations filtered through Max's head, and he knew Oliver's screaming would start in a few hours. It always did once he began begging for the woman who had left him in such torture with only one look. Tomorrow, Oliver would slip into sleep. Or a coma. Max didn't know what to call it, but whatever it was, Oliver wouldn't wake up from it until he—

Max swallowed thickly. He didn't have to think about that now. He leaned over Oliver, as close as he could without touching, and did the only thing he could do: he talked to the man. Keeping his voice low enough that Luke couldn't hear what he was saying, Max outlined exactly what he would do to their captors once they escaped. It was a list of horrors repeated so often that Max had no problem talking through it without thought.

As always, the lines around Oliver's eyes eased as he took in Max's voice. Whether it was the threats of violence against those who'd wronged them for nine years or the timbre of Max's voice that slightly alleviated Oliver's pain, Max never knew. But this was the only thing that seemed to help, and so Max would recite his plan for revenge until he went hoarse if necessary.

The list was long and took Max several hours to get through. He paused only once: when one of the handful of guards who remained in the prison tossed a dried lump of bread and discolored bladder of water through the bars. As soon as the guard shuffled away, Max continued. Rage twisted his words as Oliver's hands clenched the mattress beneath him, his back bowing, his head snapping back. The first scream of what would be many was wrenched from the man's chest, echoing around the cell loudly.

Luke sat up with a snort, jerked from sleep. He raced over to Oliver's cot as Max rose to unsteady feet. "Oliver," Luke said on a breath. "You're okay." Luke sat down where Max had been moments before. "You're okay, man, you're okay."

Max ran his tongue along his teeth and took a step back before he could strangle Luke. Oliver was most definitely *not* okay, and all three of them knew it.

Max spun around, seeing nothing but red as another scream broke from Oliver's now thrashing body. "*Fuck*!" Max bellowed. His fist snapped out before he could stop it, colliding with the stone wall hard enough that his hand broke.

Luke jumped, but didn't glance his way as Max gave a cursory glance at the cracked skin of his knuckles while it began to mend. The sight of his body supernaturally healing due to what their captors had done to him only enraged him more. He clenched his fists at his sides and let the blood from his hand drip to the floor unchecked.

As Luke leaned over Oliver, whispered prayers tumbling from his mouth, Max paced back and forth, mentally repeating his diatribe of promised revenge until Oliver's screams grew loud enough to block out even that.

Chapter Two

Nervous.

Anahita, one of the cherubim and instrument of the Most High, was nervous. She knew the emotion well despite the fact she was *supposed* to be completely emotionless. Anahita felt as though she spent a good deal of her existence wallowing in the forbidden feeling.

Though currently invisible to the human eye, she still leaned back into the cool stone façade of the makeshift prison as a human guard walked around the corner. Her heart thundered when the human passed close enough to touch, and Anahita allowed herself the small creature comfort of placing an open palm over her chest to try to calm it. No other angels were around, so the small gesture of weakness would not be witnessed by those who held her to the high standards of her kind.

The same heart that thundered beneath her palm jerked a little in the direction of the cell behind her.

She could feel him.

It was so much stronger than she had anticipated, this link to her Temptation. This close to the man she should avoid at all costs, her taboo feelings were … *intense.*

Anahita's head sank back to the stone wall, her blond waves snagging against the rough, porous surface and pulling slightly. Why—oh, why—did her first official death mission, the mission she'd fought so hard to be given, have to involve *him*? Was it a test?

Of course it is a test.

"I *will* carry out my mission," she whispered as she willed her still-thundering heart to slow. When the traitorous organ failed to comply, Anahita jerked her hand from its resting place between her breasts so she could no longer feel it. She did not have the flaming sword needed to kill the immortals, but she needed to strike now or she risked losing control of her Compulsion. She would capture them, and once they were in her keeping, she would attain the weapon.

With a quick inhalation of air, Anahita closed her eyes and focused to sink through the wall and into the cell that held her targets. The cool night breeze faded, and she knew she'd made it into the cell. Keeping her invisibility fixed, Anahita turned and cracked her lids open.

The immortals' cell was cold, and not just in temperature. The complete lack of hope, the pain, the scent of unwashed male—all combined to create the coldest environment Anahita had ever encountered. Her right hand moved up to cup her left bicep in an attempt to generate warmth.

To her right, a man with vivid red hair that not even dirt could dim sat huddled over another man with blond hair and a beautiful face knotted in agony. The face contorted even more, and the man's body twisted on a dingy cot, his mouth opening in the silent scream of an infant who'd cried hard enough to lose his air.

As she watched, the man's chest convulsed with a great gulp of oxygen, and when next he opened his mouth, the scream was no longer silent. The pain was so vivid it caused Anahita to take a stunned step back, her wings hitting the unforgiving stone of the cell's corner.

The red-headed man shivered and hugged himself, feelings of impotence pouring off of him in tangible waves. But it was the sound of a strangled groan that snagged Anahita's attention.

At the opposite end of the cell, Anahita could barely make out the broad shoulders of the third man. The man that was *hers*.

No. She shook her head, dislodging the errant thought. Not her man; he was her Temptation. And she would do well to remember that.

Those broad shoulders were tense enough to hike up into the shaggy length of his hair: hair so dark in color that it must be black, even though it was impossible to tell in the dim light. Without her permission, her eyes roamed from the broad shoulders down to the well-muscled back that the man's threadbare shirt did nothing to shield.

The man's back narrowed into trim hips that held up a barely together set of army fatigues that draped across the man's buttocks like a caress of fabric. Anahita gulped.

Here, Anahita's eyes stalled, as she experienced a brand new emotion.

Lust.

Anahita was lusting after this human whom she was charged with killing. The emotion led humans to commit unspeakable atrocities, and yet, as Anahita felt it for the first time, she could not see what was so bad about it.

Certainly, the emotion caused her belly to ache—something that had never happened before. And certainly, her heart was now thundering harder than it had been when she'd steeled herself for strength outside the cell moments before. And certainly, the emotion prodded at her, urging her to touch the man. To taste the man—

With a sharp jerk of her head, Anahita realized where her thoughts had led. So *that* was what made lust so dangerous.

Before she could have another thought, the man she'd been perusing swung around and began pacing toward her. Her eyes flew to his face, a part of her rejoicing that she would now know what her Temptation looked like.

The first thing she noticed was his vicious scowl, an expression that seemed to match his clenched fists and tight shoulders. When the thrashing man on the cot screamed yet again, her Temptation's eyes squeezed shut as his chest billowed up and down. That was when she noticed the scar.

Her fingers fluttered across her lips as she struggled to stay silent. Her Temptation's exquisite face was carved mercilessly. A thick, raised scar slashed the entirety of his features, gruesomely bisecting them.

Oh, Most High. Anahita's brows shot together as her mind raced through reasons he would be scarred. It didn't make sense; he was immortal. He had eaten the fruit from the Tree of Eternal Life. A scar like this would have been healed if he had sustained it before eating the fruit. And after the fruit, his body would never have allowed such a thing to heal—or rather, not heal—in such a manner.

The blond man screamed once more, and as the tormenting screech reached its peak, it wavered and cut off. When the air was still, Anahita's Temptation relaxed and opened his eyes.

This time, there was no preventing it. A horrified gasp escaped her as Anahita observed his right eye, the one that had been sliced. Everything fell into place.

Her gaze darted to his left eye. It was the color of rich, tilled earth: fathomless and warm. But his right eye—his right eye was nearly colorless. The thick scars on his upper and lower eyelids framed a cornea of the lightest gold, as though the color had leaked from his eye when he sustained the injury.

This was most definitely done to him after he had eaten the fruit from the Tree of Eternal Life. He would not have survived otherwise. Those vile humans, who had first coerced these men into eating the fruit and then imprisoned them for it, had used the second tree, the Tree of the Knowledge of Good and Evil, to scar him permanently—probably by administering the fruit's juice to a blade and then holding him down and slicing through his face.

Bile rose in Anahita's throat, and she audibly gagged.

Her Temptation froze, and Anahita silently cursed her weak control. She must remain silent. She was invisible, but any sound she made could be heard by all three of the humans in this cell.

Her Temptation's eyes were roving over the walls as though he sensed someone was in the cell with them. Anahita ruffled her feathers as she shrank into the corner as far as she could. Her heart began to thunder once more as that mismatched gaze got closer and closer to her hiding spot. She tried to reassure herself that he couldn't see her, but those eyes fixed directly on her and stayed.

Anahita felt her shoulders curling up toward her ears. Something was not right here. Surely he couldn't see her.

Her Temptation straightened and cocked his head to the side as his brow furrowed. Anahita heard a breath puff from his nose, and then her Temptation's hand rose to rest over his heart for a moment before it slowly, so slowly, continued its journey. He covered his right eye with his palm, and she could tell by the way his spine straightened that he had somehow seen her with the eye he now covered.

A rough sound burst from her Temptation's chest, and he jerked his hand away, piercing her with that golden stare. "Luke." The name rolled from his lips in the most delicious rumbling bass voice Anahita had ever heard, and the red-haired man sitting on the cot turned his head to look at Anahita's Temptation. With a shaking hand, her Temptation pointed directly into the corner where Anahita huddled. "Do you fucking see that?" he asked.

Oh, not good. Anahita panicked as the redhead—Luke—turned his head and squinted into her corner. Luke's eyes relaxed, and then his head turned back to her Temptation. "See what, man?" he asked, his voice low and concerned.

"A woman," her Temptation said. "With Goddamned wings." Shocked silence met this declaration as Luke's head swung back to the corner. But her Temptation wasn't done yet. He sighed and whispered, "She's beautiful."

She saw the look of utter panic that crossed Luke's face before he turned to face her Temptation once more. "Max," Luke said, "you see a woman?"

Instead of answering, *Max*—Anahita felt a thrill at learning her Temptation's name—once more stroked the center of his chest with an open palm. "So beautiful," he repeated.

Another emotion, powerful and nameless, flooded Anahita's belly, nearly causing her to moan. Her Temptation thought she was beautiful. Her lips parted, and she clutched at the stone behind her with numb fingers so she wouldn't run to him. Wouldn't trail her fingers up his arm as she wanted to. Wouldn't replace the hand rubbing his chest with her own.

"Max!" Luke said his name so sharply Anahita jumped. Max's eyes flicked over to Luke and then back to her. Luke must have taken that as permission to continue, because he asked haltingly, "Did you … *hear* anything? When you saw her?" Silence reigned while Anahita grew more confused. "Max," Luke continued, "did what happen to Oliver happen to you?" Luke stood from the cot and clenched and unclenched his fists fitfully. "Come on, Max, talk to me."

Max's eyes finally drifted from Anahita's, and he looked at Luke for a few moments before nodding once.

Even in the dim light, Anahita saw all of the blood drain from Luke's face. Anahita felt her eyes ping back and forth between the two men as she caught her Temptation staring at her once again.

The expression on Luke's face continue to grow more horrified. "Max," Luke said weakly. The next thing Anahita knew, Luke's face was no longer colorless and wane. An animal-like bellow rent the air, startling Anahita's eyes back to Luke, and she turned her head just in time to see him launch himself toward the corner where she hid. He crashed into the wall to her left, his fists flying into the stone. "You will *not* do this to him, too," Luke snarled as he continued to pummel the stone, working his way toward the corner when his fists found nothing.

It was so startling that Anahita lost her grip on her invisibility. The moment she did, Luke's eyes snapped to her. They widened.

"You're real," he breathed. In the next second, the man had redirected his attack, his hands snarled and reaching for her.

Anahita was too flustered to return to invisibility, or to sink through the wall and escape, but as it turned out, she did not need to.

Luke's renewed attack snapped Max from his stupor. "You don't touch her," Max shouted, running across the cell and tackling Luke into the wall before Luke could wrap his fingers around her throat.

The men grappled together, wrapping their arms around each other and slamming against the wall again and again. The rage pouring off of them took Anahita aback, and she cringed further into the corner, dodging the flailing limbs of the men.

In the jumble of her emotions—the ones she should not be feeling—she could not determine why Luke was so angry and why that anger was directed toward her. But Luke's anger was no match for Max's, who was functioning on a level she had never seen before in a human.

When Max tackled Luke to the ground and slammed the other man's head into the unforgiving stone, Anahita jolted forward. "Stop this," she said too softly to be heard through the two men's grunts. But the sound of her voice worked on Max like a balm. He dropped Luke so rapidly, the other man's head hit the ground once more with a *thunk* that made Anahita wince.

Max's face turned immediately toward her, and his eyes—the deep brown and otherworldly gold—roved over her face and body before returning to her eyes. She felt the quick perusal of her body as though it had been a caress, and she took a stumbling step toward him, her sandals scuffing on the rough stone floor and bringing Luke's gaze to her as well, though his was slightly unfocused.

Luke's eyes widened, and Anahita ruffled her wings in a defensive gesture she could not prevent. "Oh," Luke breathed, his eyes focusing more each moment. "A-angel?" he stuttered.

• • •

Max straddled Luke's chest and had to fight with each of his billowing breaths not to continue the beating that Luke so desperately deserved for even thinking of harming his winged stranger. No one—*no one*—would ever harm her. She was his.

The moment he'd seen her, the Voice that sometimes spoke to them all—part instinct, part conscience—whispered *The One* to him. It was a two-word phrase that he, Luke, and Oliver were very familiar with as it was what had started Oliver's torment.

Remembering how dire their situation was, how horrendous it was to watch Oliver go through what he was going through, made the worst of Max's rage toward Luke vanish. Luke was stuttering like a simpleton beneath him, and Max had to focus hard on the other man to figure out what he was saying. He was no longer looking at the winged beauty but at Max himself.

"Is she an angel?" Luke was asking Max.

Max allowed himself the pleasure of gazing at her once more. She shimmered in the dim light, her beauty was so radiant. She was tall for a woman—statuesque in height—but he guessed the top of her head would reach his mouth. She would only need to tip her head back slightly for him to press their lips together. A riot of golden waves tumbled over her shoulders and down to her waist, framing a face that made him want to weep. Her features were delicate—a direct contrast to her sturdy height. Her eyes were the purest blue, and he knew he was not imagining the golden glow emanating from them. They cast a dim light in front of her as she looked at Max. She wore a glistening white robe that fell in tantalizing drapes from her shoulders to the floor. And, of course, two pearlescent wings arched over her shoulders and flared out behind her.

Holy hell, *was* she an angel? One thing was for certain: Max and the others had learned not to discount *any* possibility since their imprisonment. It would be asinine for a human who had turned immortal by eating fruit from the Tree of Eternal Life to doubt the existence of heavenly beings.

Max still had not answered Luke's question, but that didn't keep the man from continuing his dazed monologue. Just how hard had Max hit his friend's head against the floor? Remorse tasted bitter. Had he truly been trying to harm Luke?

With a grunt, Max pushed himself to his feet and then reached down to grasp Luke's hand and help him haul himself to his feet as well. Luke swayed and brought his fingers up to his temple. He pulled them back to examine them, and Max could see the telltale glistening of blood on Luke's fingertips.

An apology flew to Max's lips, but he bit it back. Luke had tried to hurt his woman. There would be no apology.

In silent synchronicity, Max and Luke turned to face the elephant in the room: the beautiful angel.

"I can't believe I tried to hurt an angel," Luke muttered, threading his fingers back through his hair to feel his injury again.

For some reason, though the word *angel* had been bandied about many times in the last handful of moments, this time it seem to stick in Max's mind. An angel. His *One* was a fucking angel.

With an urgency he hadn't felt so strongly since first sustaining his scar, Max covered the right side of his face so fast his palm made a slapping sound against his cheek. "This has to be a joke," Max muttered to himself as he forced his left hand to remain at his side instead of covering the rest of his scar. What cosmic power would put *her* with *him*? Did angels even … *mate*? Was that the word he should use?

Bad luck for her, he couldn't help but think. He definitely got the better end of this deal.

At that moment, Oliver thrashed with renewed vigor on his cot, and another of his heart-wrenching screams filled the air. The gravity of Max's situation hit him full force.

When Oliver was conscious in between his dying bits, he spoke of what had happened to him that day two years ago. Back when this hellhole had been bustling with fervent guards, Oliver had seen a woman through the cell bars. She'd looked right at him. The Voice, which they had discovered only spoke to the three of them, had whispered *The One* to Oliver, and he had immediately wanted her in every way imaginable. Oliver described it as a mating—almost animal-like in its intensity. Within a day, the pain had started. By the third day, Oliver was in severe pain, and by the fifth day, he was in a coma. On the seventh day, Oliver died. His heart stopped; his breathing stopped. But because they were immortal, Oliver didn't stay dead. The next day, he came back to life, as healthy and pain-free as he had ever been. But then the cycle repeated itself. And it had repeated itself every week for two years.

Max's gaze focused on the angel he would be dying for. Could she disappear just as easily as she had appeared, leaving him as broken as Oliver?

No. The angel had to stay. Max flinched when Oliver screamed yet again.

He felt a muscle in his jaw clench as he ground his teeth together. Max was no prize—he knew that. But, hopefully, this connection between him and the angel went both ways. With that thought, Max tried to block out Oliver's anguished shriek and took a step toward his angel. He faked a confidence he didn't feel, and, turning his right side away from her, extended his hand.

Like magic, she took several stumbling steps toward him immediately, and the surge of something like hope that tumbled through his chest robbed him of breath. That hope dimmed, however, when the angel halted before reaching him. Max curled his fingers two times, beckoning her forward. His lips parted around the words, "Come to me."

The angel's fists clenched at her sides, and a look of utter wanting crossed over her stunning face. Max's body responded to that look in swift arousal, the sudden and powerful erection punching into the front of his well-worn fatigues. Max closed his eyes and fought for control of his body. The desire he had to close the rest of the distance between them and press her against him to grind that insistent arousal into the softness of her belly was almost too strong to ignore. The desperation behind his feelings scared Max even more, and he opened his eyes and repeated his order again, this time more firmly. "Come to me!"

The angel jumped, then swayed forward slightly. But after a beat, she shook her head almost violently.

She doesn't want me. The thought was accompanied by powerful disappointment tempered with self-loathing. Of course she didn't want him. He hadn't seen his face since sustaining his injury, but he knew how he looked. He was a monster. She was an angel.

Max's hand fell back to his side. He abandoned all finesse along with hope. He began closing the distance between them, and the angel took one step back for every one he took toward her. Lord knew what he looked like right now, but the angel's retreat was a pretty big clue.

Her back hit the stone corner once again, and Max kept coming, causing the angel to curl in on herself, wrapping her arms around her middle. She was obviously scared, but something told Max she was not necessarily scared of *him*.

He made himself stop a hair's-breadth from touching her, but he was close enough that he could feel the heat radiating from her body into his. She wasn't meeting his eyes, and Max turned his face away, allowing only his handsome side to face her, before leaning in and placing his hands on the stone walls by her shoulders, boxing her in.

"You must stay with me," Max commanded. The air of his words stirred the hair at her temple, and the angel closed her eyes briefly.

"I will," she said. It was the first time Max had heard her speak, and the melodious, husky quality of her voice caused him to lose focus before he was able to interpret what she said.

His eyes snapped to hers, and he felt his scar pucker as he frowned—a reminder to turn his face aside before she had a chance to look at his ugliness. "You will?"

Her delicate throat worked a few times before those beautiful blue eyes rose to meet his left eye. "I will stay with you," she said gravely, "because I must kill you."

Max turned his face to meet her gaze and blinked. Surely he had misheard her. His brows crashed down. "Do you want to repeat that?" Max asked.

Without flinching away from her words, the angel said, "I've been sent to kill you and the other two men. You have violated the holy Tree of Eternal Life, and your lives must be forfeited to pay the price."

Max straightened, and his hands fell from the wall to rest at his sides. After nine years of imprisonment by what had to be the world's most eccentric group of quasi soldiers, Max had seldom encountered something or someone who took him by surprise.. But this angel had caught him off guard.

Her statement was at odds with her delicate beauty. She looked as though she should be rescuing kittens from gutters, and here she was calmly and gravely stating that she was here to kill him. Could she even take him in a fight? She was tall, sure, but he was a brute. Just how did she think she was going to kill him?

"And when is this killing going to occur?" Max asked.

The angel's eyes turned thundercloud blue, and her chin tilted up defiantly. "Now."

Max raised his left eyebrow and crossed his arms over his chest. Just as he expected, the angel made no move against him. "Right *now*, now?" he asked.

And then, the angel's chin quivered. Fucking *quivered*. Max felt it down to his toes, and all of his mirth disappeared. His arms uncrossed, and he reached for her, catching himself just in time to prevent an embrace meant to comfort her.

"Alright," the angel said in a weak voice, "I shall return soon. I will bring the weapon to you rather than you to it. Prepare your souls for death, for you will not escape it." Before Max could riddle out what the hell she was talking about, she straightened her shoulders and seemed to be gathering her focus.

On instinct, Max knew she was preparing to disappear on him, just as easily as she had appeared. Panic unlike anything he had ever felt launched him into action. Without thought, his hand snapped forward and wrapped around her wrist almost brutally. He relaxed his hold when he felt the delicate bones beneath his fingers, but he did not release her. "You're not going anywhere," Max said simply. It was a fact. She would not leave him. She could not.

The screams that Max had tuned out for the first time in two years as he talked with his angel seeped back in to his consciousness, and he turned to look at Luke. "A little help here," he said, nodding toward the angel in his grasp.

Luke's head snapped up from its bent position over Oliver. His eyes swept over Max and the angel, and both of his brows rose in silent question.

"She's trying to leave," Max said, the desperation in his tone shocking him.

Luke frowned. "And you want to … what, exactly?"

"Capture her."

Luke's chin lowered. "Capture her," he repeated in dismay. "Capture an angel. Are you crazy? Or do you just have a death wish?"

Max closed his eyes and pinched the bridge of his nose. Luke's religious side was showing. Damn pastor's kid with his damn ideas about heaven and hell.

"If she leaves," Max said harshly, "I turn into him." He gestured toward Oliver with his chin, and right on cue, Oliver thrashed and moaned on his cot.

Luke stared at Oliver before muttering, "What do you want me to do?"

Max tightened his hold on the angel's wrist and began walking her across the cell to the other cot. "I need a way to tie her."

After several seconds, Max heard the sound of the threadbare sheets being torn. The angel stumbled along behind him, and Max was shocked that she was not putting up any sort of fight. When he reached the cot he and Luke shared, he pushed the angel down to the floor beside it.

She blinked up at him in the dim light. Luke arrived at his side and handed him strips of fabric. Without even looking, Max knew the weak fabric would not hold her without her consent. But it was better than nothing.

When Max knelt down in front of her and began tying her wrists to the cot, Luke shuffled his feet next to him. "I'm sorry," Luke whispered. "Forgive me, angel."

Max bit back a growl and finished securing his prisoner as Oliver's screams cut off abruptly. They all froze and Max's eyes traveled up to Luke's. The haunted expression on Luke's face must have mirrored his own.

Grief poured through Max. The screaming session was now over. Oliver was in a coma. At this point in Oliver's cycle about two years ago, guards would have rushed the cell, jeering and calling out insulting things while Luke and Max tried their best to make Oliver's last moments as comfortable as possible. Though Max felt himself brace for the shuffle of boots against stone, he knew no one would be coming now. No one ever came anymore. As Max gave a final jerk to the angel's bonds, Luke plodded over to Oliver's side to keep vigil. Max was sick with their current situation, but he couldn't decide what was worse: ridicule or oblivion.

Chapter Three

Anahita sat on the floor, the coldness seeping through her robe and rendering her bottom numb. Her arms were pulled awkwardly to the left side of her body to accommodate her wrists being bound to the cot. Her Temptation had not looked at her once in the two days since he had captured her, but she could not tear her eyes from him no matter how hard she tried. It was times like this when a little personal reflection could come in handy.

For example, perhaps Anahita should ask herself *how* she had ended up tied to a rickety piece of furniture in the middle of Afghanistan by the humans she was charged with killing. Certainly there were lessons to be learned from such an occurrence so the same situation could be avoided in the future.

She had to fight with every fiber of her being not to simply break the weak ties that bound her wrists. Had they restrained her with steel manacles, she would have been able to escape, and they thought to detain her with what amounted to a bit of string?

Yet, here she sat. As Max had charged her, Anahita had attempted to melt back through the wall and make her escape. For the first time in her existence, it hadn't worked. Anahita longed to blame it on the jumble of her emotions, but she suspected that she was unable to make her escape because she was unable to leave her Temptation. She had heard rumors to that effect amongst her brethren. That was one of the downfalls of encountering one's Temptation: you could never leave them. Made resisting that Temptation even harder, which, Anahita supposed, was part of the point.

It was working. She couldn't stand being this close to Max for much longer without touching him. She needed to flee, but beyond suspecting that she *could* not, she felt she *should* not. Now that she had allowed the humans to think they had captured her, she felt trapped into perpetuating the misconception. After all, she *did* still have to kill them. The Compulsion to do so was pressing against her skull every moment, begging her to decide on a course of action.

She tried to rub her temples but the restraints jerked her back. She wrapped her fingers around the leg of the cot and sighed. A roll of her shoulders did nothing to alleviate the tension in them.

A sudden rustle from Max's direction drew her attention. When she looked his way, those mismatched eyes of his were pinned on her, and he was scowling.

"Stop. Fidgeting."

Even from across the dim cell, Anahita could tell his fists were clenched and his jaw ticking repeatedly. Though his eyes were on her, it had been so long since he had acknowledged her presence that she looked over her shoulder to see if he was talking to another prisoner crouched in the corner. No—he was definitely talking to her. "I am fidgeting?" she asked, frowning. "I did not realize—"

"Well, you are," he snapped. "So, knock it off."

Her head drew back a little. She couldn't help it. She was a Warrior, but even among them, no one spoke to each other in such a way. "You should not allow your anger to overtake you so," she said before she could stop herself. Immediately, she wished the words back.

His expression darkened. "Are you fucking kidding?" he asked. He gestured to the surrounding cell with a toss of his hand. "You don't think I have plenty to be angry about?"

She shook her head. "That is not what I said. I said you should not allow it to overta—"

"No. You don't get to tell me that."

He was right. She was here to end him. To proselytize on top of that was probably poor taste. She gave the slightest nod of acknowledgement.

He jerked his head to the side, his hair flopping over his right eye, and he looked away from her. The same oppressive silence they had lived in for two days descended again but did not last beyond a few moments.

Max launched to his feet so quickly, both Anahita and Luke jumped. Max made a noise deep in his throat and then began to walk to one wall of the cell before turning around and walking back. They watched Max pace for a few minutes before Luke turned his attention back to the unconscious man. Anahita, however, was riveted.

As Max paced, he rubbed at the skin of his arms with rough strokes of his open palms, and while he did so, he continued to make those rough sounds of anger and distress. He was uncomfortable, that was certain, but Anahita suspected that his discomfort was passing into the realm of pain, which meant that Max had Impulse-paired with her, just as the poor man on the cot had Impulse-paired with someone and then been denied union with her.

Her grip on the leg of the cot tightened. Her shameful secret roiled within her and pushed at her Warrior Compulsion. The thing she tried so hard to conceal was acting out in response to the knowledge that Max was in pain.

Anahita was a Warrior, yes; she had inherited her mother's fierceness. But Anahita had inherited her Guardian father's nature as well. Anahita was an anomalous half-Guardian, half-Warrior angel. It meant she had two drives in play at all times—one to vanquish, one to protect—and that was a secret she had to guard with her life. If the others found out she was so untrustworthy, so unreliable, she would never be admitted into the ranks of the Warriors, and she might even be killed. Angels were too dangerous to be so changeable.

She distracted herself from Max's pain the only way she knew how: by watching his form as it moved. Her mouth grew dry as she watched the muscles beneath the seat of his pants bunch and release. That part of him looked so firm. So round. She shifted where she sat as a longing to lay her palm over one of those powerful displays of muscle grew intense enough to cause some discomfort of her own between her legs.

Max reached the end of the cell and turned to pace back, but he froze and sucked in a breath. When she looked upon his face, his gaze was fastened on her and his lips had parted. Anahita's eyes grew wide as she realized he had just caught her staring at his bottom. She jerked her eyes away and looked up into the corner of the cell, praying he would say nothing.

"Were you just staring *at my ass*?" he hissed at her.

She had never longed for the ability to lie more than she did in this moment. "Yes," she muttered after he raised his brows at her stubborn and ineffectual attempt at silence.

"What the hell kind of angel ogles a man's ass?"

Not a very good one. "I … could not help myself," she admitted.

Max grunted and fell back a little, his shoulders meeting the wall. He rubbed at his ribcage. "I, uh … don't think my body likes knowing that about you," he said on an exhale.

Her Guardian side surged. "Is it bad?" she asked. He frowned at her. "The pain?" she clarified.

His head tilted to the side. "How do you—" His body jolted, and then he straightened and began walking toward her, his eyes narrowing with each step. "You know things," he said, his tone making the simple statement an obvious accusation.

Oh, heaven. "You do not?" she asked, her heart in her throat. She had been told that the humans knew all about the side effects of the fruit. "Impulse-pairing" was a term the *humans* had coined.

Max stopped right in front of her. "They have not been forthcoming with information here, angel," he said, before crouching down, putting them face to face. "But you're about to be."

"I … I thought you knew." Stuttering? She took a steeling breath. She, of all creatures, knew the difference between a secret and sharable information. This was not a secret. "Ask your questions. I will answer them."

He rocked back on his heels, and in his crouched position, it nearly caused him to topple over. "You will?" He shook his head. "You don't know the slightest thing about war techniques, do you?"

That hit its mark. "I am a Warrior," she said, enunciating every word. "You merely assume your petty circumstances mean more to heaven than they do. There is only a need for secrecy when the information is consequential."

Even she could recognize that the bite in her words was inappropriate, and she felt immediate shame.

Max cocked the eyebrow over his left eye. "I've heard it said that one should not allow anger to overtake oneself."

Now she understood the inclination to snap at others. Many retorts perched on the edge of her tongue. "You and your sick friend have Impulse-paired," she said abruptly.

All evidence of smugness vanished from Max's face.

Anahita gentled her voice a little. The content of her words was harsh enough. "The *Impulse*, as some humans call it, was developed to aid in the world's creation at the beginning of time. That is not needed anymore, obviously, but then that is why you should not have tampered with the holy Trees. The pain you feel is a direct consequence of human disobedience."

"The pain is a *purposeful* side effect?" Max asked.

"Yes," she said simply. "It goes away when you experience pleasure with your partner, and then after that initial instance, you are able to make the pain go away on your own."

Max's face grew red at the same instant Anahita heard what she had just said and how she had said it, as though intercourse and self-pleasure were a part of her daily conversations. She cleared her throat and looked away from him.

"Then why has Luke not suffered from it?" he asked in a whisper, lowering his voice even more on Luke's name.

Her chest got tight. His worry for his friend was obvious. "He has not yet met the person who is his perfect match," she said softly.

"Perfect match," Max repeated in a mutter. He ran a hand over his face. "I'm guessing that doesn't have to go both ways with angels, huh?"

She frowned. "I don't understand."

"I used to be handsome, you know," he whispered.

Something within her melted. "Max," she began.

A noise from across the cell interrupted them. Anahita's gaze swiveled around to glance at the spot where Luke hovered over the prone form of the third prisoner.

He was no longer prone.

• • •

"Luke?"

Max froze. He hadn't said Luke's name, and that gravelly voice had certainly not come from the angel. Max closed his eyes and took a deep breath before turning to the cot that held Oliver. Blinking up at Luke, Oliver was lucid once more, as he always was moments before he died.

The end was here. Even though it had happened for two years, this part never got easier.

Luke sighed raggedly as he reached for Oliver's hand and held on tight. Here at the end, they could touch Oliver without causing him more pain. At least the poor man could be comforted as he died. It was a small mercy.

With a heavy heart, Max made his way over to his friend. He resisted looking at the angel as he passed. The baffling read his right eye gave him when he looked at her—that she was *both* good and evil—was a major distraction. It had sidetracked him so severely that he'd spewed that line about being handsome once. While he moved, even though he did not look her way, he felt her eyes travel with him to Oliver's side.

When he arrived, Max leaned over and smoothed the ragged, dirty hair off of Oliver's forehead, the skin of which was scorching hot. "Hey, Oliver," Max grumbled past the lump in his throat.

Oliver turned glassy eyes upon him. He attempted a smile, but it turned out closer to a grimace. "Max," Oliver breathed. "Hey, yourself." A dimple flashed in his left cheek. "You look like sh_t."

A sharp laugh burst from Max's lips. "Always do."

"A different kind of shit." Those glassy eyes seemed too perceptive, and Max turned his scar away.

Oliver's eyes closed and crinkled at the corners, and Max could see from the blanched knuckles of Oliver's hand that he was squeezing Luke's hand hard. "Damn her," Oliver groaned. "Why do I want her so much?"

"Shh," Luke said. "It's not your choice, you know that."

Oliver groaned again, his torso writhing slightly. "I want to hate her so bad."

"Then hate her," Max growled. God knows *he* did. That fucking woman had destroyed his friend.

"I can't," Oliver said on a desperate moan, his back arching.

Luke cast Max a black look, and Max felt the intended rebuke. He knew Oliver could never abide anyone talking down about his woman, despite what Max now knew for sure she had done to him.

"Okay, okay," Luke said softly. "You don't have to hate her."

The hell he doesn't. Max kept the thought to himself.

"I'm sorry," Oliver mumbled through dry, cracked lips. "For this."

Max closed his eyes. Oliver always—*always*—apologized to them before he died. "You don't say sorry, Oliver," Max ground out past a clenched jaw. "Ever."

"You've done nothing wrong," Luke said, leaning over Oliver more and smiling. Luke was always so calm and composed in this situation, as though he had been trained from a child to tend to others in need.

Max grimaced. Luke probably *had* been trained that way. Duties of a pastor's family and such. Luke always waited until after Oliver was gone to show any grief, and then he was withdrawn to the point of being almost catatonic. Yes, Luke was one of those bury-the-emotions people.

"Fuck," Oliver groaned. "It hurts."

"Yeah," Luke said simply.

"It'll be over soon," Max said softly.

Max's words were cut off by a pained shout that escalated in volume and pitch until it became a shriek. Oliver's body bowed off of the cot, and his head thrashed back and forth, his mouth wide open around that ungodly sound.

Luke continued to hold Oliver's hand and offer comfort just by being near, but Max felt like he was coming undone. This was his future. He'd be going through this exact same thing a couple of days before Oliver went through it again. They'd leave Luke shackled to tending to their needs, and he'd be practically alone watching over a dead body and a prone one for the rest of his life.

Oliver screamed again, and Max cursed. Max was shaking so hard, he could barely stand. He was going to commit violence if he didn't get a hold of himself, and fast.

As Oliver's latest scream died in intensity, he did something he had never done before: he began to sob. "I c-can't … do this anymore," Oliver cried as his chest heaved. Another ragged sob burst from his mouth, and he cast an arm over his eyes and broke down for the first time since this hell had started.

Max's mouth fell open. "Oh my God," he mumbled, taking a stumbling step toward Oliver, not at all sure what he could do to make things better if he got any closer. This was not something he thought he would ever be witnessing. Oliver was stronger than Max and Luke combined.

While Max just stood there like an idiot, Luke gathered Oliver into his arms and held the man against his chest.

Oliver's fingers clenched Luke's T-shirt, and even though his face was buried in Luke's chest, Max was able to hear him say, "Kill me. Please. Find a way to make this be the last time."

Max covered his mouth with a trembling hand. Luke exchanged a loaded glance with him, but simply rocked Oliver back and forth and said nothing.

Another scream began in Oliver's gut and rose to a height yet unreached. Oliver's fingers turned claw-like, and Max could see blood well up around the places where he clutched Luke's shirt and the skin underneath.

And then, Oliver's body completely relaxed as his scream abruptly ceased. His head lolled back on Luke's arm, and Max could see the flat, lifeless gleam in Oliver's wide-open eyes.

Oliver was dead. Again.

Luke laid Oliver flat on the cot once more, and then reached forward and closed the man's eyes. Heavy silence prevailed before Luke seemed to deflate, burying his face in his hands and releasing a shuddering sigh.

Not only was Max shaking where he stood, but a low, rumbling sound was rolling from his chest. His hands were clenched at his sides, and he could feel his own fingernails digging into his palms.

With a mind of its own, Max's body turned away from the tableau of Luke and Oliver. Max's bare feet shuffled against the stone floor, and the next thing he knew, he was facing the angel.

She looked stricken by what she'd just witnessed. Her knees were drawn up to her chest, and her fingers were pressed over her mouth. Her eyes were wider than he'd ever seen them, and tears swam along her lower lids, perched on the edge of rolling down her cheeks.

But all Max saw was a problem. His problem. Luke's problem. Even Oliver's problem. This angel was just as bad as Oliver's mystery woman. Oliver may never get the chance to act against his mate, but Max was here in a cell with his. She was in his power.

Max knew he could never hurt her; he couldn't even entertain the possibility. But he *could* prevent this sort of thing from happening to *him*.

Before he was quite sure what he was going to do, Max found himself stalking forward, the angel in his sights.

Chapter Four

The angel's wide eyes snapped away from Luke and Oliver and landed on him. If he were in her position, watching a perfect stranger charge him like a freight train, he'd be scared—or at the very least, apprehensive.

The angel didn't seem to be so. She calmly returned his stare, and Max again got the feeling that she was both good and evil. Not realizing what he was doing as he did it, Max leaned over and snatched at the frayed bonds that tied the angel's wrists to the cot. They disintegrated in his hands, and Max felt his eyes narrow as his gaze swung to the angel's face.

She could have escaped at any time. Just what in the *hell* was she doing here? At that moment, the evil part of her seemed to swell so greatly that it blocked out the good in Max's regard.

Max grabbed the angel around her upper arms and hauled her to her feet. As he did so, the fine muscles in her slim arms flexed beneath his fingers, and Max had to re-evaluate his thoughts of her as *delicate*. There was quiet strength beneath his grip.

She didn't fight him as he brought her to her feet, and Max regretted walking across the cell to her. Now that they were both standing in each other's personal space, Max couldn't prevent his hands from skimming down skin smoother than satin. He jerked them away with a grunt.

No caressing. That went without saying.

The angel's eyes turned up to meet his, large and luminous and rendering her the most vulnerable, innocent creature Max had ever encountered. He flexed his fists at his sides to keep himself from stroking the soft skin beneath her eyes with his fingertips.

"That poor man," the angel whispered in her whiskey voice. "He was in such pain."

The angel was treading on dangerous ground and didn't even realize it. She had no right to mention Oliver to him. Max's teeth were so tightly gritted that he feared he might break them.

"I am so sorry for you all," the angel continued at her own peril. "Are you alright, Max?"

It was the first time she had ever used his name, and he wondered how she knew it before he remembered Luke had used it in her presence. So, she was watching them and gleaning information on top of threatening to kill them. More to pile onto the list of things that made her an unacceptable risk in Max's life. "Stop talking," Max ground out through his teeth. "Now." *Before I do something we'll both regret.*

As Max had the thought, he feared it was too late. She asked if he was alright. Was she kidding? Max cursed beneath his breath, and the angel's eyes widened.

"You are not, of course," the angel muttered. And then she sealed her fate. Max watched in horror as her finely boned hand rose between them. He was so shocked at what her obvious intent was that he made no move to avoid her as her fingertips brushed over his shoulder and then made their way to his face. Max felt the whiskers of his beard stir as she skimmed over it, and then like a fire brand, her pointer finger touched his scar where it emerged from his beard on his left cheek. She traced it over the arch of his nose, and Max's eyes closed as she continued to follow it over his right eyelid and into his hairline. "So much pain in you all," the angel whispered.

It was the first time someone had touched him gently in nine years. A broken sound slipped past Max's lips, and his right hand snapped through the air, tightening around the angel's wrist and jerking it away. She gasped as Max took two quick steps forward, backing her into the wall behind her. The wrist clutched in his right hand he pinned to the wall above her head. He growled as her body arched into the awkward position, thrusting her chest into his. Her breasts were small, high, and firm, and they scorched his skin through both of their clothing.

Max realized his mistake as soon as his hips came into contact with hers. Damn his lack of control—his lack of a hold on himself. The memory of how her body felt against his was now a permanent part of him. He could never forget—never *wanted* to forget.

And then, contrary to what he expected, the angel relaxed against him. She softened, and her body contoured to his even more. Max zeroed in on her face as her eyes drifted closed, and then her lips parted around a breathy sigh.

That sigh jolted through him, and his fingers spasmed around her wrist. Her eyes opened once more, and she stared into his gaze. Heat rose to his cheeks, and before he could stop himself he snapped, "Don't look at me!"

Rather than obey him immediately, her eyes softened and swept over his entire face—scar, unruly hair, ragged beard—and then back to his eyes. "I fear I like looking at you too well to stop," she muttered.

Max dropped her wrist as though it were the vilest of things instead of something he never wanted to release. As he made to move away from her, however, the hand he'd just released sprang forward and clutched at his T-shirt. At the same time, she made a sound akin to that of a wounded animal.

Max froze. He felt his face morph into a dangerous mask of rage, and he turned to glare at her once more. "What the *hell* do you think you're doing?" he bit out word by word.

The angel shook her head, but did not release her grasp on his shirt. "I do not know," she said. "Just—" Her fingers tightened, and he felt his T-shirt pull at his neck. "Do not move away yet," she said, seemingly against her will, as the skin around her eyes tightened. "Please."

Max moved forward slowly, dangerously, until she was pinned between him and the wall once more. He fought desire and attempted in vain to supplant it with the rage that was always just beneath the surface. "I will destroy you," he said, leaning down the small bit required to put them eye to eye.

"No," the angel said. Her hand relaxed until it no longer clenched his shirt. Now her palm rested over his pectoral, and the heat of it burned. "I believe *I* will destroy *you*."

It was something she never should have said. With a groan made of equal parts grief and relief, Max lost a bit more of his control.

• • •

He was so imperfectly beautiful, Anahita couldn't catch her breath around him. That scar that bisected his face disturbed him to the point of pain, but Anahita had been around perfect beings her entire life. Beings whose lives had been too easy. She had never laid eyes on an angel that carried the physical evidence of struggle, and she found it startlingly arousing. He was so different from those she had been surrounded by since birth; he was a breath of fresh air. She shook her head. Perhaps, *fresh* was a bit optimistic.

Those disparate eyes that wouldn't meet hers for more than a handful of seconds together were so filled with anger and loathing as they focused on the stone wall beside her ear. His body was rigid as stone; she knew so because it was pressed against hers from chest to knees.

Anahita could safely say she had never been pressed to another being before, and certainly not a man. His body was so different from hers. Anahita was not a soft woman, she knew that. She had often looked upon the curvy mortals that had been the focus of her brethren's missions with envy. Where they were petite and lush of form, Anahita was taller than most men and muscled where she should be supple. But Max's body was much harder than hers. The wall of his chest was packed with muscles she could feel pressing against her breasts unforgivingly—a sensation that made Anahita weak in the knees.

As she tried to keep her hand where it lay instead of allowing it to trail down the curve of his pectoral, Max shifted and brought his hips more firmly against hers.

He leaned in until his lips were beside her ear. She felt a breeze on the sensitive skin of her earlobe as his chest rose with an intake of air. "You should not have reminded me of your intent, angel."

The words were soft, but they were not gentle, despite the fact that feeling them spoken in puffs of breath, as well as hearing them, made Anahita want to wrap her arms around the man.

"I would have walked away from you if you hadn't opened your mouth."

A trail of goosebumps broke out on the skin behind her ear and traveled down her neck to race across her chest, causing her nipples to harden into aching little points.

A rumbling sounded next to her ear, and Max pressed his chest into hers even harder until her hand almost didn't have room to rest on his pectoral anymore. "Is the skin of your neck sensitive, pretty angel?"

Anahita tried to take a breath, to exhale a breath—anything. Her lungs were frozen and felt simultaneously empty and too, too full. He could feel the effect he had on her breasts! How was his body so in tune with hers?

And, yet, hers was so very in tune with his: the way his stomach brushed into and receded from hers with every movement he made, the way his knee had shifted to come between her legs and now rubbed against the inside of her thigh. And between his stomach and knees, where their hips touched, she felt a part of his body begin to change just as her breasts had. When it kept growing and pressed into her, Anahita's lungs released their iron grip on her air, and then she gasped. Her fingers flexed on his chest, and she wrenched her hand away when she felt her nails scrape through his shirt and into his flesh. "I am sorry," she breathed desperately. She had clawed him!

Air stirred by her ear again, almost as though he had chuckled. "Don't be. No need to be sorry unless you stop."

Anahita's head snapped to the right, and she found herself staring at his ear as it peeked through his long, ragged hair. She blinked at the sight in silence. He'd *liked* being clawed?

"Your hand, angel," Max said gruffly. "Return it."

She could scarcely believe she had permission to touch him when it was what she'd been longing to do since stepping through the wall of this cell and laying eyes upon him for the first time.

Her fingers trembled as she raised her hand and placed it over the place that was still warm from her palm. The muscles of his chest jumped beneath her hand, and Anahita had to swallow another gasp.

"Now, move it around, angel," Max whispered. "You want to, don't you?"

Anahita wanted to draw her head back, to gaze into Max's eyes, but the wall at the back of her head was unforgiving. She knew there was some reason she should not be touching him, but for the life of her, she couldn't remember what it was.

He was so warm. She rotated her hand on his chest, and the changes in his body structure were a tantalizing mystery she could not wait to solve. She pulled her palm back to trail her fingertips over the pad of his muscle and downward. Max leaned away from her a little to allow her fingers passage, and Anahita was delighted to discover that his nipples had hardened as well. When she passed her pointer finger around the taut nub, Max groaned heavily, his breath stirring her hair.

The harsh sound startled Anahita, and she jerked her fingers away, her elbow colliding with the stone wall in a loud crack that sent pain radiating up her arm. That was strange. Anahita usually never felt pain. Why the change? And, more importantly, why was she fighting the feeling that she should not touch Max?

"R-release me," Anahita stuttered as she felt her brows furrow. She needed a moment to regroup—to gather her thoughts. Something important was attached to this man, and she couldn't discern it or remember it with his distracting body pressed against hers.

Rather than obey her, however, Max reached forward, and next she knew, his fingers were brushing hers. He grasped her hand and brought it back to his chest, where he pressed her palm down. "You really want me to release you?" he asked in a husky whisper. "Then ask me again."

When her lips parted to do just that, Max laid his palm over the back of her hand, intertwined their fingers, and began to trail her hand down the front of his body.

Lord of the Most High, his body was magnificent. The heavy muscles of his chest curved downward to tantalizing lines that spread horizontally across his torso—what the humans would call a six-pack. Or it very well could be an eight-pack. Anahita could not tell while he wore his shirt, and she wished his shirt gone with a desperation that bordered on despair.

She barely registered when Max removed his hand from hers and allowed her to continue to explore his body without his aid. She was too involved in the way his stomach muscles leapt to her fingers as she continued to trail her hand down the front of his body. When one of her fingers dipped into his navel, his hips flexed forward, surging that hard, prodding piece of flesh into her in a way that wrenched a moan from her lips.

But, too soon, his hips withdrew, creating space between their lower bodies. She was too overwhelmed with disappointment to realize why he had moved until he whispered hoarsely, "Continue down, angel." His tone no longer carried the casual distance it had since he'd pinned her to the wall. "Let your curiosity guide you."

Curiosity? Yes, that was all this was. She was curious about his body. She'd never felt one before, so of course she would want to when given the opportunity. She shoved aside the doubts that still plagued her and let her fingers continue southward. As soon as she reached the waistband of his fatigues, she felt the change in his body—not just physically, as his abdomen flattened out and narrowed. She'd thought him tense before, but as her fingers brushed the button holding his pants together, his body tensed even more, and in her peripheral vision, she saw his hands clench into fists where they rested on the stone on either side of her head.

She was suddenly and intensely nervous, and she couldn't say why. If this was mere curiosity, there were no stakes, and she had no reason to be alarmed. For some reason, however, she wanted him to enjoy what she was doing. What she was about to do. That she couldn't look at him and gauge if he was or not was beginning to bother her.

"Don't stop now," Max breathed. "Please." His voice broke on the single syllable, and with that, some of Anahita's nervousness disappeared. He had to be enjoying this to some degree or he wouldn't wish it to continue.

As she began to move her fingers down again, the fabric she was feeling tented outward until she ran into the turgid ridge of flesh that had been pressed into her. She closed her eyes and swallowed a moan that did *not* come from mere curiosity as her fingers traced it down, and down—she had not expected it to be so long—into the leg of his trousers where it seemed to be painfully pinned between his thigh and the constricting seam of his pants. When her fingers encountered a raised ridge of flesh several inches down his pant leg, Max sucked in a ragged breath and then cursed softly into her hair.

Her hand tried to close around what it held, but the fabric of his pants prevented her, and she felt an uncharacteristic flare of impatience that manifested itself in a breathy moan.

In answer, Max brushed his cheek against hers, the bristling texture of his beard chaffing her just right, and whispered, "You don't have to stay on the outside of my pants, you know."

· · ·

Max held his breath and cursed himself as soon as the words left his lips. *You don't have to stay on the outside of my pants*? Fucking shady. And where was this confidence coming from? He was speaking to the angel the way he'd spoken to women before his capture. Before his scarring. But that was when he had his looks on his side. He couldn't even stare Oliver and Luke in the eyes these days, and here he was pinning an exquisite angel to the wall and whispering filthy orders to her.

The skin of her cheek was so soft that Max wanted to stay here, pressing his face against it, for the rest of his miserable existence. And that unwelcome sentiment was exactly why Max jerked his face away from hers. So far, he'd kept contact to a minimum— only their clothed bodies touching—and that was the one thing that was keeping him sane. Though he ached with every ounce of his restraint to run his hands over her exposed skin, and her unexposed skin, for that matter, Max kept them firmly planted on the stone wall behind the angel.

He hadn't been touched by a woman in nine years, and the angel's heady, unpracticed sweeps of her hand were about to unman him—in more than one way. Max feared he'd spill in her palm, but more than that, he feared he'd spill tears. He'd had no idea he'd been so starved for any kind of physical affection. He found himself wishing that he'd allowed Luke's attempts at those damn hugs he was always trying to give over the years.

When the angel had brushed her fingers over the head of his aching erection, Max ground his teeth against the broken pleas that threatened to burst from him. What had slipped out instead was that little beauty about shoving her hand down his pants.

Max closed his eyes, blocking out the sight of her perfect, blond waves, as he hoped she would ignore what he'd just said. Or at the very least, not rip his limbs off with the strength he suspected she possessed but held at bay.

So, when she made a deep noise that vibrated from her chest into his and sounded anticipatory, Max nearly sprang back from her so he could see her face. He held himself very still, knowing he'd *had* to have misinterpreted that sexy noise. But then, her fingers started moving back up the inside of his thigh.

Max found himself arching into her touch as those fingers burned a trail up the front of his hips and rested at the button of his fatigues. He could feel her uncertainty radiating from her in the sudden tension of her muscles. "I may ... *touch* you?" she asked breathlessly.

Max bit back the instantaneous desire to bellow *yes* into her ear, and instead managed a bitten-off, "Please."

She sucked in a ragged breath—for courage?—and began to fumble at undoing the aged button that barely held his pants together. Something most unwelcome, almost like affection, overwhelmed him. She may have never done something like this before. It made him feel simultaneously protective and resentful. If she was new to this, he had certain responsibilities. Didn't he? He felt like normal, *kind* men were careful in these situations. Those societal expectations could go fuck themselves. And yet... He nearly placed a hand over hers and stepped away with some sort of excuse to end an encounter she may not be ready for.

But then, the image of Oliver dying—*again*—surged to the forefront of Max's memory, and any desire to be gentle with this angel's sensibilities vanished in a violent death all its own.

"Do it," he spoke into the angel's ear, resisting the urge to nibble on her earlobe. "Touch me."

Her breath hitched and then resumed in a quickened rhythm as she brought her other hand into the mix and used both sets of fingers to unbutton his pants. They breathed simultaneously as she spread the front of his pants apart, the sound of his zipper coming down echoing in the quiet cell.

Max was close enough to her that he knew she wouldn't be able to look down and examine him, and he was grateful, though he definitely wanted to feel her eyes on his cock. If she was inexperienced, she might not respond favorably to his size, and he could tell by the heaviness in his groin that he was bigger than usual.

He could see the harried rhythm of her pulse in the flutter at the base of her neck as she skimmed hesitant fingers along the expanse of skin below his belly button. Max's body jerked without his permission, and he hissed in a breath.

He'd never felt anything as arousing as this brush of her fingers against his naked skin. His head fell back, and his throat worked up and down as he resisted the strong desire to speak to her—to whisper *nice* things into her ear: call her his pretty angel as he had done once before in a moment of low resistance; tell her how much she rocked him, both in how she looked and with what she was doing; beg her for more; plead with her to wrap her arms around him and hold him. Sentimental shit that he would never say in his right mind, and that he suspected she would deliver if he did. That he could not stand. He would completely break down in her arms.

Her fingers maneuvered inside of his pants, and Max realized that as soon as her fingers had touched his skin, the discomfort—which had been steadily headed toward pain and had plagued him over the past two days, since hearing *The One* ... it had vanished.

The relief he felt was palpable, and with the relief came a renewed sense of urgency that she not stop touching him. Not until he was sure his relief would be long-lived.

For the first time since this encounter began, Max allowed one of his hands to move away from the wall. He pulled his open pants further aside to allow the angel's hand easier access to the aching erection within. Like they had coordinated the move, the angel took his cue and slipped her hand deeper into his pants.

Her cool fingers brushed against his cock at the root where it was bent sharply down, trapped as it was in his pant leg. Even that light brush nearly unmanned him.

"Soft," she murmured.

Max closed his eyes and the grip he had on his pants tightened while the knuckles of his other fist ground farther into the stone. "Take it in your hand, angel," he whispered roughly. "Free me."

She muttered a sound of assent, and then she tried to wrap her fingers around him in the confines of his pants. It took some obvious effort, and when she tentatively tugged on him a couple of times, Max's eyes rolled back into his head.

"I cannot…" the angel paused. "I do not want to hurt you."

"You won't hurt me," he muttered. Not caring if his pants hit the ground, Max slid the hand that had been holding his pants inside next to her fingers. His pants stayed put, and their fingers brushed together as Max showed her how to wrap around him and pull him free. And then she held him in her hands.

Max couldn't prevent the earthy groan that rose from his chest at her first hesitant squeeze.

"You feel…" The angel hesitated, and Max held his breath. "I am in awe," she said on a breath.

Max allowed himself to move into her grip slightly. "Move with me," he whispered, forcing his hand to rejoin the other against the stone wall when he wanted to wrench her to him and thrust with all his strength. When Max next canted his hips forward, the angel moved her fist down his length with him.

"Oh, God," Max groaned. His fists unfurled, and his fingertips grappled at the stone wall. "Please," he heard himself beg. "Don't stop, please."

The angel's breaths were near pants, they came so quickly, and she moved her fist over his length like this was a fucking dream, somehow knowing he needed her to move faster. Harder.

Max's eyes closed, and he admitted defeat. He knew he was not going to last. At all. What had begun only minutes before was going to be over in the next few heartbeats, and there was nothing Max could do to stop it. Even if he pulled her hand from his body, it wouldn't help, because the memory of her fingers on him would take him to the finish line just as quickly.

"Angel...I—" A groan cut off his words.

As though she already knew his body, she tightened her grip and increased her pace even more. And just like that, it was over.

Stars burst behind Max's closed eyes, and he heard the distant sound of rock cracking beneath his hands. He clenched his lips against words that wanted to burst from him as violently as his orgasm—words that would be endearments. The pleasure kept coming until Max wondered if it would ever end. When his skin grew too sensitive, he covered the angel's hand with one of his own, stilling her movements but keeping her hand upon him at the same time. He gulped mouthfuls of air as he tried to regain his senses, and in a moment of weakness, his other hand found the back of the angel's head. With a moan, he drew her into his body, tucking her head beneath his chin. A fine tremor wracked his body.

Thoughts bombarded him: She was magnificent. He was never going to be the same.

As soon as he caught his breath, he was going to lay her down on the cot to their right and cover her with his body. He was going to touch her so right until she was breathless and couldn't say his name until it burst from her in a scream as she came apart in his arms.

His thoughts broke off as she nuzzled into his neck. Clarity began to return as she opened her mouth and licked the hollow of his throat, her tongue so hot in the cool cell that Max jumped. And then she wrapped her arms around his waist and hugged him close.

Just before he returned her embrace, he remembered himself. He was imprisoned somewhere in Afghanistan. His best friend in the world died every week. His other friend relied on Max to keep him safe. He'd approached the angel to avoid Oliver's fate and no other reason. And he was a hair's-breadth away from losing control to the very creature who'd threatened to kill him.

With a harsh curse, Max wrenched his hand from the back of the angel's head and tried to step back. When her arms tightened, Max gripped the angel by her biceps and pulled out of her embrace.

As soon as he was free, he took two giant steps back and dropped her arms as though they scalded him. He felt himself scowl as he took her in. Her hair was disheveled from his fingers, and her lips were glistening wet from when she'd licked his neck. His orgasm marked the front of her robe.

She looked so confused by his sudden abandonment that, for a moment, he almost couldn't resist wrapping her in his arms again and reassuring her. He even took a step toward her to do just that before he forced iron into his spine and stood his ground.

She threatened to kill you. Would have turned you into a vegetable if you'd let her. With a sick feeling in his gut, he wiped all emotion from his face. Shaking his hair into his eyes and staring at a location somewhere over her shoulder, he sneered. "Was *that* part of your orders, angel?"

As soon as the words left his lips, he felt like the dick he was. In his peripheral vision, he saw the angel jolt as though she'd been struck, and Max curled his fists at his sides. She placed a trembling hand over her stomach, and Max glanced at her face through his hair. He immediately regretted it. Her eyes were wide and glassy. She took a step back, and then another one, until her back met the wall where she'd hand-fucked him moments before. Her lush bottom lip trembled, and Max felt as though he would vomit.

Then, her chin rose into the air, and she fixed him with a look of utter sorrow. In the next moment, she vanished.

Max felt his eyes widen as he stumbled forward, his hand outstretched toward the space the angel had just occupied. He stopped and forced his arm back to his side.

A sound behind him brought him up short, and Max turned around only to find the twisted face of Luke where he still sat on Oliver's cot. Max had never seen Luke look at someone the way he was looking at Max right now. Rage contorted features that were usually so quick to offer a smile.

"What the *hell*, man?" Luke's words quavered with fury.

Max closed his eyes as he realized what he'd just done in front of an audience. That Luke had deigned to swear at him was telling enough in and of itself. Max had never heard him use a word harsher than *gosh*, and they were soldiers.

"I know," Max whispered, shocking himself even more. He apologized to no one. "I know," he said again, staring at his toes.

Max heard the sound of Oliver's cot squeaking and then the rustle of fabric as Luke approached him. With a sigh, Max raised his head and didn't defend himself as Luke's fist snapped toward Max's jaw.

It was less than what he deserved.

Chapter Five

Anahita covered her mouth with her fist, biting into the flesh of her knuckles to keep from moaning aloud. From just outside her Temptation's cell, she watched through the bars as Luke punched Max. She had been able to gather herself enough to sink through the walls in the moments following Max's cold dismissal of their intimate act.

As Max hung his head and covered his face, Anahita clenched her knees together, hoping to assuage the foreign ache between her thighs that plagued her to the point of tears. The skin of her own knuckles tasted bitter in comparison to the heady honey that had been Max's neck as she'd dabbed her tongue in the hollow—an instinctual action she longed to repeat again and again.

Her head ached. All of the reasons she should not have touched her Temptation—those internal warnings she could not focus on in the heat of the moment—were now pounding through her skull. A few moments more, even one kind word, and—Anahita could not fool herself—she would have Fallen. Just like that: centuries of faithful work erased with the passionate swipe of a hand.

There were only two ways an angel could Fall: taking of the Tree of Eternal Life, and succumbing to one's Temptation, which could happen in more than one way. Temptations were not always human—Lucifer's Temptation had been pride—but they usually took the form of a human. If angels created life with their Temptations, they Fell at the moment of conception. Nephilim—the offspring of a human and angel—were dangerously powerful and not to be created. One of the other ways angels could succumb to their Temptations was making a conscious decision to Fall *for* them in order to be with them for the rest of their lives. It was the only way an angel could be with their Temptation for anything more than a short length of time: the average lifespan of a human. By Falling, the angel joined life spans with the Temptation's: the angel lived for a shorter amount of time than she would have, but the Temptation existed much longer, which was why some of the earlier humans had lived for hundreds of years.

But Falling came with too many risks for many angels to even consider the benefits of lifelong love. For one, when an angel Fell, they lost some, or even all, of the gifts given to them by the Most High. Jayden had lost his ability to turn invisible when he Fell for his Temptation, Grace, and he had been lucky that invisibility was all he'd lost. For another, Falling turned an angel mortal. Oh, angels would still live in perfect health until something external—like an attack—killed them, or until their Temptation succumbed to mortality. But once word got out that an angel had Fallen, they seemed to have a target upon their backs. Angels were among the most hated beings in the universe, and their enemies pursued them in their weakened Fallen state mercilessly. Not many angels would consider the risk to the human they loved worth the cost, since their lifespans were linked and the human died with the angel. Anahita knew it must already weigh on Jayden's mind with his own human. Yes, the Fallen could potentially live millennia with their Temptations, but Anahita knew of no Fallen who had managed to do so.

If Anahita were Fallen, she knew she would not last long. She was a Warrior, yes, and a trained one, but she had no actual war experience. Minutes ago, she'd been willing to give it all up for the man who had looked at her with disgust and spoken cruelly to her while his passion had yet to dry and was being absorbed into the fabric of her robe.

Anahita closed her eyes against the view of her Temptation. Even looking upon the body that had been pressed to hers brought on fresh self-loathing.

And still, Anahita could not leave him. She'd tried. That was why she was pressed against this wall outside the bars. She'd laid eyes upon her Temptation; she'd touched her Temptation. She was as much a prisoner of his presence as he was a prisoner of this cell.

Anahita winced at a faint pressure in her temples. The angels rarely felt pain, so it caught her attention. And—Anahita frowned—this pressure felt just like the pressure she always felt when her brother, Jayden, read her mind. Jayden's gift never hurt the humans when he used it, but the angels were sensitive to each other's powers. Jayden would have to be here—within a certain distance of her—to read her mind.

With a sudden rush of something that felt akin to shame, Anahita hoped that Jayden had not witnessed her first intimate act and the bruising rejection that had followed on its heels. Anahita covered her eyes with one hand and took in a shuddering breath. She would not be able to stand it if Jayden had seen.

She heard a telltale ruffling of feathers, and with a silent sigh of resignation, Anahita raised her head. Jayden, indeed, was here.

He walked over and stood next to her, leaning against the wall. How he'd gotten here, Anahita did not know. He would have had to walk through the compound in full sight to get here.

She felt the gentle pressure on her temples that meant Jayden was again reading her mind, and then he snarled. "I will *kill* him," he whispered. "Your emotional pain is breath-stealing."

Excellent. So, Jayden hadn't witnessed her shame firsthand, but he now knew of it nonetheless because she could not control her thoughts. Again, mental images of how Max had looked at her stole through her mind, and the bones of Jayden's fist cracked as he repeated, "I will *kill him.*"

Anahita couldn't prevent the mental plea that shot through her entire being: *No!* She could feel the tension radiating from Jayden, and she knew she didn't have much time to convince him of anything before he acted on her behalf and slaughtered Max before her eyes. She grasped at the first viable excuse she could think of. *Killing him is* my *mission. Brother, you know how much I have to prove. It must be me.* When Jayden relaxed, Anahita sighed. She gathered her thoughts. *Why are you here?*

She could feel Jayden's hesitation. Finally, he whispered, "We are here to rescue these men. To take them home."

Anahita frowned. *We?*

"The American soldiers I was tasked with killing." Jayden's feathers ruffled again. "They want their friends back."

Anahita squeezed her fists. Earlier this year, Jayden had allowed his Compulsion to set in his mission to kill the immortals in America who had tasted of the Tree of Eternal Life. Instead of killing them, Jayden had embraced them as his pseudo family after encountering his Temptation in their midst.

It was the reason Anahita had been given the mission of killing the immortals in the cell before her now: Jayden had failed, Falling rather than killing those he loved. And of course Jayden's immortals would want these men back. They had been separated almost nine years ago and had thought each other dead. If one group knew of the other's existence, their desire to reunite would be overwhelming. Humans formed lasting ties that defied Anahita's comprehension.

Anahita glanced at Jayden with this fresh reminder of her purpose. Did he have his sword here with him, hidden beneath one of his wings?

Probably. He always had the sword with him. Could she be fortunate enough to have both her targets and the weapon needed to dispatch them in the same location?

An idea sprouted like a sunflower in summer, and Anahita calmed her adrenaline before Jayden could detect it. *Jayden, I'll help you ... rescue the humans.*

She could tell that he'd felt her hesitation on the word *rescue,* but she could also feel interest pouring off of him as well. Jayden feeling emotion. Anahita almost couldn't believe it. He had always been so stalwart, and now even she, weak as her perceptions were, could sense his emotions.

"I'm listening," he whispered.

Anahita had to tread lightly. She knew how much he loved his immortals. She could only hope that that love did not extend to the three before her. *I will teleport them through the walls to you and your men. That will prevent you from having to fight your way out, thus preserving human life.* Though, the type of human who would imprison others in squalor might not be worth preserving.

Jayden grunted softly, an indication that she should continue. He knew there was a catch. *In exchange, I would ask the use of your sword in my mission.*

Jayden tsked. "Allow you to rescue them only so you can kill them?" he whispered.

Well, when he put it that way … Anahita squeezed her eyes shut. She *needed* that sword. She needed to complete this mission. She needed Max. She needed to kill him. *I will … delay the Compulsion as long as I can. That will give your humans some much-needed reunion time. And if you're near them, you know you can defeat me in a fight and prevent me from acting. You risk nothing by loaning me the sword.* It was true. Jayden had been one of her instructors. He knew all of her moves because he had taught them to her. But since he knew all of her moves, she knew all of his as well. She hid that thought before he could discern it and hoped he would not think of it on his own.

There was tense silence before Jayden whispered again. "You will not attempt to harm my immortals?"

He sounded so proprietary when he spoke of them. She looked at Max before flicking her eyes away just as quickly. She could only hope she would not be the same with her own immortals. *You have my word. I will attempt to carry out my mission to kill these three immortals. It will be enough to show the brethren that I can be trusted. I will then allow another angel to be assigned the rest of the task.*

Anahita struggled with both relief that she would not have to kill more humans and regret that she would not be given the chance to prove herself further. But she loved Jayden enough to promise not to cause him pain in this area. She only hoped that he bore enough love for her to agree to this deal. Love among angels, though an emotion, had been allowed and even encouraged in the heavens. It was the only pure emotion in existence.

"I agree to your terms," Jayden whispered.

Anahita squelched the relief that poured through her. *This is good,* she projected with as much nonchalance as she could muster. *I can deliver them to you one at a time. Where shall I take them?*

"You have been to the front gates of the prison?" Jayden asked.

Anahita could teleport anywhere in the world, whether she'd been there or not, but knowing an exact location was always helpful. *I have. But will there not be guards to witness us?*

"There will not," Jayden whispered. "There are few here. I have rarely seen such a lackadaisical operation. I avoided them easily, and I am not what one would call stealthy these days."

Anahita was unable to organize her thoughts quickly enough to reply before Jayden continued with, "The crew is waiting at the front gate in two vehicles." He straightened and made to move away, the slightest hint of impatience to get started spiraling off him.

She nodded quickly. *I will see you there momentarily.*

Jayden walked away, peeking around the corner to check for humans before disappearing from sight. With a deep breath, she focused on the three men before her and prepared to make herself visible again.

Chapter Six

Max had had the irrational feeling that someone was staring at him since the angel disappeared from his life half an hour ago.

Great. She was gone and he was *still* going crazy.

Oliver was out, Luke had not glanced at him once since decking the fire out of him, and the angel was gone. There was no one left in the cell to stare at him, and yet, that tingling feeling at the base of the back of his neck would not go away. That same feeling had served him well on the field of battle many times, and he'd learned to never ignore it, but right now, he was tempted to start. He didn't want to be any crazier than he guessed he already was due to nine years of imprisonment.

While Luke hadn't been looking at Max, Max had been looking at him. Max had never seen Luke lose his temper like that, and certainly not at Max himself. It made him antsy to do something. Something like apologize for his actions. Which was crazy and something Max never did. But as he sneaked another look underneath his hair at Luke, he saw the other man roll his shoulders, just as Max himself had been doing to alleviate the damned tingle on the back of his neck.

"You feel it, too," Max said softly, hoping whatever was staring at them would not hear.

Luke stiffened where he sat on the cot guarding Oliver's body, and for a moment, Max thought he was still so angry that he wouldn't answer. But then, Luke nodded imperceptibly.

The sound of a pebble being kicked across the floor echoed through the cell like a shot, and Luke sprang to his feet and cocked his fists at the same time that Max spun around and prepared to launch himself at their attacker.

He drew up short and heard Luke do the same right behind him. It was his angel. She was back.

Feelings Max did not know he'd been feeling since she'd left so suddenly—despair, loneliness, longing—vanished in the most astounding rush of relief Max had ever felt. "You're back."

It was said in the same deep, rough tone of voice that Max always used, but the next thing he knew, Luke was pushing him out of the way and placing himself in front of the angel. Luke assumed a defensive position, sinking into a slight crouch and holding his hands fisted out in front of him. He pinned Max with eyes that were now dark with censure. "Don't come near her," Luke commanded.

For several precious seconds, Max was stunned into silence. But then, just as quickly, the reality of what Luke had just done rushed in. He was defending the angel against *him*. She was his! "The fuck do you think you're doing?" Max said slowly, hoping to delay the inevitable attack on his friend if he didn't move out from his position between Max and his woman.

Before Luke could answer, the angel placed her hand on Luke's shoulder. The other man jumped at the contact and turned his head to the left to look up at her. The angel smiled. At Luke. She fucking smiled at Luke.

With a rumbling in his chest, Max took two steps forward without realizing it. Just when he was preparing to snatch Luke by the fabric of his shirt, the angel flicked her eyes from Luke's and looked straight into Max's. Her cool blue eyes sparked a hot fire in his chest. He froze to catch his breath, but it evaded him while he again got the impression that the angel was both *good* and *evil*. The shock of her eyes and her duality distracted him before he remembered to shake his hair more securely across his scar.

She did not seem to notice the effect she had on him or the raised flesh that slashed across his face. "Max." She paused and glanced at Luke again. "And Luke. I am here to liberate you."

It was almost as if the words, which Max completely understood, had no meaning. She couldn't be saying what it sounded like she was saying. Max frowned. "You said you were going to kill us."

Luke's head snapped around so quickly, Max was sure it should've made a sound of some kind. He gave Max another black look, and Max had to resist the urge to throw up his hands in the air and say *What?* To him, it seemed like a perfectly good observation. Because she now claimed to be their salvation, they were supposed to forget she'd threatened them?

"Would you like to be freed or not?" the angel asked.

"Just going to ignore what I said, then?" Max crossed his arms over his chest and ignored the pleas to shut up that Luke was tossing at him with those puppy-dog eyes of his.

The angel cocked one eyebrow and said nothing. *That's a yes, then.*

"We'd like to be freed, yes," Luke said, turning adoring eyes upon Max's angel.

"Very well," she said softly. She stepped around Luke and walked toward Max.

More than anything, Max wanted to open his arms and invite her to step into his body. Instead, he held out his hands and barked a harsh, "Stop!"

It worked better than he could have hoped. She stopped so quickly, Max worried that she would fall forward. A brief look—eyebrows drawn together and lush lips pursed—flashed across her face before it was hidden behind a blank façade. And that quickly, Max knew he had hurt her, probably just as badly as he feared, with his callous treatment earlier. It devastated him to a level he would never have guessed. Something that felt like physical agony knifed through his gut.

This was *regret.* Max couldn't remember a time he had felt regret—definitely not for how he had treated someone. Of course, he had never been felt up by an angel before, so perhaps his level of regret was merited.

Merited or not, Max had his men to protect, and the angel had threatened to harm them more than she'd threatened to help them. And he was *still* getting the impression from his eye that she was both evil and good. Unfortunately, life experience had taught him to err on the side of evil.

He focused on the angel in front of him. He had stopped her for a reason: she'd appeared as though she were about to touch him again. He could not have that. "Just … don't come any closer, okay?" Max said quietly. "For the time being." Now, why the *fuck* had he added that qualifier?

"Max," Luke said in a warning tone from his place behind the angel. "She wants to rescue us, man."

The hope in Luke's voice made Max antsy, and more than anything, Max wanted to make sure that Luke's weakness wasn't exploited. "What's the plan, angel?" he asked roughly.

She appeared to wince at Max's words, but spoke in the same calm, husky voice as always. "I am Anahita."

Max forced himself to frown when what he wanted to do was grin like a fool. He knew her name now. *Doesn't matter.* "Yeah, not what I asked."

Luke huffed, but Max ignored him.

The angel—Anahita—cocked her head to the side. "I had hoped that knowing my name would put you on more even footing with me," she said. "Perhaps create a tiny measure of trust between us."

"That will never happen." *It helps a little, yes.* Max gritted his teeth. His damn mind had better get on board.

Anahita sighed. "The plan is simple," she said wearily. "Your men Eli and Jericho await your arrival at the front gates of the prison. I am to transport you there."

Eli and Jericho? Optimism Max couldn't afford to feel bloomed in his chest. She wouldn't know their names unless they were really here, right?

"Oh, my God," Luke breathed, stumbling forward and reaching for the angel's arm until Max growled and stared him down. Luke's outstretched fingers dropped to his side. "Eli and Jericho are alive?"

Anahita smiled at Luke. "Very, yes."

"How?" Max gritted out between his teeth. She simply had to quit smiling at Luke. Or Max would—he closed his eyes. He'd do nothing. She could smile at whomever the hell she wanted.

"I'm sorry," Anahita said, turning her eyes on Max again. "How—?"

"How will you *transport* us to them?"

"I can disappear and reappear wherever I wish," the angel said with a small lift of one of her shoulders. "I wrap my arms around you, and you come with me."

Max tamped down the part of himself that got excited at the idea of her wrapping her arms around him. *She'll wrap her arms around Luke and Oliver, too, dumbass.* Rationally, Max decided that trying this was better than nothing. If she was a liar, and it didn't work—or worse, was a trap—they would deal with it. Anything was preferable to a day's more imprisonment in this hellhole.

"Fine," Max said. Anahita's brows rose, but then she reached for him. Max took a quick step back. "My men first."

"Max—" Luke began.

"No," Max cut him off. "You first, then Oliver, so you can watch over him until I arrive." Then, if it *was* a trap, at least Oliver wasn't alone and helpless in his current state. Luke was more than capable of defending himself and Oliver, and then once Max arrived, hopefully two would be greater than whatever force awaited them.

"Very well," the angel said softly. With no more hesitation, she turned to face Luke fully. Max watched with a clenched jaw as she wrapped her arms around Luke's broad shoulders. Before the rage that bubbled inside him at the sight could take hold, they both disappeared. That was the moment Max discovered he'd truly doubted she could do what she'd said she could do. With the realization that she could teleport and take people with her, intense worry rushed in. Luke had been gone for a handful of seconds, but a handful of seconds was all it took to carve someone up. Max rubbed a hand over his raised scar.

His chest grew tight, and his fists longed to lash out at something—anything. Before he could do anything rash, she was back, sparkling in beauty amid the dank cell. Her arms were empty.

"Tell me he's okay." The words left Max's mouth before he knew he was going to say them, and he cringed at their desperate twinge.

The angel's face softened. "He is with his friends and in perfect health. You have my word, and angels cannot lie."

Max could only hope that was true.

"Do you still wish me to take Oliver before you?" she asked softly.

Max hesitated. His longing to see Luke well for himself warred with his desire to make sure Oliver was kept safe. Finally, Max nodded curtly.

Anahita acknowledged his wishes with a quick dip of her chin, and then she spun around toward Oliver's prone form. With more strength than Max had guessed she possessed, the angel scooped Oliver's considerable bulk into her arms, cradling him against her body before they both disappeared as well.

In her absence, Max closed his eyes and counted his heartbeats, trying—in vain—to time his erratic breathing to the increasing rhythm of his heart.

This time—because she knew Max would be worried?—the angel returned more quickly. Max felt her arrive in the cell, and his eyes snapped open.

He almost jumped out of his skin. She was a hair's-breadth away from him, her nose nearly touching his, the warmth of her body flowing over his chest and stomach. He should move away. He *would* move away. Any time now.

"Sorry," Anahita mumbled, her eyes dipping to his lips. "I miscalculated."

And, yet, she did not step back. Max felt as though gravity had shifted, and he worried that he was going to sway toward her any moment. There was no room for swaying. Max felt his throat work around a convulsive swallow, and he tried to formulate words that would get her to move away from him before he did something stupid, like appease the curiosity in the gorgeous, golden-blue eyes that were *still* focused on his lips.

Just when the insistent knowledge from his eye that she was both good and evil made a dent through his lust, and he was preparing to step away—albeit reluctantly—the angel spoke. "Are you ready to join your friends?"

Her husky voice acted the same upon him as a hand stroking down his chest, and he felt his eyes widen as he realized she was close enough to get an up-close, uninhibited view of his scar. He shook his hair into his eyes and tilted his chin downward to try to hide himself as well as he could, given her close proximity. Best to end this as soon as possible. "Yes," he said gruffly.

Though he'd seen her transport someone twice, he was unprepared for her to step even closer to him. Her arms came around him, her breasts pressing into his chest. Max closed his eyes and forced his arms to remain at his sides. *Lilies.* The same scent that came from those flowers that always decorated grocery stores around Easter—that scent wafted up from Max's angel and surrounded him.

So many desires flooded him, he knew he was doomed if he didn't allow a slight alleviation of the pressure. With a sigh, Max allowed his arms to rise and wrap around Anahita, the fingers of his right hand tangling in the soft silk of her hair.

She gasped, her breasts pressing into him rapidly. "Keep your eyes closed," she whispered breathlessly.

Max felt the firm stone beneath his feet disappear. His arms tightened around her even more, and he closed his mouth to prevent a huff of breath from escaping. Before terror could take over, his feet landed upon firm ground again.

Max felt himself shaking, but there was nothing he could do to stop it. And in a move that only made him feel worse about his masculinity, the angel squeezed him and made a shushing sound in his ear. "You are here."

Max jerked away from her, his arms falling to his sides. The angel moved away from him without meeting his eyes, and for the first time, Max was able to see where he was.

They were inside a massive military blind that shielded them from any onlookers. The dappled shade cast dark shadows over his skin and provided a bit of relief from the heat of the desert. A Humvee made up one of the sides of the blind, and the back door was open. Inside, Max could see the prone form of Oliver laid out on the vehicle's floor, Luke kneeling beside him. Max's shakes vanished. The angel had told the truth.

Holy shit. The angel had told the truth. They were rescued. They were actually free!

"Max."

Max turned toward the deep, bass voice. It belonged to a blond giant with blue eyes. "Jericho?" Max noticed the dark-haired man beside him. "Eli?"

"Good to see ya, man," Eli drawled in his Southern accent

"'Good to see ya, man,'" Jericho mimicked. "It's damned great to see you!" The blond man stepped forward, his arms outstretched.

Max launched backward, shaking his hair into his face. "No hugs," he grumbled. Out of the corner of his eye, he saw Jericho stop in his tracks, but Max refused to look at his face again. "I don't … do that," Max finished lamely. He closed his eyes and mentally counted down. *And they'll notice my face in three, two…*

"Holy God, what did they *do* to you?" Eli stepped forward and gripped Max's chin, forcing him to raise his face. "Shit," Eli breathed at the same time Jericho whistled low.

Max jerked his chin out of Eli's hold and growled, the sound echoing throughout the blind in the now uncomfortable silence. "I'm fine," Max said.

"Yeah, I'll bet," Jericho said softly.

Max glared at him through his shaggy hair. Jericho looked as though he wanted to say something more but after a few moments held out placating hands. "Okay, you're fine."

A derisive sound escaped the Humvee, and Max jerked around to find Luke staring at him, not even trying to hide the fact that he'd made the noise. Max frowned at him and spoke to Eli and Jericho without looking. "Get us out of here," Max commanded. "The guards could stumble upon us at any moment."

"Actually," Jericho said, "there's really no rush."

Max froze. "No rush?" Had he somehow mistaken the definition of those words? "They'll capture us again!"

"There are, maybe, five guards left," Eli said. "I think that's what our intel said. We don't know for sure why you three were separated from us, but we think you were hidden here in case shit hit the fan back in the States. If the military didn't know you existed, they couldn't take you away. But now Taylor's dead, and they won't have the manpower to locate us and come after us. Funding got cut; everyone left. Operation: Middle of the Garden, as we knew it, is done."

Max's mouth went dry. "Taylor's dead?" After the five of them—Eli, Jericho, Oliver, Luke, and Max—had found the Garden of Eden while on tour in Afghanistan, Major Taylor had coerced them into testing the fruit from the Tree of Eternal Life for the army so their families would be told they were dead and then be compensated rather than *just* told they were dead.

Eli nodded. "Killed him myself."

Max tilted his head to the side, dreading the understanding that was beginning to dawn. "Taylor's dead and no one's left?" His revenge. God, what would his purpose be now?

The smile on Eli's face slipped. "Uh—"

"Forget it," Max said quickly, wiping all emotion away before he could collapse under the pressure behind his heart. "I don't want to be here a second more." Without another word, Max crawled into the back of the Humvee with his men and slammed the door behind him. Jericho and Eli hopped into the front along with a male angel Max had never seen before. Max did a double take, viewing the new angel's long, dark hair, broad shoulders, and vicious countenance before forcing himself to act as though this new angel were no big deal. As though Max saw fucking *angels* every day. As they drove away, abandoning the blind, Max knew he did not need to look back for *his* angel.

Though he couldn't see her because she sat on the side of his good eye, he could feel her right beside him.

Chapter Seven

Operation: Middle of the Garden Headquarters in Washington, D.C.

She could not leave him. She couldn't leave him right after he'd squeezed her tight for comfort upon gaining his freedom. She couldn't leave him when he saw his friends for the first time in nine years and his attention was directed away from her. She couldn't leave him when they drove off, and he did not even look back to see if she was still there. She couldn't leave him when they boarded a plane and flew to the States. And she could not leave him now that he was safe and sound inside the Operation: Middle of the Garden military compound that housed the Trees that had been supplanted from the Garden of Eden.

More than anything, Anahita wished she could leave him. And more than anything, she was glad that she couldn't. She had felt many forbidden emotions over the centuries of her existence, but she had rarely felt confusion. She could safely say she did *not* care for it.

She stood, now in the center of an enormous, domed room, watching with hesitant fascination as the sunlight filtering in through the glass of the dome picked up red highlights in her Temptation's hair. He stared, with a stiff back, at the Tree of Eternal Life and the Tree of the Knowledge of Good and Evil where they grew in the center of the room.

The Trees were gorgeous. Their branches stretched upwards and outwards, nearly brushing the glass of the dome. They grew on a much larger scale than typical trees, and their branches were heavy with fruit: glittering gold for the Tree of Eternal Life and swirling black and white for the Tree of the Knowledge of Good and Evil.

Most of the humans in the room were entranced by the Trees, staring at them as they walked past, and Luke and Max were no different. Eli and Jericho had brought the men straight here upon arriving at the compound, and Luke and Max had planted their feet here at the Trees' trunks and had been staring up into the branches ever since.

Anahita glanced at the Trees for a moment. Though, until very recently, she could have viewed them from the heavens when they were still in the Garden of Eden, she had never taken the opportunity to do so. The Trees were reviled among her kind. They were a physical manifestation of the Most High's partiality to a weaker race.

But she wasn't focused elsewhere because of that. She was focused elsewhere because when her Temptation and the Trees were in the same room, it was no contest as to what snagged her attention.

Heavens, he is magnificent. Anahita sighed as she eyed his broad shoulders and muscled back. She feared she was growing obsessed with this part of his body. Was that normal? Was a woman supposed to lust after a man's back? It did not seem normal to her. She had heard of women lusting after a man's backside—and Max was blessed in that area, as well—but Anahita could not tear her eyes from their current target.

To her right, Jayden cleared his throat and glowered in her direction, obviously not knowing exactly where she was since she was invisible, but able to determine her location based on her thoughts. Her lascivious, lascivious thoughts.

Stop reading my mind, brother, Anahita projected toward him, a tinge desperately.

"Stop eye-raping the human," Jayden said.

Eye-raping? Jayden was speaking more and more like a human every moment, it seemed.

Eli and Jericho turned and looked at Jayden with furrowed brows, and Anahita felt herself flush even though they couldn't see her and didn't know why Jayden had spoken so oddly.

They can hear you! Anahita thought toward him.

"Of course they can," Jayden said simply. When Eli's and Jericho's brows crinkled further, Jayden smiled broadly and waved at them with a wiggle of his fingers. Eli and Jericho glanced at each other before Eli shrugged and they both turned back.

A finger wave. Jayden, terror of the skies for millennia, had finger waved at a pair of humans. *You are much changed*, Anahita projected.

"I could say the same about you," Jayden said. This time, his one-sided conversation went unmarked by those around them.

Anahita closed her eyes, feeling every inch of censure in Jayden's words. And yet, even with her eyes closed, she could see the form and shape of Max's back against the insides of her eyelids, and a fine tremor shook her limbs.

Jayden *tsked*, and Anahita opened her eyes.

"Jayden!"

The Fallen angel's name had come from behind them, and Anahita turned her head to see who had spoken the two syllables with what was the equivalent of a vocal caress. In her peripheral vision, Anahita saw Jayden spin around. The Fallen's hand came up to his chest, where it rubbed a circle, and he breathed, "My Grace." And then he opened his arms wide.

Anahita watched in wonder as a very curvy, short human with a riot of curly, red hair raced across the distance between them and launched herself into Jayden's open arms. Jayden wrapped himself around her, and her fingers threaded through his hair, and then they were kissing so passionately, Anahita wondered how they were even breathing.

Anahita's mouth was wide open, and she closed it and turned away just as she saw what was definitely Jayden's tongue thrust into the human's mouth. Anahita ruffled the feathers of her wings self-consciously, and she caught Eli and Jericho glancing over their shoulders. They looked at Jayden and his human for maybe a second before Eli rolled his eyes, Jericho grinned, and they looked back at the Trees.

Apparently, this massive display of affection was a common occurrence.

With a heavy groan, Jayden broke the kiss, and out of her peripheral vision, Anahita could see him staring into his human's eyes.

"I missed you so much," the Temptation—Grace—said softly.

"*Missing you* does not begin to describe how I felt being apart from you," Jayden grumbled, rubbing his nose against hers.

And you accuse me of changing, Anahita projected while still trying hard not to stare at them.

"Only for the better," Jayden said.

Anahita saw Grace straighten in Jayden's arms. "Whom are you talking to?" she asked.

"Anahita," Jayden said absently, more focused on wrapping one of Grace's curls around his finger.

Grace pushed away from Jayden. "Your sister?"

Anahita was shocked when Jayden pouted. *Pouted.* "Well, not technically. We do not share the same parents, but we belonged to the brethren together, so saying so is not false." He attempted to pull Grace back into his arms, but the woman was scanning the area around Anahita.

"Where is she? I want to meet her."

Had Jayden told his Temptation of Anahita? It appeared so, if she knew enough to suspect Anahita was both nearby and invisible. Why would she want to meet her?

"Surely we can say hello to each other properly first," Jayden protested, fisting his hands at his sides.

Grace laughed and rose to the tips of her toes to brush a kiss across Jayden's lips. "Soon enough."

Jayden grasped Grace's arms to keep her from moving away and said loudly, "Anahita, show yourself."

Anahita groaned and turned her eyes to her own Temptation, who, for the first time since arriving in this room, was no longer staring at the Trees. Max's mismatched eyes were now focused on Jayden and with such attention that he had not shaken his hair into his face yet to hide his scar. Anahita used the opportunity to drink in his features. His brow was furrowed, and something akin to anger crossed his face and then was gone. Anahita got the impression he did not like Jayden ordering her about. She shifted her weight back and forth and crossed her arms over her stomach before forcing them to straighten at her sides once again. And then, like the last time Max had discovered her presence through the use of his eye, Anahita lost her grip on invisibility.

Her sudden appearance snagged the attention of Eli, who turned quickly. "Whoa," he said. In the next second, his face was a blank mask, and he was reaching for his gun.

Anahita wasn't sure exactly what happened next, but Max's glorious back was suddenly all she could see. She blinked to discover that her Temptation now stood in front of her. She peeked around his shoulder; he held his hands out in a placating manner toward Eli, who pointed his gun toward the ground rather than toward them.

Jayden dropped his arms from his Grace and moved to stand between Eli and Max. "You will not harm her," Jayden said softly.

Eli's gun shook slightly. "She's one of the good guys?" he asked.

Jayden said *yes* at the same time Max said *no*.

Everyone in hearing distance turned to look at Max, who was still standing in a defensive position in front of her.

"Uh," Eli said, "you're defending a bad guy?"

"No," Max said shortly, stepping out from in front of her and crossing his arms over his chest.

Jericho seemed to be interested in something else entirely. "*How* do you know she's a bad guy?" he asked Max.

Max looked at Anahita momentarily, swallowing hard before looking back at Jericho. "I don't really," he said. "I mean ... both *good* and *evil*..." Max tapered off and self-consciously but deliberately brushed his fingers over his scarred eye.

Jericho's eyes widened. Apparently Max's stuttered words meant something to him. "Oh, wow," Jericho said on a breath. "We have a lot to discuss."

"She's not a bad guy," Jayden said gruffly, glaring at Max.

Max raised his chin and glared right back. "She's here to kill us."

For some reason, Anahita wanted to bury her face in her hands. A muscle ticked in Jayden's jaw though he did not refute Max's statement.

Eli and Jericho now stared at Anahita again. Eli sighed. "Another one," he muttered in an offensively dismissive way while holstering his firearm.

Jericho looked at Max. "Is she yours?" he asked softly.

"The One," Max ground out, casting her a dark glance as though this were her fault. "Mine, yes." Before pride could take hold in her heart, Max continued, "Unfortunately."

"Actually," Anahita found herself saying out of frustration, "he's *mine*." They all turned to look at her, and she felt blood heat her cheeks. "My, uh, mission," she mumbled.

Jayden made a noise that sounded like a snort.

You are not helping.

The infuriating Fallen shrugged and smirked.

She wanted that look off his face. *I delivered your humans' friends. Now, deliver the sword, Jayden.*

Mission accomplished. Jayden's face grew grave.

"Grace," Anahita said, turning to the red-haired human, "it was nice to meet you." Grace opened her mouth to speak, but Anahita continued over her, "If you will all excuse us now, Jayden and I have something to discuss."

"Yes," Jayden agreed. "It appears we do." Jayden kissed Grace's forehead, not answering the question in her eyes. "I will be back soon," he whispered to her. Then he turned his green eyes upon Anahita. "Come with me, Anahita."

She made to follow Jayden's direction, but then hidden drives within her stalled her feet. She looked over at Max, her brow furrowing.

Jayden, of course, read her thoughts. "He will not go anywhere, and you are not leaving him."

Max's face grew thunderous at Jayden's words, but he did not say or do anything to refute them. With a deep breath and a mental reassurance that Max would be here when she returned, Anahita got her feet to follow the direction Jayden indicated for their "discussion."

It was not until the soft click of a door sounded behind her that Anahita saw Jayden had taken her into an office. His, if the nameplate on the desk were to be believed. This new, human-friendly Jayden took some getting used to. Before Grace, he had despised humans in the way of all the brethren. Perhaps even more, since his mission to guard the Trees from human interference kept him from battling.

"Do you work for the humans now in their experimentation with the Trees?" Anahita asked. The touch of disbelief tinging her voice sounded like scorn, which, she realized, could only help her case. Jayden would wonder if Anahita did *not* act as though she despised humans.

Rather than get defensive, Jayden surprised her yet again. "I do. They are most resourceful. It is a joy to me to help them."

"Hmm," Anahita hummed noncommittally. "Well, I am happy for you."

"*Happy?*" Jayden said with a one-sided smile. "Feeling, are we?"

Anahita ruffled her feathers and straightened her posture. "The sword, Jayden. We had a deal."

The smile faded. "We did."

"Then hand it over," Anahita said, frowning.

Jayden shifted his weight from one foot to the other. "Let us just ... talk first."

He wasn't handing it over? "You ... *lied?*" The thought that Jayden would lie had never even entered Anahita's mind. Angels could not lie. Of course, Jayden was Fallen now, but for him to lie—to have fallen *so* low. Anahita swallowed past a lump in her throat.

"No!" Jayden shouted. "I would never—" He cut himself off and thrust the fingers of one hand through his long hair. "This is a mess."

"I do not understand."

Jayden looked at her with heavy eyes. "You promise you will not harm my humans?"

Anahita clenched her fists. "*I* do not lie."

Jayden closed his eyes and sighed. When he opened them again, he was resigned. "Have you allowed your Compulsion to set yet?"

A gleam of understanding lit in Anahita's mind. This worry she could understand. An angel who had allowed his or her Compulsion to set was unstable until the mission of the Compulsion was carried out. If the angel delayed too long, innocents could be harmed when the time on the Compulsion ran out. The angel would carry out the mission blindly, harming anyone in the way.

Though it would show how weak she was, Anahita confessed, "I have not." When Jayden's shoulders relaxed, Anahita felt it necessary to remind him, "But I will. Eventually."

Jayden nodded. He would understand. He had foolishly delayed allowing his Compulsion to set for eight years in regards to his mission to kill the humans he now protected. And the delay had cost him. Once his Compulsion *did* set, he was nearly uncontrollable. "Yes," he said gravely, "you cannot delay long."

Jayden reached over his shoulder and unsheathed the sword that had been hidden by his wings. Anahita had been right: he did still keep it on his person. Millennia of habit was hard to break, and handing over the weapon that had been ever at his side was a sacrifice Anahita would not take lightly.

Her eyes widened as she saw the weapon for the first time since Jayden's Fall. *This* was the notorious flaming sword? The only weapon that could take an immortal's life?

It flamed no more. As Jayden laid it across his open palms and extended it toward Anahita, the metal of the ancient sword did not even gleam. This weapon, forged by the Most High Himself, was ... ordinary.

Anahita felt her throat go dry. "Will it ... will it even *work*?"

Jayden nodded. "I am Fallen, Anahita. Take the sword in your hand."

Anahita tried to ignore the sandpaper-like quality of her tongue and reached out a shaky hand. If this weapon no longer worked according to its purpose, Anahita's mission was doomed before it could begin.

The minute Anahita wrapped her fingers around the hilt of the sword, green and gold flames erupted along the length of the blade. The metal glowed with an otherworldly heat, and an inscription in the ancient language—which read *What the Tree gives, the Sword takes. What the Sword takes, the Tree gives.*—seemed to spark with purpose.

But that was not the most astonishing thing that happened when Anahita grasped the sword. Her Compulsion pushed at her. It knew she had a mission to accomplish and that the weapon in her hand would help her to accomplish it. For the first time since receiving her mission, Anahita felt the pressure to set her mission in stone and allow the countdown to begin. It was *strong*.

Anahita gritted her teeth and pushed it back with all of her might. And then she nearly dropped the sword, for another disparate Compulsion stretched within her. *This* Compulsion, rather than urging her to kill the humans assigned to her, pressed her to protect Max. To Guard him.

"Oh, Lord of the Most High," Anahita muttered, the sword shaking in her hand.

Jayden stepped toward her, his brows crashing together, his hand reaching for her. "What is it?" he asked harshly. How must she look to wrench such a response from her usually stoic brother? "Anahita?"

Her natures. Her cursed dueling natures. She was so ashamed of them, she had never discussed them with anyone. Who knew that each side of her—both Warrior *and* Guardian—would have their own Compulsions? Would someone have been able to tell her to expect this if her own pride had not gotten in the way?

It did not matter now. "No, no," Anahita moaned. She could feel her Compulsions swirling around each other within her— almost as though they were facing off. Her Warrior side pressed her to allow her mission to kill Max to set; her Guardian side begged her to take Max on as her Ward.

Which would win?

"*Anahita!*" Jayden grasped her by her upper arm and pulled her toward one of the armchairs in front of his desk. He exerted pressure until Anahita's knees collapsed beneath her, and she crashed into the plush leather with no grace.

But when he reached for the sword to take it from her, Anahita snapped, "No!" She jerked it out of Jayden's reach, nearly cutting herself in the process.

Jayden's eyes grew wary. "Careful, angel," he said while backing away slowly.

She could barely register the change in Jayden. She could only clench the hilt of the sword and pull the weapon in as close as the flames would allow. She needed it. She had to use it.

She had to protect Max from it.

No! She had to *kill* Max with it. Her head felt as though it would split apart as a jagged shard of pain shot through her.

"Angel, you promised to tell me when your Compulsion set," Jayden said from behind his desk, his hands held out, palms down, in front of him.

Anahita blinked up at him until he came into focus. "Why do you call me *angel?*" she asked, her voice cracking with the force of concentration it took to utter the words.

Jayden straightened, obvious hope flashing across his face. "Are you still—Anahita?"

"Of course I am," Anahita said, frowning. Her hand hurt, and she looked down to see it clenched so hard around the hilt of Jayden's sword that her knuckles blanched white. The flames of the sword had switched from green and gold to red and black. When had that happened?

Both of her Compulsions pressed against her skull again, but the momentary distraction of talking with Jayden gave her the strength she required to push them both back. She imagined forcing them into a chest and locking it.

Immediate relief flooded her, and in that same moment, the sword's flames went back to green and gold.

She heard Jayden push out a breath from across the room. Oh, heaven. She had almost allowed her Compulsion to set. *Without* thinking through her plan first. Whether her Guardian or Warrior side had won was irrelevant. Angels who allowed their Compulsions to rule them in deciding their missions were dangerous.

Jayden's expression softened. "Do not look so shocked, Anahita," he said softly. "Did you think fighting the Compulsion would be easy?" He smiled gently. "You did well."

He had no idea. She did *well?* She was going to be destroyed. If she could not join her Warrior brethren by completing her mission, what good was she? Becoming a Warrior had always been her dream—a dream she wasn't supposed to have but did nonetheless.

And now, one human threatened all of that. Max stood between her and her dream by either leading her to her Fall or, possibly even worse, turning her into a Guardian.

Perhaps she should be grateful that the man who could be her potential downfall had looked at her with complete disgust and spoken cruelly. She had never understood women who were with men who were mean to them. It was not attractive—at least, Anahita did not find it so. Enough women were with these men that maybe they *did* find it attractive.

And she *certainly* had not enjoyed the physical side of their encounter. It had left her more frustrated than she had started and feeling shame—an emotion she did not want to repeat.

Women liked sex? It didn't seem likely to Anahita. She peeked up at Jayden through the fringe of her lashes and considered him in a new light. *Does Grace like sex?*

She didn't realize she had projected the question until Jayden's face grew grave. His lips parted for a moment, and then his teeth clashed together, and he fisted his hands. "Are you sure you do not want me to kill him?" he ground out.

That same shame that had been with her since she'd touched Max lit through her. "*I* will kill him," she muttered, gritting her own teeth when both of her Compulsions reacted to the words.

Just then, she felt herself being summoned by Remiel, the leader of the Warriors. Anahita felt her eyes dart back and forth as the feeling that she needed to meet with the Warrior grew stronger and stronger—until it was nearly a Compulsion all its own. This ability to summon other angels was one of Remiel's gifts and one of the few gifts Remiel revealed to others. The angel was notoriously enigmatic, and many suspected he had myriad gifts from the Most High that he used in secret so as not to reveal any weaknesses.

He did not shy away from using this particular gift, however. Anahita had been summoned by Remiel many times, and never for a heart-warming chat.

"I, uh—" Anahita broke off to clear her suddenly dry throat. "I must leave ... go elsewhere, I mean." They both knew Anahita could not leave, not with Max located in the building. "Is there somewhere private I can go?"

Jayden's gaze grew intent, and Anahita blocked him from her thoughts. He did not need to know Remiel's arrival was imminent. "You will be staying here for a while?"

The very thought struck panic in Anahita's chest. More time with him meant more time to Fall for him. Nevertheless, "Yes."

Jayden nodded. "Then, you will need a room."

Anahita felt her eyes widen. A room? Something of her own? She had never had something to call her own. "Very well then," she said with false calm.

Jayden smiled again, and she knew she had not been as calm as she should have been. He began to walk out of the office, and Anahita knew she was to follow him. As they passed through the main room, Anahita's eyes naturally found Max's form where he was still beneath the Trees, talking in low murmurs to Eli and Jericho while Luke stood at Max's shoulder, nodding along with something Max was saying. At the sight of him, some of the anxiety Anahita had been feeling since leaving his presence loosened. Max's head began to turn in their direction, and Anahita looked away before he could catch her staring at him. Again.

Jayden was speaking and appeared to have been for quite some time. Anahita caught his words in the middle of a sentence. "—is a fully functioning military compound with medical staff, research specialists, and promising young soldiers. The other two Impulse pairs used to stay here at the compound, but both families have moved to houses in consideration of the children. Grace and I still live here, however, so should you need anything, we will be here for you."

Anahita was still puzzling over the sentimental way Jayden had said the world *children* when she noticed they were walking through what appeared to be a barracks. Jayden pressed a palm to a door in passing. "Our quarters," he said, before stopping at the door adjacent. "You can stay here."

Anahita frowned up at him. "You want children?" The invasive question escaped her before she could call it back, and Anahita wished the words had stayed in her head—though that may not have kept them from Jayden's knowledge, either.

Jayden's eyes widened. "It is that obvious?" he asked while rubbing the back of his neck with one hand.

"Jayden, it is forbidden," Anahita said in a low voice, trying to keep the censure from her tone.

One side of Jayden's lips tipped up. "And so is Falling for Temptations. I have already done that. What is to keep me from other forbidden things? I have nothing left to lose and much to gain."

Anahita's frown deepened. Jayden's reasoning made sense in a bizarre way. Yet, to create a Nephilim—it had not been done in millennia, and would not go unmarked by the brethren.

Jayden shifted his weight. "It is not in the works, by any means," he said dismissively. "In the meantime, I greatly enjoy the humans' offspring. They allow Grace and me to care for them frequently, and it makes both of us happy enough for now."

A sudden stab of impatience came with Remiel's next reminder that she was being summoned, and Anahita knew by instinct that Remiel waited for her just beyond this closed door. He was one of the few other angels that also possessed Anahita's gift of teleportation. "Yes, well," Anahita said in what she hoped was a light, lilting voice that did not betray the urgency she felt to meet with her leader. She placed her hand on the doorknob of her quarters. "I will see you later then," she said lamely.

Jayden cocked one eyebrow but nodded. "Yes, later." The sound of a door opening brought both of their attention to Jayden's quarters. Grace stuck her head out into the hall, her riot of red hair catching the light in the hallway and appearing flame-like around her head. A rumbling sound came from the general region of Jayden's chest.

"Much later," he said over his shoulder to Anahita, already walking away from her and toward his Temptation. He never looked back as he playfully pushed the now grinning Grace back into their residence, following her in and closing the door behind them with a resounding boom.

Anahita stared at their closed door for a few heartbeats, an unknown longing weighing in her heart. Then, with a shaky intake of breath, she turned the doorknob and entered the dim interior of her quarters.

Chapter Eight

It took Anahita's eyes no time to adjust to what appeared to be a tiny apartment, with a shadowed, winged form standing in the midst of a smattering of living room furniture.

"You are late." The indictment was delivered in a deep, rumbling voice, but it was delivered emotionlessly. As was to be expected, of course.

Anahita, however, found it impossible to be emotionless at the casually delivered phrase. She felt a wave of what had to be annoyance. It prickled up her spine and bit at her mercilessly. The words, "I did not know we had an appointment," left her mouth before she'd knew they were forming.

As Remiel stepped forward into a shaft of light from the nearby window, she could see that he'd raised one eyebrow, and a sick feeling collected in the back of her throat. Had she just spoken to her superior—the angel who would determine if she would join the Warriors or not—in that disrespectful tone?

"Apologies, brother," Anahita murmured, making sure to keep the sick feeling from tinging her tone. "I am feeling the pressure of the Compulsion. It is ... taxing." Truth—it had to be. However, it was not the whole truth, and she hoped Remiel would not pick up on that.

"Your Compulsion," Remiel said, nodding slowly. "Yes, that is why I am here."

Oh, heaven. This was going to be bad.

Remiel lowered himself into a nearby armchair and then gestured for Anahita to take the couch opposite him.

He was offering her a seat in her own home? Or ordering her to take it—again, in her own home? That Anahita was so proprietary over a space she had just been given was not rational. She could not, however, keep those feelings at bay, and resentment that he would do such a thing moments after she'd been given this boon burned hot in her chest.

And, yet, she walked to the couch and settled into the supple cushions.

She expected him to speak right away, but he stared at her, his blue eyes so cold and lacking calculation that Anahita found herself squirming in her seat. How could he be so calm and so intimidating at the same time?

"I have not set my Compulsion," Anahita blurted into the silence.

Remiel dipped his chin. "This I know."

Silence again. Was it warm in here? Anahita would swear that it was sweltering. "I, uh ... I need some time to organize my ... thoughts first." The words were a chore, each one requiring careful planning.

Remiel tilted his head to the side. "This does not have anything to do with your Temptation."

The words were not spoken as a question, and Anahita knew that was by design. It was quite brilliant, actually, she had to admit. By stating it as though it were a fact, Remiel had made Anahita feel shame at the simple truth that the statement was *not* fact. Thus, she felt an overwhelming desire to reassure Remiel. To explain everything to him. She tamped down that instinct. "Of course it does not," she said firmly, her hands clenching beside her thighs on the couch cushions.

Remiel blinked and steepled his fingers in front of his chin. "Hmm," he hummed.

Compassion was known widely as a tool of the Guardians, but Warriors were not completely devoid of it. Anahita found herself wishing Remiel could have a bit more of it at the moment.

Remiel was known not just for his surplus of gifts, but for the very rare instance of resisting Temptation. Remiel's Temptation had been a woman, and not only had he resisted her, he had literally destroyed her, seemingly with ease. This epic occurrence had taken place much, *much* before Anahita's time, so she did not know firsthand what had happened, but in the whispers among the brethren, Anahita had gathered that Remiel's Temptation had been a very evil woman—one who had broken some of the Most High's most important laws. And Remiel had meted out justice despite what Anahita now knew had to have been great internal struggle.

Max had broken one of the Most High's most important laws as well, and yet, she could not bring herself to do as Remiel had done.

Yet, Anahita reminded herself. It would be done. "I need a small amount of time," Anahita said, raising her chin and leveling Remiel with steady eyes. "I have only just encountered the objects of my mission, and I must make sure I proceed with caution now that more variables are known."

The words were wise, Anahita knew, and not ones Remiel could take exception to. The damage a single angel could do when under the power of a misguided Compulsion was not to be taken lightly.

"You must not wait long," Remiel said after a beat of silence. "This was Jayden's downfall." He rose to his feet, and Anahita craned her neck back to maintain eye contact. "Organize your thoughts quickly, Anahita, and get your mission underway."

"Yes, of course," Anahita said, rising as well so she could feel more on even footing with the imperial angel.

And without another word of encouragement or censure, Remiel vanished. His final words rang through the quiet of the apartment with what felt like increasing urgency, and as though in response, Anahita's Warrior Compulsion rose to the forefront to accept the challenge the other angel had laid out. But then, right on cue, Anahita's Guardian Compulsion beat the Warrior

Compulsion back and nearly convinced Anahita to Guard Max before she was able to get a hold of it.

Suddenly, the thought of organizing her thoughts seemed worlds outside of possible.

•••

Max's ear began to heat against the metal of the door that led to the angel's living quarters. Why he was even here, he had no clue. He'd been with Jericho, who had given him a name for what his eye did. It was called *Knowledge*, and Jericho and his wife, Dahlia, also had the ability, though only through touching one another. Turns out Max had been unintentionally wise to keep his eye's ability from their captors. It would have been exploited in the worst ways.

Jericho had mentioned in passing that Jayden was showing Anahita where she would stay, and after nearly having a coronary at discovering she was *going to stay*, Max had found himself right outside her door.

Where he had promptly heard another man speaking to her in near-whispers. The emotions such a discovery had inspired in him did not bear scrutiny.

Okay, fine, he'd lost his shit a little. But after punching a hole in the wall across from her door, he'd gathered himself enough to listen in on her conversation—a very mature move that he steadily stood by. Especially since it had yielded some very, very interesting intel.

Anahita's little mission of death did not seem to be her own idea. That was ... nice, Max guessed. As was the knowledge that she was hesitant to carry out her mission—at least, that's what he was able to glean from her tone of voice and cryptic answers. Reading other people was not Max's forte. That was more Luke's area of expertise with his covert ops training. Max had never seen a man who could disappear by appearing ordinary the way Luke could—a stunning feat for a red-haired giant. The things people said in front of Luke because they forgot he was even there, if they'd noticed in the first place, were uncanny. And Luke's interpretation of body language and voice patterns was almost a superpower in and of itself.

Did the others know that Anahita was under orders from a mysterious other angel? He remembered that there appeared to be an angel-who-was-not-an-angel in their midst—Jayden. Surely he knew about this in-charge angel. Could Jayden be trusted?

Max had to admit that if Jericho and Eli trusted him, then he was trustworthy. He'd found out that Eli and his "Impulse Mate," as they were called, had a small, infant daughter named Genesis; Jericho and his Impulse Mate, Dahlia, had a baby on the way and a son named Gabriel. If they trusted the angel Jayden to be around their children, Max had no room to protest the guy's trustworthiness.

And, yet, it was not Jericho and Eli who Max wanted to take this new-angel information to first. Years of being cooped up with Luke and Oliver had built up a near-family feel between them all. He could not think of two different men he would want to have his back than them. But he also could not keep this from Jericho and Eli.

Max shuffled around and began to leave the wing of the compound that housed the living quarters. As he passed through the main room with the—Holy God—*Trees* that had changed his life forever, he muttered a soft, "Come with me," to Jericho and Eli where they stood talking. He continued through the room to the medical wing, Jericho and Eli in his wake, following him without question: a move he appreciated.

He paused outside of the closed door of Oliver's hospital-like room and squinted through the metal checkered pattern of the door window to see Luke sitting beside Oliver's bedside, staring at the man's slack face. Oliver was due to wake up in the next few hours, and he was always so disoriented when his eyes first opened. Now those eyes would be opening to a whole new environment. Max knew Oliver could not be alone today. He or Luke needed to be at his side at all times to reassure him when he awoke.

Max sucked in a breath and opened the door, which emitted a soft click. Luke's head snapped around, and he smiled easily at Max. It looked like he was partially forgiven for … *playing* with the angel. But Max's expression must have been grave, because Luke's expression sobered.

Luke's brown eyes flicked over Max's shoulder to where Jericho and Eli stood. "What's wrong?" he asked, a small waver to his voice.

That waver caught Max right in his gut, and he realized he hadn't checked on Luke to see how he was handling all of the recent changes. He needed to step up his caretaking and stop focusing on the angel, who he needed to stay far, far away from anyway. He walked over to Luke's side and squeezed the man's shoulder before turning to the other two men.

"Are you aware that an angel in some sort of position of power is ordering Anahita to kill Oliver, Luke, and me?"

Eli and Jericho shared a loaded glance. "Kind of," Jericho said.

Max raised one eyebrow before he remembered to shake his hair into his face. He turned away from them slightly, showing them his left side and then saying, "Explain."

"Well, we know that she has a mission to kill you," Eli said. "We just didn't know she was under orders from an actual person." Eli shook his head. "Angel," he corrected. "I keep forgetting they're not quite people."

Max's jaw went slack. "How on earth can you forget they're not *people*?" he asked.

Jericho shrugged. "Jayden seems so normal to us now."

"Normal," Max repeated. "The huge man with a robe and wings seems 'normal.'" He dropped his air quotes and had to resist the urge to roll his eyes.

"Grumpy," Luke murmured for Max's ears alone.

Max grunted. Of course he was grumpy. What the hell? Who *wouldn't* be grumpy in his position?

"It's okay," Eli said softly, and Max was reminded that they would have extraordinary hearing just like he and his guys did thanks to the fruit. Max didn't have the good sense to be ashamed of his grumpiness. He didn't have time for good sense right now.

"He *didn't* seem normal to us when he was holding us hostage in the medical wing," Eli continued.

Max's jaw dropped again. "And you're *friends* with this thing?"

Jericho dipped his chin and leveled Max with a no-nonsense look. "Yes."

The single syllable was a challenge, and everyone in the room knew it. Max held out his hands. "Okay," he said carefully. "Obviously a sensitive subject. But *why* are you friends with something that tried to kill you?"

Eli smiled lopsidedly. "For all of his bluster, he's really just a big softy."

Max knew this did not merit a reply. He settled for raising one eyebrow, the pull of skin across his forehead reminding him he was displaying his scar. He resisted hiding his face with all of his might.

"An angel around his—or *her*—Temptation is just about the most conflicted being in existence," Jericho said, pointedly emphasizing the word *her* for Max's benefit, he was sure.

Max grunted, but Jericho was already continuing. "Once Jayden saw Grace, there was no chance he was going to kill us. We knew it, even if he didn't. It was just a matter of waiting him out until he knew it, too."

Max opened his mouth to speak, but Eli cut him off. "The real danger is in the Compulsion. Angels have no free will, so if they fall into their Compulsions, they complete their missions blindly.

It was the only challenge with Jayden, and as we understand it from him, Anahita has not allowed hers to set yet. She's no threat."

Enough. "I disagree with you there," Max said. "You're both overconfident. You've encountered one angel—*one*," he spit out. "To say you know that all angels who encounter their Temptations are no threat is not only naïve, it's damn ignorant, and it could get my men killed."

Eli and Jericho leaned forward simultaneously, but before they could speak, Luke said quietly, "I agree with Max."

All three of their heads snapped to Luke's direction. Max tried to hide his surprise.

"*You* think Anahita's a threat?" Eli asked with both brows launching into his hairline. "The creature you've been following around like a puppy dog since we arrived?"

"Hey, now," Max said, not sure exactly what he was protesting.

"I agree that you don't have enough intel to judge this situation correctly," Luke said, his eyes darting to Max's in what could be described as a guilty move.

Tense silence filled the room. Finally, Jericho sighed. "So, it's two against two in the angel-threat area."

"*Three* against two," Max corrected.

"Oliver's still out," Eli said. Max had fully disclosed the man's situation, and both Jericho and Eli knew what a soft spot Oliver's condition was.

"He's with us," Max said firmly. "Trust me."

Luke nodded his agreement.

Eli blew out all of his air through pursed lips. "Hell, what a clusterfuck."

"It doesn't have to be," Max said. "Luke here," he clapped the man on the back—perhaps a little too roughly, "is the best at collecting intel. *And* he and the angel already seem to have a ... friendship of sorts in the works." And that did not bother Max at all. Fuck no.

And because they'd been imprisoned together for so long and knew each other so well, Luke picked up Max's train of thought right where he left off. "I can find out about this other angel," he said, straightening with the excitement of a new plan of action. "Put feelers out as to her intentions *and* this other guy's intentions. Then, and only then, will I feel comfortable deciding Anahita's not a threat."

Max wanted to take it all back. When he'd developed this plan for Luke to talk to the angel, he hadn't fully comprehended that Luke was going to have to *talk to the angel*. Spend time with her. Alone.

A cold sweat broke out along Max's spine. He had yet to look in a mirror, but he knew there was no contest in the looks department between them. Though Luke had the kind of talent that allowed him to disappear into the walls and keep women from noticing him, if one ever got close enough and Luke let his guard down, they would discover that the red-haired man was freaking attractive in this obnoxious I'll-always-protect-you way that Max just couldn't manage himself. Not even when he had been handsome. Max was the kind of man who put women on edge, and now, with a scar carving up his features, he was the kind of man who repulsed them.

This was a bad idea. Bad, bad, bad. The word pounded through Max's skull, but just as he opened his mouth to call it all off, Eli beat him to the punch.

"That's not a bad plan," he said begrudgingly. He looked at Jericho who nodded his agreement. "But we cannot," Eli continued, returning his attention to Luke and Max, "under any circumstances, let Jayden know. To say he would be ... peeved ... is an understatement."

"I thought you said he was not a threat," Max said.

"Not to *us*," Eli said with an apologetic smile that only tipped one corner of his lips.

Jericho turned toward the door, but then turned back just as quickly. "You should probably know," he said, looking directly at Max, "that Jayden can read thoughts. Sooo," he drew the word out, "lusting after the angel he considers a sister in his presence is probably not a good idea."

Max ran a hand through his hair. "Fucking great."

"We're leaving now so we won't know the plan and Jayden won't get it from our thoughts, but you should avoid him until we have the information we need since hiding your thoughts takes some practice." With that final directive, Jericho and Eli exited the room, leaving Max and Luke alone with Oliver.

Luke wasn't quite meeting Max's eyes, and Max knew Luke well enough to guess that it had something to do with the angel. Alarm sprang through him instead of just mere annoyance. Just how hung up on the angel *was* Luke?

Max cleared his throat, which brought Luke's eyes to his face. Max didn't try to hide his scar this time, feeling more comfortable with Luke than all of the new faces he'd seen since they'd arrived here at the compound. That he'd ever felt the need to hide it from Luke now seemed laughable. The man had been there from the beginning. Hell, maybe Max should do the right thing and let Luke have a chance at the angel. He deserved it, and he'd be much better to her than Max could be.

Upon having the wayward thought, every fiber of Max's being rebelled against the idea. Max clapped his lips closed around the *She's mine* that threatened to burst from his chest. Instead, he managed a barely civil, "Do we need to talk about something?"

Luke's eyes shifted to the left, and his unease was palpable. When Luke opened his mouth to speak, Max felt something heavy land in his stomach, because the look on Luke's face said he definitely wanted to "talk about something," and Max probably wasn't going to like it. But it was almost worse when Luke closed his mouth and shook his head, his shaggy red hair swishing around on his forehead. "No, man," he said in a gravelly voice that rivaled Max's own. "Nothing we need to talk about."

Max shook his head. *Yeah right.*

Luke sighed and ran a hand through his ragged, knotted hair. "Okay, if I'm going to do this talking to the angel thing…" He paused and looked at Max as though asking if he was still sure this was the path he wanted them to take. Max nodded, albeit reluctantly, and Luke continued, "Then I need to get cleaned up. Get back in my game so I'm as nonthreatening as possible. Cut this mop of hair off and shave."

At this statement, Max's eyes drifted to the en-suite bathroom at the other side of Oliver's room. His first shower in years. He desperately wanted one. The thought, though, was damned depressing. He'd get in the shower, get clean, and still come out one ugly son-of-a-bitch. *Clean* wasn't going to help him any.

Luke looked at Max fully for the first time since Eli and Jericho left. "Do you want me to cut your hair, too?"

Max had taken two quick steps backward before he caught himself and halted. The abhorrence Max had felt at the suggestion had been swift and surprising. The idea of having his face fully exposed … He couldn't prevent the shudder that wracked his body.

Luke's face fell and blanched simultaneously, and Max felt a new flare of panic that he was so discomposed as to freak his very dear friend out over something as simple as *Do you want a haircut?*

"Max," Luke said softly, reaching toward him. "Man, it's okay. You're okay now."

Max shook his head once and felt a muscle tick in his cheek that matched the pressure between his molars. "I'll never be okay," he muttered before he could stop himself. At least if he always expected the worst, he'd never be caught off guard again by life's little fuck-yous. Luke looked as though he wanted to speak again, but Max cut him off. "Go ahead and do your thing. I'll stay here with Oliver until he wakes up. Maybe I'll catch a shower." *Try to do something to make myself more presentable.*

Luke's brows drew together in the center, but he nodded and left the room without another word. Max fought down the urge to follow him out into the hall and warn him to remember that Anahita was his.

The silence in the room was oppressive, and Max couldn't stand still in it for long. With one quick glance at Oliver's still form on the bed, Max decided it was time to face the music, so to speak.

He walked to the bathroom and turned around immediately upon entering to shut the door so he could avoid the mirror above the sink. As he psyched himself up for his first glimpse of himself since the scar, he turned to the shower stall, opened the glass door, and twisted the knob all the way over to hot.

He listened to the ceramic sound of the water hitting the stall for several moments before he acknowledged that if he waited much longer, the steam from the shower would obscure the mirror, and he wouldn't get to see himself for a longer stretch of time. And while that thought was tempting, Max didn't think that he could ratchet up his courage again.

Max let his head hang down as he shuffled around to where the sink was. He walked forward on dead feet, and when he arrived at the sink, he gripped the sides with both hands and leaned forward as some of the strength abandoned his legs. With a shuddering sigh, Max raised his head and met his reflection.

He froze. His breath abandoned him, and stars dotted the horrific vision before him. Steam began to fog the mirror over, but just before Max couldn't see himself anymore, he caught the sight of a tear tracking down the ravaged skin of the ugliest face Max had ever seen.

He raised a hand to his face and touched the droplet with disbelieving fingertips. He drew it away again and stared in horror at the sign of weakness. Weakness he had promised himself he would never encounter again.

With a snarl, his fist launched forward and shattered the mirror. Glass fell down and splintered further around his bare feet, and without giving the broken shards any thought, Max turned and stalked over them to the shower, shedding his clothes as he went.

Chapter Nine

Gathering my thoughts. Gathering my thoughts.

Anahita sat in her living room and attempted to do not only what she had told Remiel she'd planned on, but what he had *ordered* her to do. Her thoughts were proving elusive. At least, the thoughts she was *supposed* to be gathering were proving elusive. Certain other thoughts were proving to be present in abundance.

She ran her fingertips along the fine leather of the sofa on which she sat and tried to allow herself to feel the joy she'd first felt at discovering she was being given her own space to live in. But that joy was long gone.

Max—her brave, wounded, stalwart Max—was going to die, and Anahita was going to deliver the blow. And while that thought appeared in her mind every few seconds, it interrupted a senseless stream of other thoughts that were preventing her from organizing herself and allowing her Compulsion to set.

Namely, how close she'd come to finding out how Max's lips tasted. She'd been so close to him—had already been able to taste the skin in the hollow of his neck. She'd only needed to tip her head back and press her lips to his. Would she have been allowed to touch them with her tongue to get a better taste of him? Would he have permitted such a thing, or was she depraved?

She wished she knew more about what happened—what was considered *normal*—between lovers. She had never paid close attention to the humans she'd encountered in such situations because she'd had to be so focused on gaining her Warrior status, such matters had been inconsequential.

Anahita dug her fingertips into the couch and gripped with all of her might as she shoved thoughts of Max and his treacherous lips aside.

Her mission.

Oliver, Luke, Max—who was guiltiest? Who needed to die first? They had all eaten the fruit at the same time and voluntarily— though under heavy pressure—so no seniority ranked one over the other. They had all been imprisoned for the entire duration of their immortality, so none of them had committed certain deeds that would make them more viable as a threat. So, really, it did not seem to matter who died first; they were all equally guilty.

Unfortunately, Anahita was suffering from partiality. No Warrior would ever admit to such a thing. Max—of course she would not want to kill her own Temptation. That was the base of their functions: to Tempt angels away from their callings. Luke, however, Anahita *liked*, which was more than she could say for her cruel Temptation. Luke was sweet. Innocent, but for the grave error of eating of the Tree of Eternal Life. And he had been raised with a healthy respect for the Most High, one that she could not help but admire.

Anahita hung her head and looked at her lap. Why couldn't Max be more like Luke?

Her head snapped up. Thank *God* Max was not more like Luke. One word of kindness from Max, one soft touch, and all would be lost.

A knock sounded from the direction of the door, and Anahita looked toward it and frowned before she remembered this was how humans announced a desire to visit one another. What was she supposed to say? "Come in?"

Despite the fact that the words had come out as a question, the door cracked open and a tall, red-haired man with tortoise-shell glasses peeked in.

"Anahita," he said with a smile. "Hi."

Anahita narrowed her eyes. Did she know this man? As she looked closer, she noticed his eyes crinkled at the corners behind his glasses, just as—"Luke?" she asked, straightening in her seat.

Luke ducked his head and rubbed the back of his neck as he laughed. "Yeah."

Anahita took him in in amazement. His long, shaggy hair was gone. Now he wore the haircut of a businessman. He was clean shaven, and as he entered the room and shut the door behind him, Anahita could see that he was dressed in slacks and a short-sleeved, collared shirt ... a polo shirt, she thought they were called. He certainly looked different. Would Max have undergone a similar transition? How she longed to see him and see for herself.

"I thought I'd come by and check to see how you're settling in," Luke said. Anahita must have been staring at him in silence for quite some time, because Luke shifted from one foot to the other. "Is it alright that I'm here?" he asked.

Anahita straightened and made herself focus. This was good, that Luke was here. Perhaps she could learn about him through conversation and find out where on the chain he should fall in her mission. Now, if she could remember the manners of the humans. "Will you sit down?" she asked, gesturing to the chair across from her that Remiel had vacated earlier.

Luke smiled that easy-going smile once more and made his way over to her where, instead of sitting in the chair she had indicated, he sank down onto the leather sofa beside her. He ducked his head and glanced into her eyes. "Are you okay?" he asked gently. "You seem concerned about something."

Anahita laughed without humor. That was putting it mildly.

"That's putting it mildly, huh?" Luke said, the corner of his lips tipping up.

Anahita jolted in her seat. "I, uh, was just..." Anahita shook her head. "Yes. I guess you could say that."

"Is it anything I can help you with?" he asked, looking so earnest something pulled in Anahita's chest.

She felt herself smile. "No, unfortunately." She had the urge to pat his hand. "It is something I must figure out for myself."

"Hmm," he hummed. His brown eyes seemed to gain warmth, and Anahita had to fight the sudden struggle to unburden herself to him. He just seemed so trustworthy and harmless. "Is there a way you can talk it out without revealing any details?" he asked. "I'm a great sounding board."

Anahita tilted her head. "Sounding board?"

His smile grew sheepish. "Uh, yeah." His hands moved in front of him as he visibly struggled for words. "A person who just kind of listens while you work to figure something out." His hands fell to his lap. "Would that be helpful?"

Anahita smiled. "That would be helpful, yes, but it is a luxury I cannot afford." Why, *why* did she have to kill this man? "I have several constraints on me at present, unfortunately."

Luke's eyes crinkled at the corners a bit. "Is that so?"

Anahita's smile slipped. She got the sudden feeling that she'd just revealed everything she was supposed to keep secret.

Luke's smile once again grew easy. "I may as well tell you that Max overheard a man talking to you in here." He chuckled while Anahita's shoulders tensed. "He sent me to make sure you were okay."

Now that felt like an outright lie. "I doubt that."

Luke chuckled again. "Okay, maybe *I* just wanted to make sure you were okay after he told me." He shrugged. "So, are you? Okay? Is this man anything we need to do something about?"

Anahita felt the urge to laugh herself. As if they *could* do anything to help against Remiel. As she gave in and a soft laugh escaped her lips, she noticed that Luke's eyes crinkled again, and she silently cursed and reminded herself to remain emotionless. The man before her seemed to glean much from little. She hoped she was mistaken in that supposition. "Remiel is perfect," she said. "Not a threat to me at all. In fact, he would never do anything outside of his calling. He's the only one I know who was able to thwart Temptation."

"Thwart?" Luke asked with a smile. "Sounds easy enough. Like resisting hamburgers?" His eyes twinkled. "Maybe not easy enough, come to think of it." He leaned forward. "Burgers are definitely *my* temptation," he said in a conspiratorial tone.

Now Anahita laughed outright, and it felt so good. Had someone ever made her laugh? "No, not like hamburgers," she said. "And not easy at all. He sent her—" Anahita caught herself right before the words left her mouth, and she sobered. "Well," she said, staring at her hands. "It is not my story to tell. However, it is my aspiration."

She looked at Luke again to find that his face was still close to hers after he'd leaned forward to whisper and joke with her. Something in the back of her neck relaxed. Unlike with Max, Luke brought an ease to her. A genuine feeling of closeness without the complications of lust, anger, and shame that seemed to hang over her each time she even thought Max's name.

"You're so beautiful," he whispered, and her tension returned along with her frown. "I wish you were mine," he muttered.

Anahita straightened and sat back from him a little, but not nearly as much as she should have. His words were like a balm to her. She'd had the same thought, after all. She'd mesh much better with Luke than Max. But the Most High must disagree with her, she remembered as she looked into Luke's kind eyes. For it was *Max* who was her Temptation, not this man before her. And, as Luke's fingers reached forward and brushed a strand of hair from her cheek, she noticed the marked lack of any flare of heat—heat that would be an inferno if it were Max's fingers reaching toward her face.

"He doesn't deserve you," Luke said as his fingers brushed across her cheek and moved to tuck the curl behind her ear. It was such a familiar gesture, and Anahita felt her first burst of unease. This didn't feel right. Almost like a betrayal of all things.

Yet, still, Anahita did not move away. Her cursed curiosity was striking again. She knew from the intent way Luke was now focusing on her lips that he was considering kissing her. And Anahita had so wondered about kissing. Max would *never* look at her this way. Would probably never even kiss her—he seemed to despise her with such vigor.

When Luke's eyes widened behind his glasses, Anahita realized that she'd said at least part of her thoughts aloud. What was *wrong* with her? Angels were never this indiscreet!

"I could help you with that, you know," Luke said softly and urgently. "If you really want to know what it's like."

He was leaning in closer as he spoke, and that was when Anahita knew she'd crossed a line. She really, truly liked Luke, but even with her inexperience, she knew that Luke liked her in a different way, *and* that he had delicate feelings. As Luke's lips softened, she recognized that she was in a mess.

•••

Why was he doing this?

Max watched his feet as they inexplicably took him down the hall, away from Oliver's unconscious form so close to regenerating. He had a feeling they were taking him to the angel.

Ah, hell. Who was he kidding? He *was* walking to the angel's quarters. To interrupt Luke as he did what he did best. Like he didn't trust his friend.

He *didn't* trust his friend.

The realization struck him painfully, and guilt flared behind it. Max didn't know of a person more trustworthy than Luke.

But something primal roared within him whenever he thought about Anahita. He was no more in control of his feelings for her than he had been of his situation in prison. And, honestly, the lack of control over his feelings was much, *much* worse than his lack of control in prison. He'd gotten through his imprisonment by assuring himself that he'd never be naïve again. No, his rose-colored glasses were shattered beyond repair, and, yet, here he was stalking down the hallway toward an angel he didn't want but somehow needed.

He was resentful as hell.

He felt the eyes of Eli, Jericho, and especially Jayden as he walked through the main room of the compound. He pointedly ignored them. If they spoke to him, he did not know what he would do or say that might be embarrassing, so not making eye contact was his only recourse.

He shook his head as he neared the angel's doorway; this was the second time he'd come here uninvited and with some half-cocked idea of "claiming his territory"—a sentiment he was beginning to realize the angel resented if her reaction to him saying she was his in the main room was any indication.

As he stalled in front of the angel's door, he frowned. When he'd been here before, he'd had no trouble hearing the other man's voice through the door. And that had been a low-volume conversation.

He couldn't hear anything now.

For the first time since leaving Oliver's side on this stupid, *stupid* mission, Max wondered if his concern was actually merited.

Yours, the Voice whispered to him. Max jolted. The Voice had not spoken to him since telling him Anahita was his One. Its sudden reappearance was both acknowledgement that Max should be worried, and the prod he needed to act.

He swallowed hard as his hand reached for the doorknob and turned—it was unlocked. The door swung inward with barely a sound, which seemed to mock the volatile effect of what Max saw.

Luke had his fingers in Max's angel's hair. *In her hair.* The hair that was as smooth as silk and smelled of lilies. But what nearly sent Max to his knees was the fact that Luke's lips were a scant breath away from the angel's, and getting closer by every thundering heartbeat in Max's chest.

Something in the back of Max's mind exploded, sending sharp shrapnel through every thread of affection Max held for Luke.

"I am going to kill you," Max said calmly.

He was still present enough to notice that both Anahita and Luke stiffened on the couch, and that Anahita launched herself away from Luke, her body hitting the arm of the sofa with an audible thud. But Luke simply sat there; his usually kind face was defiant, and his eyes flashed behind the glasses he wore in order to appear non-threatening to targets. It was that defiance that launched Max into action.

His boots pounded the floor and his fingers wrapped around Luke's neck, hauling the man to his feet. Anahita's gasp fell on deaf ears as Max's blood roared through them, blocking out all other sounds. "Anahita is *mine!*" Max roared into Luke's reddening face. "Not yours," he continued. "*Never yours.*" He threw Luke to the floor, and the man skidded a couple of feet, his eyes never leaving Max's.

"Don't you think that's for her to decide?" Luke rasped, his hand coming up to rub the red marks Max's fingers left behind.

"No!"

Anahita spluttered from her position on the couch and launched herself to her feet, and for the first time since seeing them together, Max tried to rein in his runaway temper. He could only do so—and, still, almost totally ineffectually—by maintaining eye contact with Luke. And to Max's further ire, Luke smiled wryly, the message clear: Max was digging his own grave without Luke's help.

"Fine," Max gritted out, bracing himself and turning to face the angel. Her face was twisted with a range of emotion, but anger and a hint of shame vied for the place of prominence. "You were going to *kiss* him?" he spit out. Immediately, he cringed at the level of hurt the simple question contained.

Anahita apparently heard it too, much to his horror, because her twisted face relaxed and the anger blanched away. Her hands twisted in front of her, and she looked down at them. "N-no."

"You ... *wanted* to kiss him?" *Please, God*, he found himself thinking, *let her say no*. He could feel the tension radiating from Luke on the floor as the red-haired man waited for the same answer that would either give Max back his breath or steal it forever.

"I ... wanted *a* kiss," Anahita said in halting syllables, her eyes still focused on her clenched fingers.

Luke hissed in a breath in the silence that followed the angel's declaration, and the man's disappointment was heavy in the air. But Max could also feel Luke's reluctant surrender.

"Get out," Max said. His eyes were still locked with Anahita's, but no one in the room was fooled as to whom he addressed.

With a soft groan, Luke struggled to his feet, and Max felt his first stab of regret that he'd struck his closest friend and ally. He bit back the apology that formed on his tongue, however. There was no need to get crazy.

As Luke shuffled toward the door and closed it behind him, Max clenched and unclenched his hands, hoping the constant motion would keep him from grabbing the angel to his chest and going primal on her.

A kiss. His angel wanted to experience a kiss and, apparently, was willing to go to someone else to do so.

The fact that he had not met one of her needs bit at him. But at the same time, panic ate at him, too. He'd vowed to himself that he would maintain an emotional distance from this creature. He was *never* going back to the place where he trusted people not to hurt him.

A kiss was ... *intimate*. Breathing for each other. Tasting each other. Could he kiss her and keep distance?

He brought his eyes to hers and looked through his lashes, convincing himself it did not quite count as eye contact this way. His mind brought forth the image of Luke leaning into her, his lips about to touch hers, and Max decided: It didn't matter if it was difficult to maintain distance. He was going to kiss her.

He raised his chin and locked eyes with her for the first time since entering the room, and he was again reminded that the angel was both good and evil. With this reminder came another: His face was carved up like a pumpkin. It was because of his twisted eye that he was even able to get a read on the angel at all.

He'd washed himself, had trimmed his beard a little, but not enough that it did not still hide a good deal of his scar. With all of these changes, his hair was just as long as it had been, and now, with a mind of its own, his hand rose and shuffled his hair over his lacerated eye. Immediately, the knowledge that the angel was good and evil disappeared. Instead, the very ordinary and instinctive knowledge that he wanted this angel bloomed within him, suffocating even his shame at his looks.

He kept his hand over the ruined half of his face and moved toward Anahita. Her head tipped back as she watched him approach, and he saw the pupils of her eyes expand and take over the beautiful blue.

When they were toe to toe, Max whispered, "Let's get one thing straight, angel." His words rustled the tighter, golden waves that surrounded her face, and he was so captivated by the sight that he forgot what he was going to say. He shook his head to clear it and narrowed his good eye at her. "You got any needs, *I* meet them. Understand?"

She said nothing, and unease itched at the base of Max's spine. She was staring at him so hard. Could she see beneath his hand to the horror it covered? She tilted her head to the side and spoke. "Does the same paradigm apply to you?" she asked.

His head rocked back, and he felt his brows crash down over his eyes. A million retorts perched on his lips: *No!* and *It's none of your damn business!* among them. What came out was a breathless, "Do you want it to?"

Fuck. He wanted to call the words back. He did *not* know that question had been brewing in there.

With her head still tilted to the side, Anahita smiled softly. He saw her hand move, and the next thing he knew, she'd placed her open palm over the hand that still covered his eye. "Yes," she whispered. Her fingers tightened over his, and she began to pull his hand away from his face.

A ragged noise nearly choked him, and the muscles in his arm tensed as he fought to keep his hand in place. "No," he said roughly.

Anahita's hand stilled. Her smile slipped, and disappointment filled her eyes. Her hand dropped to her side once more, and she broke eye contact, staring at a spot over Max's left shoulder.

He felt the absence of her gaze, but schooled himself not to react. This is what he wanted. What he *needed*. Distance.

With his free hand, he reached up and grasped Anahita's chin with his thumb, turning her face. Her eyes crashed back to his, and he could see himself in them as they widened. He looked pathetic: his fingers sprawled over most of his face, his visible eye desperate. He wanted to shrivel up and crouch in a corner to lick his wounds. Instead, he whispered, "A kiss. You want, I deliver."

Her lips parted, and her eyes darted down to his mouth. Perfect. *Here goes nothing.* He lowered his head slowly, giving her plenty of time to understand what was happening.

His grip on her chin tightened as her breaths crossed his lips. It dawned on him how badly he wanted to do this when that grip trembled slightly. All the more reason to distance himself. He closed his eyes so he wouldn't see her and crossed the remaining distance needed to press their lips together.

A thousand thoughts exploded like stars in his mind. *Soft.* Her mouth was so damned soft. And warm. *Comforting,* of all damn things, while at the same time revving his engine so fucking much he thought he would die if he was not inside her in the next handful of moments.

Their lips were barely touching.

Distance!

She gasped, and the action pulled him further into her, interlocking their mouths so that the tip of his tongue got the briefest taste of her lush bottom lip.

His hand fell from his face.

Chapter Ten

Anahita's mind reeled. Was that his *tongue* brushing across her bottom lip?

So, tasting each other this way *was* acceptable. At least, it was acceptable between Max and her, apparently. That single, velvet caress of his tongue across the sensitive skin of her lip was going to be her undoing, for that action made her want to commit a dozen more actions: embrace him, press her breasts into his chest, feel him between his legs again, return the lick.

It was too many ideas at once, and her mind grasped on the easiest of those at this moment: return the lick.

Anahita tilted her head and jumped when her nose bumped into his. Heat flooded her cheeks. That wasn't supposed to have happened, was it? Most High, she was an idiot.

"'S okay," he muttered against her lips. And then he grasped her face with both of his hands and tilted it the way she had been aiming to do so herself.

That was when she realized he'd dropped his hand from covering his face. Her eyes popped open. She wanted to *see* him. To see all of him. The few glimpses of his face he'd afforded her since entering the room had been tantalizing to the extreme: a groomed beard, hair that was clean and looked so soft.

With her eyes now open, she could see the scar that he'd attempted to hide from her. His eyes were closed, and the scar crossed his face uninterrupted by the glowing eye that saw so much. He had thick lashes for a man, and they rested against the skin right beneath his eyes.

He was beautiful, and at the same time, he was not. That scar prevented him from being pretty—which, from this close, Anahita could see he had been before his injury.

And he took her breath away.

Physical longing panged low in her belly, and her eyes slid closed once more. She could not look at him and keep her composure. She was not sure she could keep her composure *now*.

Max was pressing his lips to hers again, and when she felt that same, wet lick along her bottom lip, she was reminded of her plan to return the favor. His top lip nestled between hers, and she slid her tongue over her teeth and touched the tip to his skin.

Mint. Smooth as silk. As addicting as she had feared.

Her lungs felt too full, and she breathed out all of her air, not realizing it would enter his mouth. She felt his chest billow out as he took her air into his own lungs, and she grew dizzy at the headiness of something that had been in her body entering his.

She licked him again, this time less tentatively, running her tongue from one side of his lip to the other. Some deep, rough noise sounded from his gut, and the fingers against her face spasmed, gripping her tightly before they relaxed once more.

Oh, no. None of that. She liked him desperate for what she was doing to him. That noise, that flex of his fingers—they had made her feel powerful and like she knew what she was doing for the first time since clapping eyes on her Temptation.

She opened her lips wider and lapped his top lip into her mouth to bite at it with her teeth, rolling it back and forth and sucking on the flavor of his skin.

Max jerked back, snatching his lip from her teeth so quickly she did not have the chance to loosen her bite. Her eyes flew open, and worry crowded out her heartbeat, causing it to hasten. She had probably just hurt him.

He was staring at her, his brows drawn together and almost meeting in the middle. His brown eye and golden eye darted over her face almost quicker than she could track, and she could see that his top lip was red and swollen.

She had slipped up. Done something untoward. Horror flooded just beneath the surface of her skin, bringing with it an almost unbearable heat.

And then, Max's eyes slid closed almost lazily, and he sucked his own top lip into his mouth. She could see his jaw moving in a way that could only mean he was nibbling on it, just as she had done. His mouth opened once more, and he breathed, "Oh, *fuck.*"

The next thing she knew, she was in his arms, crushed against his chest, and his mouth was upon hers with a force she had not known was okay but was thrilled to find out was allowed. His lips pried hers apart, and his tongue thrust into her mouth, running into her own tongue and tangling with it before pulling it back into his mouth where he sucked on it hard.

Every muscle in Anahita's body simultaneously clenched and went liquid, and she pulled her arms out of the embrace where they were pinned to her sides so that she could slide them around his shoulders, her fingers seeking the hair she just had to touch.

He continued to suck on and caress her tongue, showing her by example how to thrust and parry with his, but just as her fingers reached the nape of his neck, his arms abandoned their crushing hug. His hands clasped her wrists like manacles and pulled them from his shoulders to behind her back where he gripped them together with one of his hands, rustling the feathers of her wings while doing so in such a delicious way that it almost distracted her from the fact that he'd just prevented her from touching him.

She pulled her wrists apart, trying to release herself, but his grip held. She could force it to give way, but instinctively knew such an action would end the kiss here and now, and she could not bear such a consequence. She let him restrain her.

For now.

His fingers clenched and unclenched on her wrists, and just as she was wondering where his free hand was, she felt it wander over the feathers of one wing. A moan was wrenched from her chest so loudly, she heard it echo throughout the room. It was so embarrassing, she was preparing to pull her lips from his.

But then he whispered against her lips, "You like that?" and did it again. So, obviously, her moans got her rewards. She relaxed again and leaned into his chest with hers—the only way he seemed to allow her to touch him, for he clenched her wrists once more and then used them to push the small of her back, pressing her into his body more fully.

Her body was reminded that it had only been a handful of hours, a full day maybe, since Max had worked her up to the point of lunacy and then left her body aching. It now rushed back to meet the point at which it had been left, and she moaned again as her breasts grew full to the point of aching against his chest and heat flooded the juncture of her thighs.

She felt his hand clench in the fabric of her robe next to her shoulder. His lips drifted from hers to her cheek, and then her neck, and Anahita thought she would die if he didn't finish things this time. "Max," she muttered, tipping her head back to allow him better access to her neck. "You can't—" Her words jumbled in her throat. "Please don't do what you—"

His kisses slowed on her neck, and she thought she would choke. He rested his forehead on her shoulder. "I won't," he said roughly. "I promise."

In her panic, she wasn't sure what he meant. Was he stopping now? His words could mean that. She didn't want him to stop. At all. That panic crawled up her throat as she said, "Max?" To her horror, her voice cracked on the simple syllable.

With his head still pressed into her shoulder, he took in a gigantic, shuddering breath and muttered something to himself that she couldn't quite hear but sounded like, "Distance." Then he turned his head, and she could feel his breaths on the still damp skin of her neck. Was his breathing faster than it normally was? His lips brushed upon her pulse point, and she realized that not only was *she* breathing just as fast as he was, her pulse was racing beneath his mouth. Lust had many side effects, it seemed. Many *delicious* side effects.

His lips moved back up her neck, and goose bumps broke out in the wake of his open-mouthed kisses. When he arrived at her jaw, he licked and then nibbled her skin before moving to her ear. "You want more?" he whispered.

She moaned, and her head fell back. "*Please.*"

And then he, blessedly, released her wrists. But before she could reach for him, clutch his skin, he wrapped his arms around her waist and lifted her. Her lips parted. No one had *ever* done such a thing. She was not considered delicate, by any means, at nearly six feet tall and packed with muscle.

He began to walk backward with her pinned against him and her sandaled feet dangling above the ground, but she was distracted by where he was going when his lips returned to hers. His kiss was now more familiar but nonetheless devastating to her senses. She moaned around his tongue, and his arms tightened.

Then, her equilibrium tilted, and next she knew, she was being laid down on a hard surface, her wings finding something unforgiving and slightly chilled. She pulled from the kiss to look over her shoulder. She was lying on the short-legged table that sat in the midst of the living room furniture. A stack of magazines dug into her shoulder, and she shifted uncomfortably. She was about to protest when Max followed her down, resting on top of her and between her thighs while simultaneously sweeping the stack of magazines from the table to scatter on the floor.

Her breath left her, and not because he was oh so heavy upon her. She couldn't catch her breath because it was the best thing she'd ever felt. With his lower body nestled between her thighs, she could feel that he was aroused again. So hard was he against the juncture of her thighs that she wondered if he hurt like she hurt.

However, as soon as he laid upon her, he was up again, and a very un-angel-like word flashed through her mind at the loss.

He shoved a hand through his hair, revealing his scar to her, as he stood between her sprawled knees and looked at her through tortured eyes. "I c-can't lay on you like that," he gritted through clenched teeth. "I'll lose it."

Anahita didn't know what *it* was, but she couldn't bear for things to stop now. "You promised," she said while rising to her elbows so she could reach for and detain him if he fled. She felt her wings flare behind her back in their freedom, and his eyes caressed their lines before returning to her face.

"*Shit*, Anahita," he said, flexing his hands.

"Max," she pleaded.

He tossed his head back and stared at the ceiling while he muttered to himself, but Anahita was too engrossed in the way his throat moved to pay attention to what he was saying. She wanted to lick up that throat the way he had hers. Would it affect him the same way?

"Okay," Max said, leveling his gaze at her again. "I'll touch you. Just touch you." He appeared to be still speaking to himself.

Anahita's wings ruffled at the promise in his rough tone. "Yes," she said, reaching for him with one arm while remaining balanced on the other against the table.

His eyes sharpened. "You don't touch *me*. Understand?"

Anahita felt herself frown and her outstretched arm shook.

"It's all I can offer, angel, so take it or leave it."

She felt like crying. *No*, she corrected herself. She felt like fighting him for the right to touch him. Restraining him as he had done her and then laying her hands all over him. His eyes narrowed, and he seemed to know what she was thinking. If his expression was any indication, she'd better not try it.

"Fine," she said ungratefully. "Touch me."

His Adam's apple bobbed up and down. "Lift your robe," he said, his chin tilting up as though the words were a challenge.

Before another second passed, Anahita grabbed a handful of her robe and wrenched it up her legs.

A sharp noise burst from Max's lips. "Not shy, then," he muttered with his eyes riveted to the space between her thighs. Anahita could feel his gaze like a caress and brazenly widened her knees. *"Holy Hell,"* Max gasped, his open hand slamming over his heart. The look on his face right now—Anahita had never felt more beautiful. He raised his eyes to hers so slowly it appeared as though he had to drag them away. He cocked one eyebrow, and the tiniest lift appeared at the corner of his mouth. "Angels don't wear underwear?" he asked.

She felt her own lips tilt at the corners, and she pulled her robe higher, feeling empowered by the lust in his eyes, while shaking her head.

"Damn, woman," Max said. "You sure you're not a devil?"

Anahita felt a flare of worry. Was she acting too brazenly? She *liked* the way she was acting. It felt great. And she'd thought that Max had liked it, too…

Max made a sound with his tongue and teeth. "Your face is too damn expressive, angel," he said, as though it were a bad thing. "Don't you dare act any differently than you are right now. I *do* like it. I was just trying to flirt with you. Apparently really badly." He frowned down at his shoes.

She felt her smile grow again. "Not *that* badly."

He laughed, but there was no humor in it, and Anahita felt a pang in her heart. "What am I doing?" he asked, and Anahita instinctively knew he wasn't asking *her*.

She answered anyway. "I thought you were going to touch me. Isn't that what you're doing?"

His head raised slowly, and his eyes roamed her face, that golden eye seeming to glow even more. "You sure you want me to do that?"

Oh, yes. She was sure. "Just so you are aware: I've never done things like this before." His laugh had a little touch of humor in it this time, but she didn't feel as though he were laughing at her. "I do not really know what I am doing. I never watched the humans do this sort of thing… Never thought I would need to…"

A dimple flashed in his right cheek. "You're doing just fine," he said, as though it were the understatement of the decade. "Trust me."

Confidence poured through her once more. "Then what are you waiting for?" she asked, spreading her knees again.

Max smiled broadly. It was the first time she'd ever seen him do so, and it stretched his scar, flattening the raised flesh so that it blanched and almost disappeared into his features. *Oh, my heart*, she thought as her lips parted. With every moment, she was finding him more and more attractive. More and more Tempting.

She closed her mouth. She could do this. She would not Fall. She had no plans to create life with this man who barely tolerated her, and she was certainly not going to Fall to be with someone who despised her. Things were going to be fine.

She jumped when she felt something brush her knee, and it made Max jump, too. Her eyes snapped to his face, and he was wearing a wary half-smile. Her eyes darted down, and it was his fingers that were brushing her knee. "Okay?" he asked.

Her world narrowed down to that light brush of his fingertips, and as she watched, he did it again. Heat shot straight up from his caress to the juncture of her thighs. "Oh, yes," she said breathlessly.

She heard him swallow roughly, but she was busy staring at his fingers as they brushed ever higher, making small circles above her knee, and moving to the inner thigh. When they reached the place where her inner thigh met her body, they stalled, and Anahita heard herself whimper. "Do not tease me," she said, her tone begging.

"Didn't realize I was," he said, but there was a smile in his voice. With a boldness that surprised her, she reached for his fingers and moved them to where she wanted them: directly cupping her.

Max sucked in a breath and choked slightly. "Okay, then," he muttered, flexing his fingers. Anahita moaned and arched her hips into his touch. "God, Anahita," Max whispered reverently.

Anahita placed her hand over his, intending to move it against her, but he lightly slapped it away with his free hand. "I can take it from here, angel," he said, and her eyes shot to his face once more. He was smiling down at her, his free hand now planted by the curve of her waist on the table. "You've got some control issues, pretty baby."

Pretty baby. She was surprised by how much she liked that. She wanted to fist her hand in his shirt and pull him down to her, but he seemed to panic each time she touched him, and now he was ordering her not to take charge. Her only recourse was to whimper and undulate into his palm.

He chuckled huskily, and then his fingers began to move. His palm was fully covering her: the heel of his hand pressed against the top of her cleft, his fingers along her opening. Those moving fingers brushed up and down, and she felt him spreading moisture. It felt so good, in that moment, she would have gladly Fallen to make him continue.

He groaned, and she heard the fingers of his free hand scrape along the table beneath her. "So damn wet, angel," he whispered. "You won't last long at all, will you?"

She wasn't quite sure what he was talking about, but she shook her head anyway, agreeing more to the promise in his tone than the words. The heel of his palm lifted, and Anahita whimpered a protest. But then, his fingers, slick with how much he had made her want him, brushed upward and over that same spot.

She cried out, her head craning back on the table, and her hips rising so sharply his hand was almost displaced. His fingers brushed her again, and her thighs fell completely open. Her hands shot down, and she wrapped both of them around his wrist and thrust his hand onto her hard while canting her hips up at the same time. As his fingers rubbed her just right, Max hissed in a breath. He straightened and grabbed her hands with both of his.

"No," Anahita sobbed, already missing the touch of his fingers on her sensitive flesh.

"I said *no touching*," he whispered, wrenching her hands above her head and pinning them to the table. "I meant it!"

"Yes, fine," she said quickly, staring up into his face, which was now a breath away. "I won't do it again. Just ... *please*." She gulped back the sob that was tinging her words. "Do not stop, Max." His eyes glittered down at her. "*Please*."

He looked at her for several hard seconds, and then he adjusted his hold so that her hands were pinned with one of his. His index finger brushed a curl off of her forehead, then trailed down her nose and over the curve of her lip before coming to rest between her parted lips. "Lick it," he said brokenly.

She felt her brows pucker, but after a slight hesitation, she obeyed. She tasted herself on his finger. Her eyes closed, and she moaned as she sucked it further into her mouth, laving it until the flavor was gone.

He pulled it out of her mouth with a little pop, and when she opened her eyes to gaze up at him, his eyes were swimming with a new level of lust. "You're gonna be the death of me," he whispered.

He was right, of course, and the sudden reminder was unwelcome and harsh. Her eyes searched his face until he broke eye contact. Before she could become too embroiled in the sudden dark turn of her thoughts, the fingers gripping her wrists tightened, almost as though he were warning her to live up to her promise not to touch him. Then, his finger, wet from her mouth, landed right on the spot that drove her wild and began moving in tight, fast circles that showed her no mercy.

Her legs jerked with each pass of his skin over hers, and tiny, breathless noises burst from her mouth faster than she could catch them. It felt as though a string were being pulled tighter and tighter, and any moment she would snap.

His name became a litany she said in hoarse, pleading whispers. After the first few repetitions of his name, Max looked into her eyes. His face was tense; his eyes were tortured. He never let up on the pressure and speed of his finger, and as her cries grew louder, his expression turned expectant. "Do it for me, pretty baby," he groaned. "Let me see your face as you come apart."

For the first time since he'd pinned her hands, she tried to get free. She was unraveling. Her skin felt too tight for her body, and she wanted to hold on to him, to have him ground her. He pressed her hands more firmly against the table and tsked at her, but blessedly, he did not let up with the brushes of his finger, because Anahita finally found out what that snapped string would lead to.

"Max!" she said, throwing her head back and bowing off of the table to ride wave after wave of pleasure as it shot through her, radiating out from where his finger had now slowed and brushed over her gently.

When she whimpered and her hips fell back to the table, his finger slowed to a stop. As clarity became more accessible, she noticed that his fingers were trembling where they clutched her wrists. His breaths were exploding out of him, puffing across her face and stirring her hair. His face was a mask of utter longing.

Anahita remembered the physical torment she'd been in when they'd done this before and Max had left her wanting. She would not do the same to him. She must have caught him unaware—or he simply wanted it too badly himself—for Anahita was able to free her hands from his hold.

"Your turn," she whispered up to him. And then she placed her palm over the front of his pants. She gasped at the same time he did. She could *feel* him throbbing through the fabric. His length was so long and so hard, she almost hurt for him. But just as she was about to undo his pants and bring him to pleasure the way he had showed her to do, Max exploded into an upright position.

He stumbled back, almost tripping over his feet. His eyes roamed, touching her and quickly sliding away to her surroundings. He muttered to himself in an unbroken stream of self-recrimination that Anahita could not quite hear, except in snatches.

Then he turned and ran. Anahita was still gasping from the heights he had taken her body to when the door slammed behind him.

All of the good feelings he'd wrung from her body dissipated into the air. This—this was almost worse than how she'd felt when it had been *him* who'd received the pleasure, and she who had gone wanting.

She felt dirty. Used. *Again.*

Who was she fooling? This *was* worse.

Chapter Eleven

Distance. Distance. Distance.

Max careened down the hall, his raging erection preventing movement without pain, and all the while, that damn word was a litany inside his head, mocking his complete failure at maintaining it.

Distance. Distance. Distance.

He made it all the way to the end of the hallway before he broke. With a roar, he spun into the wall, kicking the plaster hard enough to make a plume of dust explode out and cover him. "*Fuck* your distance!" he bellowed.

He heard a snort and spun around again to find that his little mantrum had taken place right where the hallway met the main room. Eli and Jericho stood a handful of feet away, both wearing wry grins. Max's brows crashed down over his eyes. He didn't know which of these bastards had snorted, but he was going to find out and punch him in the throat.

Before he could act, however, Eli raised an eyebrow and said, "Problem, Casanova?" And then he pointedly flicked his eyes down to Max's waist.

Max's eyes followed, and there it was: the biggest hard-on he'd ever sported pushing obviously against the front of his trousers. "*Shit,*" he muttered, crossing his hands over his fly.

"I hope to God you left her in a better state than you," Jericho said, "because Jayden will straight up take this out on your hide if he finds out."

"I can take the angel."

Jericho's smile faded. "Uh, no. You really can't."

Eli nodded. "Truth."

Max wanted to throw his hands up, but he still had a pants problem, so his hands stayed right where they were. "Where's

Luke?" he asked in a piss-poor attitude that even he could recognize was obnoxious.

"Came out here looking like someone had kicked his puppy, and then took off for the medical wing like his britches were on fire," Eli said with a shrug.

Medical wing. "Ah, hell," Max said, dropping his hands and taking off in a sprint across the room.

"Everything okay?" one of the men shouted after him, the Southern accent indicating it was Eli.

Max didn't bother to answer, just kept running. Everything *wasn't* okay. He'd left Oliver alone. He'd left Oliver alone!

"Shit, shit, shit," he muttered under his breath, tearing past people who stopped to gawk at him.

He heard the explosive noise coming out of Oliver's room from the beginning of the medical wing, and immediately, Max knew he'd messed up in a way that he could not compensate for.

Oliver's voice came roaring through the hall, nearly bowling Max over. His friend was screaming—not obscenities, but in *fright*. Max had never heard him make that noise before, but he instinctively recognized the desperation of Oliver's fear.

"Put him *out*," Luke begged.

Max skidded into the room, not having to pause to open the door because people in scrubs were rushing in and out. Luke was standing at Oliver's side, clinging to the man's hand as he thrashed on the cot and continued that dreadful screaming. Without breaking stride, Max hurried over to Oliver's other side. Oliver's blue eyes found Max's face, and Oliver's panic increased. "Where *are we?*" Oliver shouted, gripping Max's hand so tightly he heard some cracking.

"We're safe, man," Max said quickly. "We're safe."

But Oliver's screams drowned Max out. A man in blue scrubs shoved Max out of the way, and the light gleamed off of a syringe right before the nurse plunged it into Oliver's thigh.

Almost immediately, Oliver's screams faded and then went out completely. His blue eyes slid closed, and his breathing evened out. Most of the medical staff left the room with only two staying behind to make notations on charts and check Oliver's vitals and make notations on charts.

Max stared at Oliver through eyes that were growing dry from a lack of blinking. "He woke up alone," Max said under his breath.

"No," Luke whispered gently. "I was here."

Max's head snapped up, and he blinked at Luke until he came into focus.

"But you know he needs *you* when he first wakes up."

Max nodded silently, guilt pouring through him almost more severely than he could handle.

"Stop your bitching."

Both their heads swiveled in Oliver's direction. The gravelly statement had come from Oliver, who was staring at Max through bleary but calm eyes.

"I don't need anyone," Oliver said. "I'm a regular fucking rock."

A half-laugh burst from Max's chest motivated by relief. Oliver's face was completely relaxed. All evidence of the torture he'd been experiencing was absent. "Oh yeah," Max said. "Your screams: very rock-like."

"Damn straight," Oliver muttered, his eyes drooping. "Just call me Alcatraz."

"That's terrible," Max said, edging closer to Oliver's cot as the remaining medical staff left.

"Of course it is. You geniuses roofied me."

"Your screams, remember?" Luke said.

"Oh, yeah," Oliver said, his words slurring. "This shit's great." Luke and Max glanced at each other before focusing on Oliver once more. "I want pudding," Oliver muttered, and then his head drifted to the side.

Luke cleared his throat and gestured for Max to join him out in the hall. With one last look at Oliver's peacefully sleeping face, Max followed Luke out.

Jericho and Eli were leaning against the wall opposite the door. They straightened when Max and Luke came into sight. "Everything okay?" Jericho asked.

"Yeah," Luke said, clapping Max on the shoulder. "Everything is okay." And for Max's ears alone, he added, "Truly okay, my man. You understand me? He's fine. No harm no foul."

A tiny fraction of Max's guilt dissipated from his shoulders. A *tiny* fraction, but a welcome relief nonetheless. He nodded to Luke and turned his attention to the other two men. "Luke will want to debrief us," he said.

"Really?" Eli said, his brows rising. "He was barely in there with Anahita. He had time to learn something?"

"Prepare to be amazed," Max said. He could see Luke duck his head and knew the man was blushing.

"Follow us to the meeting room," Jericho said, turning on his heel and walking out of the medical wing in giant strides that they all had to work hard to match, despite the fact that they were all taller than average themselves.

Jericho led them to a room that housed a long, mahogany table surrounded by a dozen leather chairs. They all naturally congregated at the far end where they could watch the door easily—old soldier habits die hard.

"Okay," Max said to Luke, knowing from experience that he had hit intel pay dirt. "Lay it on them."

"You were wrong about angels not being threats around their Temptations," Luke said to Eli and Jericho in the quiet confidence of a man who knew he was right but didn't want to hurt anyone's feelings.

Max frowned and saw the expression mirrored on Jericho's and Eli's faces.

Luke continued, "The man Anahita was talking to was an angel named Remiel, and he did something to his Temptation—I'm fairly confident that he killed her."

"No," Jericho said, shaking his head. "Are you serious?"

"Very," Luke said. He placed his hands on the table and stared at them rather than at the other men. "And Anahita looks up to him. It wouldn't be remiss to call it 'idol worship.'" He flicked a quick glance at Max, and then returned his eyes to his hands. "Max isn't safe from her, and if *he* isn't safe—"

"None of us are," Eli finished for him.

"There is *some* hope," Luke said softly. Max found himself swallowing hard. "Anahita is definitely ... *conflicted* where Max is concerned. But she is also resolute. She wants something—very much wants something—that only our deaths will bring about. She doesn't take this goal lightly, and neither should we."

Luke raised his head and pinned Max with a heavy look. The *and you treating her like a booty call will not help our case* was heavily implied in that single moment of eye contact. Max's eyes shifted away, and he tried as surreptitiously as possible to finger-comb his hair over his scar.

"You got all of that?" Jericho asked. "From a five minute conversation?"

"Well," Max said, "a conversation and an ill-conceived pass."

He could *feel* Luke's discomfort, and Eli's and Jericho's brows shot up. They looked at each other and then back at the two of them.

"Along that vein of thought," Max said, examining his fingers casually. "The angel and I—we've come to an agreement." He looked directly at Luke. "An *exclusive* agreement."

Luke's face fell. "You're in a relationship?"

"I wouldn't say *relationship*."

Either Jericho or Eli coughed uncomfortably, but Max didn't look away from Luke.

Luke's jaw went slack. "You're *friends with benefits* with an angel of the Most High God?"

Max frowned. Luke had been watching too much television while staying with Oliver in the medical wing. "Well, when you put it like that, it sounds douche-y."

"How would you put it?"

"…I wouldn't say *friends*…"

"I'm going to punch you again. You want me to punch you again."

"Do you guys, uh, want to be alone?" Eli asked.

Both of their heads snapped in his direction. "No!" they said simultaneously.

The door opened and bounded off the wall with a crash. Silence reigned as all four of them looked at the doorway that housed one irate Jayden. His green eyes flashed. "Do I want to know what *friends with benefits* is?" he asked.

"No," all four of them said in unison.

"I tried to visit Anahita," Jayden said as he walked into the room, his eyes never leaving Max. "She would not even see me. Kept assuring me she was fine. From the other side of a *closed door*."

Remembering what Eli and Jericho had said about Jayden's ability, Max imagined a wall surrounding his thoughts and tried his best to make sure Jayden couldn't see through it.

Jayden narrowed his eyes and tilted his head to the side, but after a tense moment, he merely pointed his finger at Max and said, "If I find out this casual agreement you two seem to have is anything other than Anahita's greatest wish, you will be destroyed."

"See," Luke said beneath his breath. "They are anything but predictable, even when around their Temptations."

"You have no idea," Jayden said, the threat in his tone clear. "Now, who wants to tell me why we are using Anahita as bait?"

Eli sighed heavily. "Told you guys to stay away from him," he said.

"He came to us!" Max protested.

"I gleaned this plan from *your* thoughts," Jayden said, turning his attention to Eli.

Jericho laughed outright before catching it and trying to disguise it as a cough when Eli glared at him.

"I'm distracted, okay?" Eli said, running a hand through his hair. "Genesis doesn't sleep much, and I miss my wife, if you know what I mean. We've been stretching the Impulse pretty thin these days."

Jericho definitely looked like he knew what Eli meant. Genesis was the first child born of an Impulse Pair. She was still a newborn, so if she had any special powers or there were any effects on her life, no one could tell yet. Apparently, she was normal in the keeping-her-parents-up-all-night sense. And Eli and Abilene would have to continue to see to each other's physical needs on a regular basis or face the same effects that plagued Oliver. The Impulse didn't take vacations, even for new babies, as it turned out.

"Yeah, that's the part I'm not looking forward to myself," Jericho said, slapping Eli on the back. "Worth it, though, right?"

Eli's eyes seemed to twinkle. "You have no idea," he said with a wide, lopsided smile.

Max turned to look at Jayden again and caught the angel looking at the two fathers wistfully before blanking his expression entirely. Jayden walked over to them and took the vacant chair at the head of the table. "So, Anahita," Jayden said, most of the ire gone from his voice. "Why have you chosen to spy on her?"

Luke spoke up first. "She's meeting with another angel who is directing her mission to kill Max, Oliver, and myself. We figured some intel would not be remiss."

Jayden nodded. "Remiel," he said.

All attention, already focused on Jayden, sharpened in a nanosecond. "You know him?" Eli said, his words measured.

"Come on, humans," Jayden said. "Anahita has taken over *my* mission. It stands to reason I know everyone she knows, *especially* the head of the Warriors."

"Jayden," Jericho said, leaning forward, "why wouldn't you tell us this before?"

Jayden straightened and seemed to glare down his nose at Jericho. "I did not know if it was pertinent yet."

Max scowled. "*Everything* is pertinent."

Jayden turned his head and narrowed his eyes at Max. "Indeed."

Max had the urge to stretch the neck of his shirt away from skin that suddenly itched.

"Before you get your feathers ruffled," Jayden continued, "you should know that I was telling you everything I thought you needed to know as soon as I knew it. For example, I told you the location of these two." Jayden gestured to Max and Luke with a wide sweep of his hand. "I have my suspicions about Remiel's motivation, but I was saving judgment until I was sure."

"You have *suspicions*?" Eli asked, straightening.

Jayden sighed. "Do not speak to me as though I owe you all I know," he said softly. "I have gained much in Grace, but everything else I have known for my entire existence is now lost to me. I cannot betray my brethren lightly. You must know that."

Max felt the slightest softening toward the angel, but refused to allow it too much hold.

"Will you tell us your suspicions now?" Jericho asked.

Jayden looked at the man, then opened his mouth with obvious reluctance. "I am not sure my mission—now Anahita's—comes from the Most High," he said.

He saw the others lean forward in his peripheral vision, and Max made himself slouch in his seat, though everything in him perked up, telling him the angel knew much more than the simple words promised.

"I first suspected when I discovered that He spoke to you all. That He spoke *fondly* to you all. You've dubbed it *the Voice*," Jayden said. "Some of you embrace it, others spurn it"—his eyes flicked to Max briefly—"but it is always constant on His side. He *likes* you. Why would He order me to kill you? And this *Knowledge* Max, Jericho, and Dahlia have…" He paused to glance at Max. "You sense that we are evil whenever we get close to killing you, correct?"

Max nodded and saw Jericho do the same.

Jayden smiled wryly. "Angels are not evil, are they." It was not a question, and Max frowned. That was an excellent point. "We would only be *evil* if we were pursuing a mission outside of the Most High's will," Jayden continued. "I was given the order to guard the Trees from all human interference when Adam and Eve were banished from the Garden of Eden. But I was only given those orders that once. The Most High never again repeated them." He paused and looked at the table. "Remiel did," he finished softly.

"What does that mean?" Max asked, finally leaning forward. "Spell it out for us, angel."

Jayden's eyes flashed. "Much has changed since the humans' betrayal in the Garden of Eden. Anger has had time to abate. Humanity has again become a favorite with the Most High. It is a fact that some of the brethren—who have *always* remained faithful to the Most High's commands—resent. It is … *possible* … that some of those brethren would have organized themselves to mete out the punishment they believe is due."

"I thought angels didn't have free will," Jericho said. "How would they be able to organize themselves into a rebellion?"

"That is true," Jayden said. "There are two possibilities: this could be the Temptation of several of the brethren, and they are facing their Falls by doing this; or, this could be the manifestation of some of the brethren obeying the Most High's initial command to the letter, disregarding His changing feelings toward humanity. He has not spoken to us on the matter since the beginning, and that allows us to assume His original order still stands. Though," Jayden said, looking across the room at nothing, "I'm beginning to see such beliefs are ignorant at best."

"Then why not disregard these beliefs?" Max asked.

"No free will, remember," Jayden said. "We are limited in our actions. Only those who approach their Fall have leeway in this, and even then, that leeway leads to destruction, so most avoid Tempting themselves by following laid down edicts to the letter if not the spirit."

"Great," Max muttered. "Beings with nearly limitless power who are a bunch of yes-men."

Jayden looked at Max. "And women."

As if Max could forget.

"You have to admit," Luke said, "that such a thing could lead to problems."

Jayden smiled at Luke. "I think you will find that I do not *have* to do anything. But in this situation, yes, I can allow myself to admit that one of the brethren could do much harm."

"A rebel faction of angels," Jericho muttered to himself.

Jayden's head tilted to the side. "Unfortunately, I fear that is exactly what we face." He let out a sigh. "They will make a formidable opponent."

Max laughed. "Are you being serious?" he asked. "A *formidable opponent*? We're dead. That's basically what you just told us."

Jayden frowned. "That is a great possibility," he said, as though he'd just considered it. Max clenched his fists in his lap to keep from throttling the obnoxious being. Jayden turned to Luke. "What did you hope to gain by talking to Anahita?" he asked, for once sounding as though he did not think the plan had been totally repugnant.

"Who she was answering to. If she was a threat"—Luke paused and looked at Max briefly before returning his attention to the angel—"to Max or any of us."

Jayden tsked. "I could have answered both questions, human," he said. "You are wasting our time and resources by seeking to do things that do not need to be done."

Eli leaned forward. "Well, then, is she a threat to us?"

"Oh, yes," Jayden said almost before Eli had finished his question. "Very much so."

Max tightened his fists. "Care to elaborate, or are your words so wise they encompass everything we would ever need to know?"

Jayden stared at Max for several seconds. "I do not like you," he said finally.

Max put his hand over his chest. "Break my heart, why don't you."

"Ladies," Eli snapped. "You can slap-fight this out later." He focused on Jayden. "It isn't a *terrible* question, Jayden."

Jayden took a big breath. "You say *ladies* as though it is an insult to call us such, but I tell you now, Anahita is a *lady* who will happily slit your throat. She is much more motivated to complete her mission than I ever was, and I was motivated indeed."

Max leaned forward; he couldn't help himself. "Why?" he asked. "What is her motivation?"

"Anahita is an outsider," Jayden said, looking Max square in the eye. "Completing this mission will admit her to the ranks of Warrior."

Max cocked an eyebrow at the angel.

"That is all you will hear from me," Jayden said firmly. "If you want to know more, I suggest you ask her yourself. She is *yours*. Do you not want to know everything about her?"

The words were a clear challenge, and Max refused to rise to the bait. But the truth was, Max *was* curious. He found himself wanting to know what made Anahita tick. It was very un-frenemies-with-benefits.

"This ... *observation* of Anahita is not the worst plan I have ever encountered," Jayden said with a sigh. "I, myself, cannot tell you what the angels under Remiel's command are up to since I have Fallen. Anahita could be a useful tool." Jayden thrummed his fingers on the tabletop. "I will allow you to continue to use her thus for two reasons. One, Remiel's rebel faction poses a threat to my Grace and to the children." He looked at Max again. "And two, when Anahita finds out—and it will be *when* not *if*—she will not forgive you for using her. You will no longer be in her life, and I will not have to find a way to put you there myself."

"Forgive me? *She* is planning to kill us!"

"Tell yourself whatever you need to, but even without knowing exactly what you have said to each other, I know Anahita has been forthcoming with you. She will not abide duplicity. I will be lucky if she forgives *me* for allowing you to do this, and we have loved each other for centuries. You are not even kind to her. You do this, you are doomed never to have her."

Max snorted and shook his head. "I don't *want* her, remember?" But Jayden's words had wormed their way into his heart, and Max felt sick to his stomach.

Jayden smiled gently at Max for the first time since they had met and said nothing. If Max was not mistaken, there was pity in Jayden's eyes.

Max shook his hair into his face and turned his eyes away to glower at the tabletop.

"Grace and I will watch little Genesis for you tonight if you wish," Jayden said.

"Yes," Eli said quickly. "Yes."

"You will want to ask Abilene first, of course," Jayden said.

"Oh, yeah," Eli muttered. "Thank you for offering."

Jayden chuckled. "I am selfishly motivated," he said. "Your pornographic thoughts are distracting to more than just *you*."

The angel rose to his feet and walked out of the room, but Max never looked up from the table, afraid that if he did, everyone would see the inappropriate anguish written across his face. He took a breath to speak, and the Voice whispered urgently, *Do not do this*, right before Max said, "We do it. We use her."

Chapter Twelve

Anahita sat on the edge of the coffee table where she had been sitting since Max tore out of her living quarters forty-five minutes ago.

She needed to move. She needed to do something. *Anything.*

Instead, she sat here, the hard edge of the table putting her bottom to sleep, reliving those final few moments with her Temptation. And with each remembrance, the weight in her gut grew heavier and heavier until Anahita had the strongest desire to lie down in the comfortable bed in her bedroom and never rise again.

She did not like this *man* business. It was much too complicated, and the pleasant feelings were much too short-lived and did not outweigh the feelings of despair that every encounter thus far had caused.

"Anahita."

She jerked to the side, nearly sliding off of the table. Her eyes widened. Remiel sat in the same chair he'd been in—was it only two hours ago?

"Remiel," she said. She had to clear her throat before talking again. "Back so soon."

"I—" He cleared his throat. "I never truly left."

Anahita felt the blood drain from her head, and she fought dizziness. "You ... *watched* us?"

Remiel's lips twisted and a flash of annoyance crossed his face—rare emotion for him indeed—and then was gone. "Why the concern?" he asked. "Did you do something shameful?"

The sudden urge to hang her head was strong, and Anahita tipped her chin up to counteract it. "As a matter of fact, no," she said. "As you can see: not Fallen."

"Hmm," Remiel hummed, his gaze penetrating. "I did not *watch*, as you so delicately put it. When I saw the direction things were headed, I called a quick emergency meeting of the brethren. We have already met and made a decision."

Anahita swallowed hard. All abandoned her except the sharpest despair. She knew she could not stop Remiel's words, but she wished with every fiber of her being that he would delay telling her the result of that meeting.

"We are not confident that you are focused enough for this mission," Remiel said.

"I am!" The words burst forth, childish and wild.

Remiel's eyes traveled from Anahita's face to the table on which she sat, the movement pointed and condemning.

"That was ... nothing," Anahita mumbled, the words barely auditory and tasting horrible in her mouth, though they were the truth, as evidenced by her ability to speak them. "I was—" She swallowed again. "Curious. He sated my curiosity. That is all."

"Sated it poorly, it would seem," Remiel said, returning his eyes to her face.

With the last of her strength, Anahita cleared her expression. "Well then, all the better to assure you I will not be Tempted further, yes?"

"Perhaps," Remiel said after a long pause. "But we know of something else that would assure us even more." Remiel narrowed his eyes. "Set your Compulsion."

Anahita's stomach bottomed out even further. "I have not had the opportunity to think clearly—"

"I was not finished," Remiel said, cutting her off. "Set your Compulsion ... or die."

Anahita's head felt loose on her shoulders. "What?"

"I believe I was more than clear," Remiel said.

"*Why?*" she asked, her hand creeping up to her throat.

"We have already lost Jayden, and now he fights for the wrong side. We cannot risk you defecting to the side of the abominations." Remiel leaned forward in his seat, looking suspiciously like he was feeling some very strong emotions indeed. "This was not my decision, you understand," he said, "but the decision of the group. So, I repeat: set your Compulsion or die."

The flaming sword was concealed beneath her wing, and for a fraction of a second, she pondered how long it would take as she reached over her shoulder to grab it before Remiel would catch on and defend himself. The moment she had the thought, she was appalled. Had she truly sunk so far that she would consider harming her leader? The head of the Warriors? "I will do it," she muttered, the words tumbling out of her mouth and over each other in her haste to get them out.

Remiel leaned back in his seat slowly, a small smile tilting his lips. "I will wait while you do."

That he did not trust her—at all—finally penetrated Anahita's skull, and she was so ashamed of herself, she could hardly breathe. She nodded absently, and then, because she could not think while sitting on the table where she had experienced her first orgasm— disappointing though the aftermath had been—she stumbled to her feet and shuffled over to the sofa. She sank down, releasing a sigh as she did so. Just before she closed her eyes to focus her thoughts, she saw Remiel observing her through narrowed eyes, the smile he'd had moments before absent.

With her eyes closed, she focused on the three men: Oliver, Luke, and Max. She must decide on the order they should die. With reflexes that felt fueled by anger, Anahita pondered killing Max first, but immediately, a hidden part of her brain warred with it, and she admitted that she could not make so important a decision based on something as trivial as anger. If she were both honest *and* compassionate, Oliver should be first. His constant cycle of anguish needed to end, and she instinctively knew he would be grateful to her. Luke was the most innocent human she could imagine, and ending his life would cause her much pain. He would be last. That meant her Temptation would be second. The order was complete: Oliver, Max, Luke. She pulled in a slow breath and set her Compulsion. She felt it click into place, and immediately, the urge to find Oliver, to begin her mission, overwhelmed her.

She opened her eyes. Remiel was smiling once more. "It is done," she said, though it was obvious she did not need to. "I will begin right away."

Remiel was rising to his feet before Anahita was even done speaking. "This is wisdom, Anahita. You are showing wisdom, and it will aid the brethren well when you join our ranks officially." He nodded at her and said, "Godspeed," before disappearing.

As soon as he was gone, Anahita, too, got to her feet. She could feel the flames of the sword heat with intent along her back. She was three trivial steps away from achieving her life's ambition.

It was time to take the first step.

Anahita walked to the door, entered the hallway, and headed toward the medical wing and one Oliver Phillips.

As she walked, the world faded to black and white, shadows and light. She paid no attention to the people she passed, even when one or two of them—she did not stop to identify who— attempted to talk to her.

When her feet met the floor of the medical wing, the sword grew even hotter. Her palm itched to snatch it, but she made herself wait, knowing that if any of the humans saw her wielding the sword while her eyes were the solid black of a Compulsion-driven Warrior, she would face difficulty in ensuring there were no unnecessary casualties.

Someone was leaning up against the wall beside her first target's door, but she paid him no mind.

However, that someone straightened and spoke. "Anahita?" he said.

Anahita continued walking toward the door.

"Fuck, pretty baby, what happened to your eyes?"

Something in that question made her pause. Anahita frowned and turned her head to examine the person who had spoken. Long, tousled black hair; compelling, mismatched eyes; trim beard that she knew was softer than it looked.

How do I know that?

"Anahita?" the man asked again, a scar that crossed his face stretching as his brows met in the middle.

A swirl of color snaked its way through her vision before expanding and driving away the black and white focus she needed to complete her mission. She blinked at the man before her. "Max?"

Max blew out a breath, his shoulders falling while doing so. "There's my angel," he muttered.

Pretty baby. He'd called her pretty baby again, and it had distracted her enough that she had been pulled out of her mission.

Temptations were strong stuff. Nothing should be able to do that. *Nothing.* "I cannot talk right now," Anahita said, her tone distant. "Or whatever it is you wish to do with me this time. I am in the middle of something."

Anahita turned to walk into Oliver's room, the world already shifting to black and white again, but Max's hand shot out and lightly wrapped around her upper arm. As light as his touch was, Anahita froze on the spot, her gaze finding his fingers against her skin.

"About that," Max whispered. "I owe you an apology."

The black and white vanished once more. Anahita let her eyes travel from his fingers up his forearm to where his bicep stretched the shirt he was wearing to the point of breakage. Finally, she looked at his face. She could tell she was staring, but she could not make herself stop. How had this man's face become so precious to her in such a short amount of time *and* when they could not seem to be in a room together without catastrophe?

Max dropped his hand from her skin and raked his hair over his golden eye and most of his scar.

"I wish you would not feel the need to do that."

Max's eyes shifted to the floor. "Do what?"

"Max," Anahita whispered, but he would not look at her again. Finally, she placed her finger beneath his chin and directed his face up until she could see it again. "I think you know what," she said.

His hair fell from his face, and his eyes widened with a vulnerability that she had not seen in them before as he visibly struggled not to hide behind it again. As he vibrated with tension before her, Anahita slowly and meticulously looked over every plane, raised line, and hollow of Max's scarred and beautiful visage. "There is nothing here to hide," she said finally.

Max swallowed hard—she could feel it beneath her finger—and pulled back until Anahita's hand perched awkwardly between them. She let it fall back to her side.

"Anahita, I—" Max rubbed the back of his neck with one hand. "I don't know what to do around you," he muttered.

Anahita blew out a quick breath. "Nor I," she admitted. As she looked at him, a sudden surge of her Guardian side nearly toppled her over. Her set Warrior Compulsion roared within her skull, and she swallowed a moan as they battled with each other. She felt her eyes widen as her mind recognized she *still* had two missions in the man before her: one to kill him, one to protect him. But her Warrior Compulsion was set. She should be able to put aside this undesirable feeling that she needed to protect Max.

"Anahita?" Max said, reaching toward her arm again.

She jerked it out of his reach, and, blessedly, her vision snapped to black and white again. Focus poured through her. She reached over her shoulder for the hilt of her sword. She had work to do, and if this human before her inhibited that, she would simply dispatch him now rather than later.

"No," the human muttered. His fingers stretched toward her face, their obvious aim her cheek. "Your eyes. Anahita, talk to me."

Anahita turned, giving the man her shoulder. Her fingers were nearly to her sword.

"What's *happening* to you?" the man beside her shouted. And then a horrible crunching sound rent the air.

Anahita paused, an undeniable pull upon her. With reluctance, she glanced in his direction, her eyes passing over a crater in the wall before finding him cracking his right fist in his left hand. Blood marred his knuckles.

Her lips parted. Her black and white vision vanished within one heartbeat. And before she could stop it, her Guardian Compulsion struck. As she looked at Max's wounded hand, the Compulsion to Guard him—to keep him from *ever* being harmed again—set as firmly as though it had been carved in stone.

Her vision went into shades of gold, everything cast in the shimmery aura, with dangers to Max's safety glowing especially bright—such as the wall upon which he had just broken his hand.

"No," Anahita moaned. "Oh, God, what have I done?" She had never once, in her entire existence, used the name of God so lightly.

A horrendous pain burst through Anahita's skull, and she irrationally thought for a moment that it was because she'd used God's name in vain. But the pain grew worse, and Anahita knew it was something else entirely. A groan was ripped from her chest, and she clutched her head with both hands, pushing in with all of her might to keep it from exploding as it felt it was about to do.

"Anahita!" Max said. He grabbed her by her upper arms and shook her. "What's wrong?"

Anahita couldn't speak, but another moan poured from her

"Open your eyes, pretty baby. Come on. Open your eyes for me."

She forced her eyelids open, feeling as she thought those who sleep must feel when they were attempting to pull themselves from a horrid nightmare. When she succeeded in getting them open, her head burst with a new supernova of pain. Her vision was cast in two: her left eye seeing black and white; her right eye seeing gold.

Max's face, right before her and bizarre looking in the multihued competition of her inner self, blanched, and his lips parted. "Okay," he said quickly, bending at the knee in the next moment and scooping her up into his arms. "You're gonna be okay."

He began walking down the hall with her resting her cheek on his chest, and every one of his harsh, booted steps reverberated up his body and through hers. She moaned again and clenched her eyes shut. "My head."

He cupped her head with one of his massive hands and pressed her face more firmly into the pad of muscle beneath her cheek. "Shhh." He paused, but then she felt him twist his hips, and with a mighty crash, he kicked a door open and strode into a dark, cool room. Through her closed eyelids, she could already appreciate the lack of lighting, and she felt her rigid spine relax slightly.

The world tilted, and she felt the crisp sheets of a bed beneath her wings. She adjusted them so they would not be crushed, and Max lowered her until she was lying down completely. He brushed her hair from her forehead with a rough, calloused palm, and Anahita opened her eyes again. Her vision was still split in two, and she saw Max wince when she looked into his eyes. "That can't feel good," he whispered, brushing his hand through her hair again.

"Does it look that bad?" she asked.

"You have one completely black eye, one completely golden eye," he said. "It doesn't look like it feels great, that's for sure."

Anahita moaned and turned to her side, curling into a *C*. "I am ruined."

She felt Max straighten. "I'll go get help."

Before he could step away, Anahita's arm shot out, and she grabbed a fist of his shirt. "No!"

Max froze and blinked down at her before placing his hand over her fist and squeezing gently. His brows rose, an undeniable question.

There were two reasons he could not leave. She could not bear for anyone to know that her Guardian side had been strong enough to set its Compulsion. And as an unfortunate side effect of that Compulsion, she could not let Max out of her sight. She had to Guard him. She felt so helpless. "Do not leave," she said, her voice breaking. "Please."

Max's nose wrinkled, but, blessedly, he sank to the bed's surface, sitting in the curve of her body. He patted her shoulder awkwardly, and Anahita blew out a breath and relaxed some more, though her split vision kept her from relaxing completely. She gazed up at him, knowing her eyes were wide and displaying her weakness for him to see, but unable to look away from him. She suspected that it was for a different reason than that she needed to keep an eye on him, to keep him safe.

Max's mismatched eyes roved her face. "What's wrong?" he asked.

She would never tell him.

"I am half Guardian," she muttered.

Immediately, she gasped. Her back straightened; her jaw clenched. She had *told him*! She moaned and placed a hand over the ache in her belly. She had just made a very, very grave error.

Max patted her shoulder again, this time leaving his hand. It was warm and large and altogether wonderful against her skin. "You didn't mean to tell me that, did you?"

Anahita closed her eyes and shook her head just a fraction of an inch.

He sighed. "Your secret is safe with me."

Anahita cracked her eyelids and looked up at him through her lashes. She thought she saw something in his face, but when she blinked again, it was gone, and she knew she must have imagined it.

"Half Guardian, huh?" he asked, one side of his lips tilting up. "I'm guessing that's this half." As he spoke the words, he brushed a fingertip across her right eyebrow—the one above her golden eye. "This doesn't sound like the end of the world," Max said, his finger continuing its trail across her cheek. "Guardian—as in 'guardian angel'?"

She nodded once.

"That's actually ... pretty cool," he said. "Don't you think?" His finger trailed down her throat. "Who doesn't love the idea of guardian angels?"

His finger was as good as scorching her skin. "I am *yours*."

The finger stopped. Max frowned. "What?"

"I am *your* guardian angel now," she whispered.

• • •

Every part of Max's body froze, except for his eyes, which darted back and forth between Anahita's black and golden eye. This was the strangest thing he'd ever seen. Her left eye was wall-to-wall black—no pupil, no gorgeous blue, no white. Just black. Her right eye was glowing golden, wall-to-wall, just like her black eye. Every time he looked at her black eye, his own freakish eye told him Anahita was *evil*. When he looked at her golden eye: *good*. Her brow was furrowed, and her teeth were clenched, and he knew by the tension in her body that she was in some pretty intense pain. And he had a job to do: get as much information out of her as possible. He'd barely been able to say *Your secret is safe with me* past the guilty lump in his throat.

But none of that compared to the bombshell she'd just dropped. His fucking *guardian angel*?

He cleared his throat. "Anahita, I may regret this question, but how does that mesh with your mission to kill me?"

She moaned and curled into herself tighter, her thighs touching upon his back and sending a spike of heat through him. "It does not," she said on another moan. "It cannot *mesh*."

"Oh," he said lamely. Inside his head, information fireworks were going off like crazy. His angel was literally split in two. He patted her shoulder once more and gave a squeeze he hoped was reassuring.

"It hurts," she whispered, pressing her forehead into his knee.

A swell gathered in his chest, and most of his thoughts abandoned him, except for one: make her feel better.

"Shh. I know, pretty baby," he muttered, leaning forward so that he was hovering over her more. His hand left her shoulder and threaded through her hair. "I know," he said again.

And he did. He was suffering from the world's most epic case of blue balls—his call-to-halt from earlier coming back to bite him in the ass, and not in the sexy way. He'd reached orgasm after initially Impulse-pairing with her, and Eli and Jericho had told him that was a vital step—the one that Oliver had missed. But that didn't mean the Impulse wouldn't demand its due on a regular basis, it just meant that he could ... handle it himself, so to speak. And with her body cocooning him as he sat within her huddled form, the Impulse was demanding its due like a motherfucker.

Even *he* could tell his thoughts were inappropriate as his Impulse mate was curled into the fetal position because of pain, and for once in his life, he was fighting that inappropriateness in order to help another being. It wasn't something he was used to, and he was finding it hard—literally—to succeed.

Anahita reached out and clutched his thigh with clawed fingers, and Max jumped for more than one reason. He brushed his fingers through her hair, hoping against hope that he was managing to keep his touch friendly. "Anahita, try to relax," he whispered.

She gave a breathless, humorless laugh, and Max cringed. *Yeah, relax. Easy as pie.* "Sorry," he muttered. "I just ... maybe if you relax, the split inside you will, too?"

She stiffened even further. "What if it does?" she asked, panic overtaking her. "What if the Guardian side takes over?" She tilted her head to the side and stared up at him with wide, black and gold eyes. "Oh, heaven, what if it *does*!"

"Okay, okay," Max said, grabbing her by her upper arms and hauling her up until she was curled into his chest, her lower body still wrapped around him, just now even more tightly. He wrapped his arms in tight bands across her back, tucking her face into the hollow of his throat. It felt so natural, so right, he had to fight his own moan. "Would that really be so bad?" he asked.

"Yes!" she shouted into his skin, causing goosebumps to erupt all over his neck.

Ouch, kind of. The thought of being his guardian angel was that abhorrent, huh?

She pulled back and looked up into his face, their lips nearly touching. "I hurt you just then, didn't I?" she asked, her breath tracking across his suddenly dry mouth.

Max snorted and attempted a one-shouldered shrug—a nearly impossible feat, he discovered, while clutching her to him as though his life depended on them becoming one.

"I *did*," she moaned. "And I feel *bad* about it! Because I am supposed to protect you from hurt!" She curled back into his chest and clutched the shirt on his back with desperate fingers. "Oh, this is just the *worst* possible thing."

"Okay," Max said, patting her back. "Easy with the ego there, pretty baby."

"I did it again!" she said, her voice muffled against his collar.

For some reason, Max felt a belly laugh brewing. His shoulders started to shake, and the next thing he knew, his mouth was falling wide open and the most unpracticed, unattractive, laugh-sounding *thing* was pouring past his lips.

He clutched her closer, holding on for balance as the laugh grew and grew, his head falling back slightly.

Anahita ever so slowly unfolded from her curled position beneath his chin and drew back to stare at him with those mismatched eyes that apparently spelled so much disaster to her entire existence. One of her brows was arching toward her hairline—the one over her black eye—and her lips were parted and slack.

And, of course, he found this even more hilarious, and he brushed a strand of hair from her cheek, tucking it behind her ear, as his laughter continued.

Then, magic happened. Her lips tilted at the corners; her eyebrows relaxed. She blinked her eyes twice, and when they opened again, they were the amazing baby blues he was becoming obsessed with. The slightest giggle slipped from her mouth. She gasped, and her eyes shot to his.

A feeling of accomplishment filled Max's chest. He had never completed so important a task as bringing this angel relief. "There now, see?" he whispered. "Feeling better?"

"It worked!" she said breathlessly. "Relaxing actually worked." Her brows crashed down, a furrow appearing in the smooth skin of her forehead. "Oh, heaven what if it comes back? It *will* come back."

"Hey, hey," Max said, giving her a quick squeeze, a sense of urgency overwhelming him at the thought of her panic bringing back the split. "Don't think about it, pretty baby. Okay? Just ... don't think about it."

She looked at him through dubious eyes.

"Distraction," Max said beneath his breath. "We need a distraction."

Anahita's eyes sparkled a bit, and her eyes dipped to his lips. Max's entire body jolted, and the sudden urge to throw her back down on the bed and lay atop her was almost a plan in motion before he got a hold of himself. *Distance*, he coached himself again, realizing they were touching entirely too much for distance of any kind to be maintained. Distance *and* distraction? Max frowned as he straightened and settled Anahita upon the pillow once more, those glorious golden waves fanning out around her head like a halo. His fingers itched to touch her silky hair, and he fisted his hands on his thighs, ignoring the look of hurt that had flashed upon Anahita's face when he'd separated them.

"Distraction," he repeated, smiling weakly at her. "Care to tell me more about this Guardian thing?"

Anahita's eyes slid from Max's face, and, oddly enough, it was the lack of her focus that made Max self-conscious about his scar, realizing in the absence of her blue-eyed warmth that he'd been interacting with her with the appalling state of his looks in full view. As sneakily as he could manage, he brushed his hair over his eye, silencing the cacophonous reciting of *good* and *evil* that had once again begun to clash with the disappearance of her dual-colored eyes.

"I should not have told you what I did," Anahita said, her eyes darting anywhere but his face. "You are not trustworthy."

Fucking ouch, again. She was right, of course. He was anything but trustworthy. *Especially* concerning the information he'd just requested. Still. Ouch.

"Well," he said, pausing to clear his throat. "Don't think about that either."

Her eyes returned to his face once more, and she frowned as she took in the hair covering his eye. She reached forward, her fingers trembling as Max's gaze zeroed in on them like a cornered animal, and brushed the hair out of his eyes. He couldn't help himself: he turned his face into the touch. The feeling of her fingers in his hair was just too divine. He barely caught the groan that threatened to erupt.

"That is terrible advice," Anahita whispered. "You are truly bad at administering guidance."

Another bubble of laughter gathered in his lungs somewhere behind his heart, but he swallowed it down. "A common complaint," he said, allowing the corner of his mouth to tip up.

Her fingers stroked through the hair behind his ear again, and Max felt his eyelids grow heavy. He hadn't slept in ... well, it was more than twenty-four hours and less than a week. Beyond that, he couldn't narrow it down.

"You are tired."

Max's eyes snapped open as far as they could, which, at best, was half-mast. "Exhausted," he admitted after a moment. "I should go catch some zzzs."

Her eyes widened a bit. "You cannot leave!"

Max frowned. "I can't?"

"I mean…" She looked away. "I—my head still hurts, and I must stay with you, and I ... just." She exhaled heavily. "Max, just, please do not leave yet. Please?" She slanted her eyes at his. "You can sleep here. I will watch you."

Max looked at the narrow space beside his angel on the bed, and a longing so intense he could taste it poured through him. *What could it hurt, really?* he rationalized. "No touching?" he asked, the words quicker than he'd intended.

Another flash of hurt in those blue depths. "If that is what you wish."

Max sucked in a breath. "You probably need to sleep, too. At least here I know you're safe."

Anahita shook her head. "Angels do not sleep. Not unless we ... Fall." She looked away again. "Or are about to Fall."

Max felt his eyebrows rise. "Well," he said slowly. He looked at the space beside the angel again, his body feeling heavy and on the verge of dreams.

They both stayed frozen in the awkward silence as they waited to see what Max would do. With a sigh that felt like surrender, Max let his body ease down beside Anahita. The firm mattress beneath him felt like a cloud compared to the cot from his prison cell. And the company was much, much prettier as well. They lay facing each other, Anahita's eyes so big and beautiful. Max scooted back from her as far as the small mattress would allow, his back crammed against the rails on the medical bed. Still, it was close enough for her lily scent to waft over him. He longed to wrap his arms around her, pull her in close, and bury his face in her neck so he could fall into sleep with that scent filling him.

"Rest and feel better," Max whispered, a yawn following the words. "I'll sleep here for now." His eyes closed and sleep rushed in, but just before he allowed it to overtake him, he repeated once in sleepy murmurs: "Remember, no touching."

Chapter Thirteen

The urge to touch him was so strong it robbed Anahita of breath. In sleep, he was beautiful to her. His face was relaxed of his default expression—something between disdain for all humanity and self-loathing—and she wanted to lean in and press her lips to his parted ones.

His lips were so contrarily soft when compared to everything else about his body and personality. They were vying with his back as Anahita's favorite part of him, though she imagined if she ever got a glimpse of his body unclothed, priorities would change.

No touching. This man's no-touching rule was becoming her bane ... which was saying a lot considering her current predicament . It did not even make sense! They had touched plenty! It felt as though his hands were constantly upon her, and she loved it when they were. *Loved* it.

But the touching was very much one-sided now—a swift and not welcome change from their first intimate encounter in that dirty prison cell. She was discovering that being denied the pleasure of laying hands on her lover was just as bad, if not worse, than being denied the culmination of her desire.

His breaths were slow and steady, and each time he exhaled, the warm draft of his air crossed over her face, scented of mint. As his eyes were closed, and he could not protest, she found herself edging closer to him with each of his exhales until they were nose to nose, though not touching. She suspected the moment she touched him, he would burst to wakefulness and be very unhappy.

His face filled her vision, and she was enraptured. Eyelashes black as coal spread across his cheeks; his hair fell onto his forehead, but not—as he so often ensured it did—into his eyes, covering his scar.

Her eyes traced that scar now, seeing in it all of the physical pain he must have endured receiving it and the emotional trauma he had obviously experienced since. That Guardian Compulsion writhed within her, trying to rise to the surface and protect.

She shoved it back down, but it did not go far, and she knew this was going to be a constant struggle for her until she completed her mission.

At the thought of her mission, of harming the man before her, that Guardian Compulsion charged to the front, overthrowing her tenuous roadblocks and tossing her right into Guardian mode.

Her entire vision turned golden—no trace of black and white this time. Her body and mind were clearly not split on where their priorities lay.

Anahita closed her eyes tightly, not willing to look through the golden haze that spelled her doom. The possibility that she could hurt Max, let alone kill him, seemed distant and far-fetched.

Max's breaths quickened, and Anahita opened her eyes a fraction. His face was no longer relaxed. His brows were low and drawn together. His lips had tensed, a firmer *O* appearing between them. Behind his eyelids, she could see his eyes darting back and forth.

A whimper left his mouth.

Before she'd had time for a second thought, her arms were around him. She pulled him into her body, wanting to wrap her entire self around him and cursing her robe for constricting her legs. She tucked his face into the curve of her neck and threaded the fingers of one hand through the hair on the back of his head. With her other hand, she made what she hoped were soothing circles across the wide expanse of his shoulder blades.

His breaths immediately settled, but she felt his body stiffen as he woke up.

"You are safe," she whispered to him, bending her head to bury her nose in his hair.

She felt him draw in a breath and hold it, and then, almost tentatively, his arms went around her, one burrowing between her ribcage and the bed, the other wrapping around her waist.

That held breath left him on a shuddering sigh. His hands clutched at her back, fingers digging into her skin through the fabric of her robe, and he pressed his face so firmly into her neck that she feared he hurt his nose.

His breaths kicked up again, and they sounded like pants—a sound that an animal would make upon realizing it had escaped a trap. They were an odd mix of residual fear and relief.

"I fucking hate that dream," he murmured into her skin. She could feel his lips brush her neck as he spoke, and she hoped the effect it had on her body was not apparent in the way she continued to stroke his back.

"What dream?" she asked.

He shook his head against her and held her tighter. Just when she was sure he would not answer her, there was the slightest whisper: "I tried to escape."

Anahita stiffened before she could stop herself, then quickly resumed stroking his back. "Hmm?" she hummed as noncommittally as possible.

"Back in prison," he continued. "I tried to escape. Constantly." His arms tightened. "My face was punishment."

Anahita tried to pull back to look in his eyes, but he would not release his hold on her. She had to settle for rubbing her cheek against his hair. "That is terrible."

An odd, humorless laugh brushed against her neck. "I killed someone. One of the guards who tried to stop me. His brother took his retribution."

Anahita closed her eyes.

"They had only recently guessed that the fruit from the other Tree may scar us. It took ten of them to hold me down, but they did it. And then that fucker sliced me up and threatened to do the same to Luke if I ever tried to escape again." His big body shuddered in her arms. "And I was so scared for him, I agreed," he said in a voice so small she could barely hear it. "Promised anything as long as they wouldn't touch him." His voice surged. "I was a coward. We didn't know that their funding had dried up when Eli killed the original head of the Operation. Most of the guards left after they stopped getting paid, and I *still* didn't try to escape. I gave up. It's disgusting."

"No," Anahita said, squeezing him tighter.

"What's worse," Max said, cutting her off, "is that I can't even take my revenge now. There's no one left to take it against but a couple of guards who stayed because they're zealots."

"Then we will take your revenge against those few," Anahita vowed. "It is important to you, it is important to me." A haggard puff of breath caressed Anahita's ear. "It is over now," she said, tenderness welling up within her and nearly bringing tears to her golden eyes. "I will never let anything hurt you again."

As the words left her mouth, she was startled that they rang true. She fought the urge to panic. She had to hurt him. She *had to.*

His breathing froze, and he pulled back. She loosened the hold she had on the back of his head and tipped her chin to look upon him.

Their faces were nearly touching. His eyes skipped back and forth between hers, and she could see in his mismatched eyes that he understood the implication of finding two golden eyes. She reached up and brushed the back of her fingers across his smooth cheek, wanting more than anything—even more than getting her Warrior side to come to the fore—to taste his lips once again.

His eyes drifted closed, and he moved in closer. A thrill shot up Anahita's spine as she realized he was going to grant her unspoken wish. His arms tightened around her back.

And then, suddenly, he was gone.

His arms had left her. She was lying on the bed, alone, the cold breezes of the medical wing pouring over her.

She looked beside the bed to find Max standing across the room, one of his hands plowing through his hair.

He glowered at her with agitated and tortured eyes. "I said *no touching*," he hissed, as though in pain.

Anahita shot upright, her hands fisting. "This is nonsense," she hissed right back. "You needed it and you liked it, so do not snap at me like a child on the verge of an irrational tantrum. Are you a man or are you a boy? Take responsibility for your actions. This was not my fault. There *is* no fault, Max. It was only comfort."

In the aftermath of her tirade, they blinked at each other in stunned silence. If she had not gotten so angry, she would have laughed at the look upon his face. He wore the same expression he would have if she had smacked him in the face with a beam.

Finally, Max exhaled heavily "I cannot get close to you, angel." He dipped his chin and looked up at her through his lashes. "And keeping my distance becomes harder with each second we're together."

Anahita tilted her head to the side. "I understand completely." Even now, her fingers itched to touch him again. To hold him and sooth both of their feelings in the wake of their confrontation.

"I want to touch you again," Max whispered, stealing the words from her thoughts and bringing Anahita's eyes snapping back to his. She hoped that was a plan of action.

"I want to touch you *always*," Max groaned, shoving both hands through his hair and throwing them down to his sides once more. "It's fucking maddening."

Anahita swung her legs over the side of the cot. "I want that too," she said, reaching toward him with her right hand. "So much I ache from it."

Max looked at her hand before taking a shuffling step toward her. He bent forward at the waist and tentatively laced his fingers with hers. He gave her fingers a squeeze. "What do we do?"

It felt as though she could not breathe. "I know what I would *like* to do," she whispered. "I know what I cannot do," she finished, feeling as though they were perched on a precipice.

"Cannot do," Max parroted. With a frown, he dropped her fingers and stepped back. "Yeah, me, too," he said without meeting her eyes.

Sorrow knifed through her. "I have hurt you again, haven't I?"

Max grimaced. "I'm not a fucking moonflower, angel. I do not *hurt* as easily as you seem to think."

Anahita ducked her head, trying to get him to meet her eyes. "I do not think that is exactly true, Max," she said softly. Her Temptation "hurt" *very* easily. He was in a constant state of hurt.

"Don't," Max pleaded beneath his breath. "Don't go there. Please."

His voice had cracked on the last word, and Anahita nearly burst from her skin with the desire to wrap her arms around him. To shield him from the world that had been so cruel to him. She stood slowly to give him plenty of advance warning that she was going to move, and then she took the two steps needed to close the distance between them.

"Max," she whispered.

His shoulders stiffened.

"Well, hello," a new voice said.

Anahita's head snapped around. Oliver stood in the doorway of the medical room, pinning them both with a bemused look.

Max sucked in a breath beside her, and when she looked back at him, he had distanced himself from her. "Hey, man," Max said after clearing his throat. "You look all better!"

And he did. The beard was gone. The long hair was trimmed so that it was tousled and a little longer in the front than back. Looking at him, you would never know he was on a constant death cycle. He sported a cocky grin and leaned against the doorframe. As Anahita watched, Max gave the man a genuine smile that brought a lump to her throat. He was so obviously important to her Temptation. Oliver's suffering weighted heavily on Max. Perhaps, when Anahita killed the remaining guards who had tortured her human, she could look for the woman who had set Oliver on his current path…

"Yup," Oliver said. "Got my pudding." He held a package of plastic cups aloft before cradling it against his chest again. He pointed at Anahita with a black plastic spoon that oddly enough had tines on the end of it. "You're an angel." Those blue eyes of his roved over her form before returning to her face. "A very *pretty* angel. Want some pudding? I would share with you."

"Oliver," Max said, the simple word a warning.

"Not him though," Oliver said, gesturing toward Max. "He's surly."

Max stepped in front of Anahita, effectively blocking Oliver from her view.

"I was sent to find you," Oliver said. "Something about a meeting. And a plan?"

Anahita leaned around Max's shoulder in time to see Oliver give Max a look laden with meaning. She frowned.

"Right," Max said quickly. He turned on the spot, giving Anahita a look that couldn't quite meet her eyes. Her frown deepened. "Uh, bye," he said, shifting his weight.

Anahita leaned around him again to look at Oliver, and the moment her eyes clapped on him, her vision split: half black and white, half golden. The sword beneath her wing heated. Reason narrowed.

Her mission.

Her sword hand was in motion, reaching over her shoulder.

"Anahita!" Max yelled, his nose an inch from hers.

Unwillingly, her eyes left her target for a moment to stare at the man before her.

"You hurt him, you hurt me," he said urgently. "Badly. Understand?" He gripped her shoulders tightly with both hands. "I love this man more than I love myself," he whispered for her alone.

Something panged behind her heart, and when she next blinked, her double vision cleared. The world was straight color, as it should be. No, as it should *not* be! She gawped at Max in wide-eyed horror. Her Temptation could wrangle her Compulsion!

"Huh." The sound came from Oliver in the doorway. "That was weird."

Max took her in with one last look, then spun on his heel. "Out," he barked at Oliver. "Now."

"But she never answered me about the pudding."

Max grabbed Oliver by the back of his neck and pushed him out into the hall, slamming the door behind them with a resounding crash.

Anahita stared at the closed door while her knees gave out and she sank to the floor. She felt her dreams crumbling within her.

• • •

Max kept his hand on Oliver's neck as he marched him down the hall since the idiot was *still* trying to turn around and go back to Anahita.

Max had about had a heart attack when the angel had looked at Oliver and her eyes had snapped into that kill-mode of hers. Never once since he'd been around the angel, who had repeatedly told him she would kill him, had Max been scared for himself. But Oliver had definitely been in her sights; Max's friend had been in danger. And then—

"Holy hell," he muttered. He could snap Anahita out of her fucking "angel craze" or whatever that black-eyed thing was. Her *Compulsion*, she'd called it. He might be able to save their bacon!

"Man, you can let go of me now," Oliver said, twisting out of Max's grip. He continued matching Max's frantic pace as they walked through the main room with the Trees. He pried a pudding cup out of the cardboard holder and peeled the lid off, giving it a lick before tossing it into a trash can as he passed, winking at the brunette sitting beside it as he did so. "You know," he said, before shoving a spork heaped with pudding into his mouth. "I think you're making a mistake," he said around the pudding.

Max grimaced. "That is fucking disgusting. *Swallow*, man. Damn."

Oliver snorted. "That's what she said." He frowned. "He said…" He shook his head. "Whatever it's supposed to be. Still figuring that one out. Chick named Dahlia taught it to me."

Max had met Jericho's wife briefly. "Can tell you right now, she hears you call her *chick*, and she'll teach you a lot more."

"Naw, she loved me," Oliver said, spooning up more pudding. "All the ladies love some Oliver." He looked at Max out of the corner of his eye. "But *you*. The ladies don't love you, man. Not because of your scar," he said, talking louder just as Max opened his mouth to object. "It's more on account of you being a massive asshole and stuff. But that angel. *She* likes you. And you're gonna use her?" Oliver shook his head. "Only tail in a bajillion-mile radius you *ever* have a chance of getting, and you're ensuring she hates your guts. Typical."

Max growled. "She's not *tail*."

"Ah," Oliver said, pitching the empty pudding cup into another trash can. "So you're treating her well and shopping for rings. My mistake."

"Shut up." Max ground his teeth before saying, "Seems you've had a thorough debriefing then."

"That's what she—"

"Nope. You're done," Max said. "We're here." He nodded toward the meeting room. But Oliver was too busy prying another pudding cup out from its package, so Max sighed and went into the room first, hoping his friend would follow sometime this century. Eli, Jericho, and Luke were already sitting around the table. Max sank down into the chair at the head of the table that they seemed to have saved for him. Because they were expecting him to tell them all he had discovered of the angel.

Oliver sat in the chair to Max's right with a sigh. "I'm gonna have three squares of this shit every day until I've scratched my itch," he said, staring lovingly at the pudding cup he held in his hand.

Jericho leaned across the table, his hand outstretched. "Sugar free?" he asked. "Can't you eat pudding like a man?" When Jericho's fingers were an inch away from claiming a cup, Oliver stabbed the back of his hand with the spork. Jericho snatched his hand back. "Damn! That actually hurt!"

Oliver pointed his spork at Jericho. "Sugar will kill you, man," he said, the words gravely serious. "It's not a joke."

Jericho had been on the verge of smiling—the corners of his lips were still tilted up—but then he looked more closely at Oliver's face. The man's bottom lip actually trembled—fucking *trembled*—before Oliver seemed to get control of himself and paste his signature cocky grin back into place.

"Oliver," Eli said softly, leaning forward himself. Max knew a little of Eli's story. He, too, had died repeatedly. Although his experience was much more gruesome than Oliver's—someone had actually murdered Eli over and over again in a sick, twisted experiment—he was the only one who had any idea what Oliver had to be feeling. "Maybe you'd like some more time before we do this," Eli said, gesturing toward Max's place at the table, confirming once again why they were here.

"Nope," Oliver said, his chipper persona back in place as he opened another pudding cup. "We have no time to waste. Max, here, has to completely alienate the woman who could love him." He turned toward Max. "Right, buddy?"

They locked eyes, and Max ignored the feeling he got that Oliver was *good* as he tried to choke down the feelings that were crowding his chest. Did Oliver think this was fucking easy? It wasn't! But the damn man had nearly cried over the sugar content of pudding. If Max could do anything to keep him safe—to keep death away—he was going to do it. He *owed* it to him. To them all.

There is still time to stop this, the Voice whispered. *You have not betrayed her yet.*

"Anahita's a half-breed." The words left Max's mouth firmly and loudly. Almost as though he was not in conflict with himself at all. "And I can keep her from killing us."

All of the men around the table straightened. "Whoa," Eli said, placing both palms down on the table. "Maybe back up a little."

"That's a lot," Luke said, his voice modulating between admiration and sadness.

"Mistake," Oliver stage-whispered before shoveling more pudding into his mouth.

Max shook his shoulders slightly, hoping to shake off the feeling that Oliver was right. "Jayden alluded to her wanting something very badly, which killing us would provide. It's because she's half Warrior, half Guardian that she is so motivated. I can tell you personally that she loathes her Guardian side." He paused. "But right now, that's the side that's winning." Big breath. "She's my Guardian angel. She can't kill me, and I just found out that she can't kill anyone else, either, if it will hurt me in some way."

"So you just, what—" Eli gestured in the air. "Follow her around and tell her *ouch* every time she tries to kill someone?"

"Essentially," Max said. "Yes." He nodded his head toward Oliver. "He seems to be her primary target right now, but I'm pretty sure he's safe at present since I've already told her I lov—" He broke off as a blush crept up his neck. He looked down at the table for a moment, hoping against hope no one guessed the sentimental crap he'd just about flung.

"We're registered at Target," Oliver said. "Don't be cheapskates."

Max raised his head and frowned at him, but Oliver just blew him a kiss. Max was pretty sure some pudding went flying. *Nice.*

"Well, if she's focused on Oliver, she won't be able to move on lightly," Jericho said. "Jayden told us the Compulsion sets up an order of action that angels are mostly helpless to follow."

"Good to know," Max said, slapping the table as he pushed to his feet.

"Hey, where you going, lover?" Oliver asked, reaching for yet another pudding cup and discovering only empties scattered on the tabletop. "Fuck a duck. Those went fast."

"Maybe if you ate something other than a kid's snack, you wouldn't be so hungry," Luke muttered.

Max spun around just as Oliver flipped Luke the bird. "She'll be coming for me," Max said over his shoulder as he started toward the exit. "Her Guardian side won't let her stay out of my presence for long, and I'm sure you have things to discuss with what I've told you." He paused at the door. "Just ... find a plan that doesn't..." He shoved a hand through his hair. "Forget it. Fill me in later."

"That's what she said. Hah! Works in every situation."

"Still not funny," Max said, reaching for the door.

"Disagree!"

Max closed the door behind him. In the silence of the hallway, he deflated a bit. Damn. That had been harder than he'd expected. And he had the worst taste in his mouth. It made him want to find Anahita and replace it with a much better taste. Like her skin. Or—even better—that sweet spot between her legs that he hadn't gotten to taste yet.

And, just like that, he was hard as a beam. "Great," he muttered, the dull ache in his belly, which had been his constant companion since earlier today, growing to the point that he grunted.

He needed to handle things. And soon. The Impulse pain was already getting borderline distracting.

He spun on his heel to head off to his quarters and sucked in a breath, his hand shooting to cover his heart. "Anahita," he said.

The angel had been standing right behind him.

"Uh, hey," he said slowly, resisting the urge to look over his shoulder and make sure the door behind him was truly closed. God, he hoped she hadn't heard anything.

She tilted her head and looked at him. Her eyes were crystal blue, so Max tried to relax. "Are you well?" she asked. "You seem ... flustered."

Max stood straight and pulled his damn hand from his chest. "Men don't fluster, pretty baby."

"Oh," she said, a small smile tipping her lips. "Of course not."

She was teasing him now? God help him. But at least he could relax. She would definitely not be smiling at him if she'd overheard him spill her secrets. Behind the door, the sound of male laughter boomed, and Max shot into action. "Come with me," he said quickly, reaching out and grabbing her upper arm before setting out for the main room like a man on a mission. And he was. It was called "Get the angel the hell away from the plan to betray her."

"Where are we going?" Anahita asked, easily keeping stride with him. "Your fingers are so warm," she said immediately after, almost beneath her breath.

Max skidded to a stop, his fingers clenching against her soft, soft skin. He looked down at her to find her face tipped up toward his, smile still in place.

"I stayed away from you as long as I could," she muttered, her smile fading. "It was so hard. Is that not wretched?"

Heat flushed his entire body. That was the most amazing news he'd heard all day. "I don't think it's wretched at all," he said past his dry mouth. "I was already coming to find you, too," he admitted.

"You were?"

She looked so damn hopeful, Max wanted to cry. Why couldn't this work for them? *Why* couldn't it work? A web of itchy, hot pain shot out from his gut, and Max couldn't prevent a grimace as he bent sideways slightly to scratch his thigh.

Anahita's eyes flashed golden for a moment before returning to blue. "You *are* hurting!"

How many times could he blush in one day? "It's nothing," he murmured, surreptitiously looking around to make sure no one was eavesdropping on them. "I was just headed to my quarters to take care of it. I'm fine. Really."

Her eyes widened. "You're hurting because of *us*?" Her words were startlingly loud, and several nearby heads turned in their direction.

"Shh, Ana," he whispered, ducking his head. "Come on now."

She jolted at the shortened version of her name, and Max silently cursed himself a fool. But something in her eyes made him wonder if she *didn't* mind the epithet. He tried to rotate his hips so that he could adjust himself in his pants without anyone seeing, but eventually gave up. They had too much attention. Max settled for shaking his hair into his face. In an odd moment of clarity, he discovered it'd been longer than normal since he'd done such a thing. He looked back at Anahita. Were her silly words of encouragement actually having an effect on him?

"It seems as though no matter what I do, I hurt you," Anahita said below her breath. "I'm not a good Warrior. Not a good Guardian."

"For what it's worth, I think you're a good Anahita," Max said even before he realized he'd meant to utter the words.

Anahita looked up at him and rolled her eyes. Great, so she was having a good effect on him, and *he'd* driven an angel to learn the habit of rolling her eyes.

For some reason, this made Max's chest warm and his palms itch to touch her even more, and the corresponding pain shooting through his gut took his breath away. He was unable to capture a grunt before it escaped. "Okay," he said. "I really do have to go." He turned his back and began to walk toward the living quarters, but after a few steps he still had an angelic shadow. He stopped, and she skidded to a halt, too. "Are you ... coming with me?" he asked haltingly. A certain part of Max's body liked that thought way too much.

Anahita looked at her toes where they peeked through beneath the hem of her robe. "Well, I cannot leave you again so soon. My entire being rebels against it. And ... I find I do ... maybe ... want to come with you. Maybe."

The word *yes* wanted to launch itself from Max's mouth, so he clenched his jaw and covered his mouth with his fingers. "Hmm," he hummed. With more self-control than he thought he possessed, he turned around slowly and once more made his way toward the living quarters. The journey was a blur as he spent most of his time distracted by the riot of reaction in his very-not-quiet mind. When he stopped again, it was to find that he was standing in front of Anahita's door. He'd led them to her quarters instead of his. The place where he already felt more at home than anywhere else in the world.

Ah, hell. He wanted to punch himself in the face. What was he doing?

But then, her lily scent wafted over him and he felt the heat of her body in his back as though she had stepped closer to him in anticipation, and he reached out and twisted the doorknob, stepped out of the way, and ushered her into the room beyond.

He leaned in to catch more of her scent as she brushed past him, and the ache within him grew to the point he wondered if he was going to be able to walk on steady legs and not have to sit down.

He trudged into the room and walked right up to where Anahita had paused in front of the coffee table, where he'd touched her before. He stepped in even closer, her wings brushing his chest, and pressed his face into the crown of her head. The soft, cool silk brushed his cheeks and closed eyelids and caught in his beard. He nuzzled his way down to her shoulder where he pressed a brief kiss to the surprisingly hot skin at the juncture of shoulder and neck. She jumped and then sighed, leaning back into him slightly.

He took it as an invitation to continue. He kept his hips away from the tempting curve of her ass, though he could feel the heat of it penetrate the front of his pants. A distant, primitive voice was screaming in his head to thrust against that part of her. To clutch her hips with both hands and yank her to him. He shoved it aside.

Distance. He *had* to have it. He felt on the verge of shattering as is.

He ran his nose up the delicate slope of her neck until his lips reached her ear. He pressed a kiss there as he wound one arm around her waist and grabbed a handful of her robe. With the other hand, he unbuttoned his jeans and lowered the zipper: a sound that echoed in the quiet of the room. As he eased his hand into his pants, he began pulling Anahita's robe up by the fistful, desperate to touch her.

His breaths were pants now and stirred the hair around her ear. "God, Ana," he groaned. "I feel like I'm already losing control."

His hand found the hem of her robe on its next desperate grab, and she made a hoarse exclamation as his fingertips brushed her thigh. He breathed a groan into her ear and swept his fingers up, brushing against the soft curls that hid his most favorite spot. With his other hand, he wrapped his fingers around an erection that throbbed painfully.

With a sharp nip to her ear, he cupped her fully, sliding a finger between her lips to stroke her.

He froze.

"Ana?"

He pressed his finger between her lips again in the hopes that he had been mistaken, and his ability to breathe left him.

She was not even remotely wet for him.

Every doubt in his mind came crashing down at once. With reluctance, he eased his hand from between her thighs, gripped her by her shoulders, and turned her to face him. She would not meet his eyes, and he wondered again just how ugly he really was and how it must affect how she felt about him.

He placed his finger beneath her chin and tilted her head up. When she still refused to look at him, he said, "Ana, look at me." He winced at how vulnerable his words sounded. He couldn't believe he *wanted* her to look at him.

She shook her head and took in a huge, shuddering breath. "I cannot do this casually anymore," she whispered. "I find I am not curious any longer." Her breath left her just as shakily as it had entered her. "I am just sad."

And then, God help him, an actual *tear* hit the finger that was propping up her chin.

"Oh, no," he breathed. "No. You can't, Ana." He felt as though someone had pitched a bowling ball at his stomach. He thumbed away another tear and threaded his fingers through her hair to cup her cheek.

"Everything I almost had is gone, and everything I *could* have with you we both deny ourselves." She made a noise that sounded suspiciously like a sob. "I am just so *tired*."

More of those tears spilled over from her eyes, and Max was undone. He pulled her into his arms, stroking her wings while winding himself around her, and tucked her face into his neck. "Okay, pretty baby. Okay," he muttered to her, not knowing what he was offering or—God help him—agreeing to.

"*Why* is my touch so abhorrent to you?" she asked in a near wail.

This. This was why he was an asshole. His stupid distance rule had driven her to the point of tears. And he would bet his life that nothing had managed to wrench such a reaction from her *ever*. He felt his well-laid plans to keep away from her crumble into dust along with his theory that he was anything but a gigantic fool.

Did he think he was maintaining distance? She was here in his arms, crying into his neck. And he'd brought her pleasure with his hand, as she had done to him.

What distance?

With half a mind that he couldn't believe what he was about to do, and the other half more than eager to get on with it, Max drew away from his angel slightly. He gathered her hands in his. "I don't know why anyone would want to touch me," he said. "But if it's truly what you want, I'm an idiot to deny you."

Finally, *finally*, she raised her eyes to his. *Blue heat.* The irrational thought filtered through his mind. Her eyes were simultaneously hot and cold, but they were all blue—no black or gold in sight. *She* was here with him, not some unthinking version of Anahita.

Unable to look away from those eyes, he raised their hands together and, after only a slight hesitation, pressed her palms to his chest.

She sucked in a breath, and he dimly thought he heard himself do the same. Even through the fabric of his shirt, her touch was life-altering. He spread his hands across the backs of hers and pressed them further into his pecs, rubbing his fingers across hers while doing so. Now that he'd decided to break the no-touching rule, he seemed ready to do so with a vengeance. Since she could not seem to do anything but gaze into his eyes with shock-widened ones of her own, Max gripped her hands a little tighter and moved both of her palms in a small circle.

His eyes slid closed momentarily, and all of his breath left him in a whoosh.

God. To think he'd wasted time without her hands upon him. "Ana," he murmured, opening his eyes once more. She was no longer looking at his face. Her eyes were zeroed in on where their hands intertwined and pressed against Max's body.

With a convulsive swallow, Max relinquished his hold on her. His hands returned to his sides, and he watched the top of her head to see what her next move would be.

With her right hand, she stroked his chest, running the palm across the pads of muscle until it ran into her other hand, and then passing it back.

Max's eyelids grew heavy, and he sucked his bottom lip in between his teeth to bite on, worried that he would grab her or scare her in some way with the intensity of the reaction that was brewing inside of him.

His erection, which had gone away upon finding that he was in arousal *alone*, was now back with a vengeance. It was trapped painfully in his pant leg and seemed to be begging to be the next thing Anahita touched in silent but insistent throbs.

Her hands trailed down his chest, fingers brushing over his nipples, and a quick burst of air from Max's mouth stirred Anahita's curls. Her head shot up once more, her eyes finding his and bearing a wary question. Her lips parted; his gaze focused in on the tip of her pink tongue. She hesitantly stroked his nipples with her fingertips again, and when this time Max couldn't contain a groan, he felt confidence pour from her.

"So sensitive," she whispered, licking her bottom lip.

Max clenched his fists. He wanted that lip in *his* mouth. He wanted *his* tongue licking it.

She pinched both of his nipples between fingers and thumbs, and Max was done. "Fuck, *Ana*," he moaned. His hands launched from his sides and grabbed her hips, pulling her in. With their heights so evenly matched, his erection ground against her mound, and he could *feel* her heat. She was burning up. "Oh, God," he whispered, thrusting his hips forward to come into better contact with her. "I want you so bad, I can hardly breathe, Ana."

Her breathing hitched and then returned at a quicker rate. "Want?" she asked breathlessly. "What do you want?"

"*You*. Naked and spread out underneath me." His hands wandered the curve of her hips until he was able to palm her ass. He thrust against her again, his cock grinding in exquisite torture, and at the same time, he used his grip on her ass to thrust her lower body into his. Her eyes widened and her breathing increased even more. "I want to be inside you. God, Ana," he said, feeling frantic and as though he were going to burst into a million pieces from frustration. "I can't—"

Anahita whimpered, cutting Max off. Was that the sound she'd make as he entered her and began to move inside her as deeply as he could? Her hands fisted in his shirt, and she began pulling on it almost fretfully. "Skin," she breathed. "I need to touch you." She began pulling his shirt up. "Max," she pleaded.

He pulled his hands from her firm ass only long enough to reach behind his shoulders and haul his shirt up and over his head. He tossed it toward the sofa, and then reached for her again, pulling her into his arms and palming her rear end to pull her into another thrust.

She gasped. "Your body," she whispered.

Max paused mid-thrust, alarm shooting through him until he noticed that her eyes were *caressing* his torso, not wide and fixed with disgust. They were tracing every line and ridge of muscle Max possessed. She moaned and raised her hands.

Her palms hovered over his pecs, and Max found himself holding his breath. When her hands finally landed over his nipples and he felt her skin upon his for the first time, a shudder wracked his body. "Touch me," he begged. "Touch me everywhere." He tried to catch his breath, but every muscle—lungs included—in his body was frozen. "Ana," he said, her name a prayer.

"Everywhere," she repeated. "Yes." She traced her fingers along one of the ridges of his abdomen and then followed the center divide down to his pants. She began to work his open fly even more apart, and Max felt something in his world shift. She was unclothing him—would soon have him...

"Pretty angel," he whispered. "If you take off my pants, I'll be naked."

"Yes," she breathed.

He groaned. "Ana, hold on." He placed a hand over hers to still her movements, though it took all of his willpower to do so. "Baby, if I'm naked, I'm going to lose my control with you."

She flicked his hands away. "That had better be a promise," she said, returning to her work and wrestling his pants wide open.

As her words registered with his lust-ridden brain, Max realized they were at the point of no return, and he had no intention of turning back. With one more try, he said, "Be very sure, Ana, because I can't handle it if you ask me to stop. It will destroy—I *will* stop, of course—but, Ana—"

She stilled and laid a finger across his lips. "Max," she said softly, looking into his eyes. "I want *you*. I do not want you to stop. I want to touch you with my hands—with my body—until we are both sated."

Max's mouth went dry. *Sated.* An image of them intertwined, sweaty, and breathless floated through his mind, and he knew *sated* was going to be an elusive concept. He would always want more of her.

She was still looking into his eyes, and he got the impression that she was waiting for some sort of acknowledgement—maybe even permission—from him. One of her hands was fisted on the waistband of his pants.

Knowing he was changing things forever, he gave one curt nod. She smiled up at him. She pulled her finger from his lips and, with both hands, worked his pants down his hips.

They both watched as more of his skin was revealed. With his cock pinned the way it was, it took a little more time than normal for that part of him to make an appearance, but when it did, she paused. With an index finger, she traced the indention at the point where his erection met his body, and Max's eyes nearly rolled back into his head.

He hummed from between closed lips, and she repeated the movement.

He needed his pants off. *Now*. "Ana, please," he begged. "The rest of the way."

He could see the corners of her mouth tip up, but blessedly, she grabbed his pants once more and worked them down to the middle of his thighs. As soon as his erection was free, it sprang to attention between them, and she gasped.

He bent at the waist a little to lay his hands over hers where they were still knotted in the fabric of his pants, hoping in some way to garner what she was thinking and to offer reassurance if she was panicked.

She stared at his cock so long that Max actually grew uncomfortable. "Ana," he said, squeezing her hands. "My eyes are up here, pretty baby."

When she still stared, he reached for her chin and prompted her gaze upward. It clashed with his. Her eyes were wide. Max swallowed, and put the question out there. "You're a virgin, aren't you?"

She did not nod. She didn't have to. She was a fucking angel for Christ's sake. They probably didn't sleep around.

He reached up with his thumb and stroked her bottom lip. "Does the sight of my—does it ... scare you?" he asked. He held his breath.

"My reaction to it scares me," she whispered.

Max clenched his teeth, preparing to pull his pants aright again. But she wasn't done.

"I want to do so many things to it," she murmured, running her fingers up and down the front of his thighs. Goosebumps lined his legs, and his cock jerked.

"What, pretty baby?" he rasped. "What do you want to do to it?"

Her eyes darted away. "It is probably wicked."

Oh, he hoped so. He pinched her chin until she looked back at him. "We're done with limits," he said to her fervently. "You want to do something to me, you do it. Standing permission, Ana, you hear me? Nothing is off limits, and nothing is embarrassing. Not between us. That's over."

"I can ... touch it with my t-tongue?"

Holy God. A fine tremor set into his legs, and he reached out and pulled her into his arms, burying his face in her hair and holding on for dear life so he wouldn't hit the floor. "Any damn time of the day," he said, his voice a husky rumble.

Her hands caressed his back, her nails biting the skin over his shoulder blades just right as she dug her fingertips into him. "It is very pretty," she muttered. "That part of you. I ... like it very much."

His eyes slid closed, and he tightened his hold on her body. She was wrecking him here. "It likes you very much, too," he said. "You have no idea."

She began to lower, trying to go to her knees. He pulled back and gripped her by the elbows to keep her close.

"I want to—"

"I know you do," he cut her off. "But, I..." His eyes roved her face—her wide-open eyes, her parted lips, the blush that tinted her cheeks. He felt himself slipping into something with her that was powerful and lasting. "Ana, if I don't get to see your body, too, I'm not going to make it here," he said.

A wide grin split her face. "Truly?" she asked.

He brushed the back of his finger down her cheek. "Truly." Her eyes sparkled, and then she stepped away from him slightly. She reached down, grabbed two handfuls of angel robe, and pulled it up and over her head. His jaw dropped as her robe floated to the floor. "You really don't have any embarrassment, do you?" he croaked.

In his peripheral vision, he saw her cock her head to the side, but he was too focused on the body she'd revealed. "Why would I be embarrassed?" she asked without pretense.

"Why, indeed?" he muttered. He'd never seen a woman look the way his Ana did. She was an Amazon, and he realized when his cock wept a drop at the sight of her that his type was Amazon all the way. Her height did her so good, with toned legs that went on for miles and a long torso that was trim and packed with delicate muscle lines. The dip that started in the middle of her stomach just below her breasts and trailed down to her belly button called to him like a Siren, and he wanted to trace this space between muscle with his tongue. Her breasts were high and perfect, tipped with nipples the palest shade of pink, and they pebbled before his eyes. He took a stumbling step forward, closing the small distance she had put between them to disrobe. His erection met her before the rest of him did, sifting through the golden curls between her legs and folding up between them to become trapped between their bellies.

Her eyelids drooped. "Oh," she breathed. She then writhed against him, rubbing his cock with her body. "That feels…"

He groaned and steadied her movements by clutching both of her hips. "Too good," he finished for her. "Oh, God."

She looked up at him, and their lips were so close he had only to lean down the fraction of an inch it took to taste her mouth. Her lips parted beneath his, and she flicked out her tongue, stroking before opening wider and biting into his bottom lip.

She may as well have slapped his ass. A beastly sound broke from his chest, and next he knew, he was hauling her up by the back of her thighs, guiding her legs to cinch around his waist. He began shuffling toward her bedroom as fast as the pants around his thighs would let him, and at the same time, he sucked on her neck hard enough that he knew he was leaving a mark.

She threw her head back and the sexiest, huskiest feminine chuckle rolled out of her. "Are you trying to walk with your pants half on?" she asked, her fingernails biting into his shoulders.

She was laughing at him. They both seemed to realize it at the same time. Her head snapped down again, and she looked at him with worry-filled eyes. "I was not laughing at—"

"Shh." He hugged her tighter. "This is *supposed* to be fun, pretty baby. Laughing is a good sign." Granted, he couldn't remember a time he had ever laughed with another lover, but it *had* always felt like it should happen.

"It is supposed to be *fun*?"

His gut bottomed out. He pressed a kiss to her chin. "Yes, Ana." He kicked himself internally. "Believe it or not, it is." She looked at him dubiously, and he silently promised to make sure it was nothing *but* fun for her from now on. He began moving again, shuffling along exaggeratedly enough to get a smile from her once more, and soon they reached the bedroom. "I'm going to lay you down, okay, Ana?" he asked.

She shimmied in his arms. "Wings," she said quickly as he began to lower her.

He cursed, twisted around, and shifted his hold on her so that he plopped to the bed on his back with Anahita straddling his stomach on her knees. Her wings flared behind her, and she looked down at him. "Oh, wow," she breathed, planting her hands on his pecs and leaning her weight onto them. "This, I like very much."

"You ain't kidding." *Holy shit.* He gripped her hips for a moment, then smoothed his hands up her sides and back down, wanting to touch every part of her at once, but desperately wanting to avoid scaring her.

She arched her back into his touch and hummed. As she arched, the hot liquid center of her rubbed back and forth on his belly, and Max groaned. He wanted to raise his knees up so that he could press his cock against the firm swells of her ass, but as he tried to do so, he ran into the problem of his pants still around his thighs. "A little help, Ana," he said, trying to wiggle his pants off. "The pants, please."

She twisted to her right and reached behind her to grab his pants and help him wrestle them off, but he was distracted by the flicks of muscle in her torso such a maneuver put on display. "Aw, *fuck*," he breathed, placing his hand flat on her lower belly and sliding it up to her ribcage, stroking those flickering muscles.

She sucked in a breath and turned back around to him, his pants finally on the floor. Her eyes were sparking heat. "Do that again."

With pleasure. He stroked her stomach again, and she arched back, thrusting her breasts to the ceiling and giving him more wonderful things to watch. With his legs free, he was able to prop his feet on the bed as he wished and move his lower body enough that his heavy erection prodded her ass. She jumped, and he wondered if he should have maybe kept his feet on the floor, but then she leaned back, her wings brushing the tops of his thighs, and ground her ass into his now-trapped cock.

His eyes rolled back into his head, and his fingers clenched her skin where he held her just beneath her breasts. And then, like the quick study that she was, she ground forward, pressing her sweet clit into the muscle of his stomach, before sliding back, grinding against him once again.

A very unmanly noise escaped Max's lips, and he clenched them tight, but not before Anahita heard him and smiled. "Like that, do you?" she asked with a teasing glint to her eye.

Before she could do it again and unman him, he spread his palms over her breasts, freezing her on the spot. He squeezed them both gently. "Lean over, pretty baby, and kiss me." His words were composed enough, and even contained a hint of cool seduction, but inside, every nerve ending was screaming for her to put her mouth upon his, so when she did lean in, he wrapped his arms around her back and between her wings and crushed her to his chest to plunder her mouth.

She whimpered and met the thrust of his tongue with one of her own. Her breasts were pressing into his pecs so hard he could feel every ridge of her pebbled nipples. She began squirming in his arms, and it rubbed the slick heat of her center all over his stomach.

He was going to lose his ever-loving mind if she kept it up.

She broke the kiss, whispered his name, and kissed the corner of his mouth, his cheek, his jaw. By the time she nibbled on his neck, Max could no longer hold back his groaning. He let his hands drift over the lines of her back, brushing the feathers his fingers found along the way, and dug his fingers into her ass to press that molten place between her thighs more firmly against him. When he gripped her hard and rocked her hips so that that place slid along him, she gasped into his ear and stiffened in his arms before moaning his name.

Hearing his name on her lips did something to his heart. He flexed his fingers and moved her on him again, and this time, she followed his lead and canted her hips in his hold in such a way that when she moaned again, he joined her. The play of muscle beneath his fingertips was going to be the end of him.

"Pretty baby," he rasped into her hair, "keep doing that." He'd meant it to be an instruction, but it came out more plea than anything.

She continued to nibble on his neck, and when she moved her lips upward to pull his earlobe between her teeth, he tilted his head to the side to give her better access.

She was rubbing herself on him faster and faster, and by this point, his dick was throbbing so painfully, he was worried that he was going to come, and soon. He was not ready for this to end. He was preparing to use his grip on her ass to slow her down a bit, to draw things out, when she repositioned herself. Suddenly, all of that slick heat that had been sliding along his abs was now on his cock.

She was sitting on him, his dick folded up and trapped between his stomach and the outside of what he could already feel was the sweetest place in the world. He bit out a low, quick curse and internally begged himself to behave. To *not* move the slight amount needed to slide into her.

She pressed her forehead into his shoulder and dug her fingernails into his biceps. "I can *feel* your heartbeat," she moaned. "You are so hard. And hot." She made the same sliding motion she had been doing against his stomach, but this time she was riding his dick.

As she sucked in a breath, Max panicked. "God, *Ana*," he groaned, tightening his grip. "Stop." His voice cracked on the word. "You have to stop."

He could feel his orgasm climbing up his cock. She felt too good.

She paused and raised her head. "Stop?" she asked. "Oh, no," she said, her eyes widening. "*Please* no."

Max gritted his teeth, the muscle in his jaw ticking. "I can't … *not* be in you if you keep…" He closed his eyes and opened them again helplessly, words escaping his grasp.

"*In me*," she breathed. "That is bad?"

Oh, God. "It's … not something … you can take back," he stuttered, swallowing down the lump in his throat that came with the realization that she was acting as though she would allow him inside her body.

He so desperately wanted to be inside her body.

She looked down into his face, her eyes tracing his features—scar included—before returning to his eyes. "I will not want to take it back," she said gravely.

He held himself back. "Your Fall?"

Her eyes grew dazed. "Oh," she said. "*Children* come from this." She spoke the words as though she had just comprehended this most fundamental law of nature.

Another laugh percolated. He'd never fought laughter so hard in this decade, and it was while he was in bed with a woman. *Never would have guessed.* "Yeah, pretty baby, they do."

Her brows drew together before her face relaxed and she grinned down at him. "You have things to prevent children, though, correct?"

A pang hit him in the chest. "Not on me," he said. *Yeah, that was stupid,* he thought to himself as he made a mental note to stock up on condoms. A previous conversation with Eli about the importance of protection between Impulse mates flickered through his mind. "Unless…" Wrapping his arm around Anahita's waist, he leaned far over to his right to pull open the drawer of the nightstand. The lamplight flickered off of a roll of shiny foil packets. "Oh, God bless everyone," Max muttered as he snagged the roll and pulled it close enough to tear off a square with both hands.

When he looked at Anahita again, she was staring at the foil square in his hand with a furrow between her eyebrows. She looked so curious, he wanted to crush her to his chest again and kiss her until she was breathless.

"*That* prevents children?" she asked.

He nodded. "Know how it works?"

She shook her head.

"Want to?"

In answer, she reached out and plucked the condom from his fingers and flipped it over on her palm. "I will need to, will I not?" She raised her eyes to his. "For the future."

Max's stomach clenched. Two warring responses battled for supremacy inside him. One was borderline panic: the future? The other won. "Only if we're talking about with me, pretty baby."

A slow smile started to spread on her lips, and before they could both examine their words any more closely, Max reached out and grabbed her hips, lifting her up from him for only as long as it took to sit her on his thighs. His erection lay heavy on his belly right in front of her, and he pulled the foil packet from her hand and held it up for her to see. Her eyes were riveted elsewhere. "Ana," he said, fighting back a smile. "My eyes are up here."

Her eyes snapped up, and she raised one brow. "I like looking at it," she said unapologetically.

A quick burst of air that sounded like a chuckle passed his lips. "Business first," he said, waving the condom. He went through the process of opening it and placing it with exaggerated moves, and once he began rolling it down his length, she slapped his hand aside and took over. He grunted as her fingers moved over him.

When he was covered, she looked back at his face. "I can put you inside me now?" she asked, raising her brows.

Max choked a bit before his throat relaxed enough for him to suck in a mouthful of air. "Um, you ... want to be on top ... or... ?" *Okay, man, get it together*. He just ... hadn't expected her to be so confident. Or so ready. Or so take-charge.

She tilted her head to the side. "Should I be somewhere else?"

He shook his head. "No," he said, his voice cracking. "Top's good."

She stared at him, then she straightened. "You are *nervous*," she said.

He groaned and scrubbed his face with one hand. *Jesus God, Max, who's the fucking virgin?* "It's just ... been a while for me, Ana. I don't know how to do this with you." He looked up at her. "I mean, we've spent most of our time laughing and talking about condoms. It just feels ... a little unromantic ... or something." As soon as he heard himself, he wanted to kick his own ass.

Anahita frowned. "I *liked* the laughing."

"I ... actually, I did, too," he muttered.

Her lips scrunched over to one side, and she propped her weight up with her hands on his hip bones. "Romance," she said, seemingly to herself. Her shoulders and wings drooped. "I do not know romance." She looked dejected; his heart cracked a bit. "I am not good at this either, am I?"

He jerked himself upright and wrapped his arms around her, crushing her chest against his and pressing her head into the space between his shoulder and neck. "Stop that," he said, more to himself than her. "You're good at this. You're *really* good at this," he said while thrusting his still aching cock into her firm belly. "It's me who's not doing good right now."

He pulled back from her slightly, and she met his eyes with those big blues he was learning to love so much. "I mean ... *look* at me, Ana." He gave her a little shake when her brows drew down in obvious confusion. "Look at my face. My looks. And look at yours! You fucking take my breath away every time I *glance* at you! I just ... " He broke off with a curse and stared over her shoulder at the wall. "Why would you even do this with me?"

Her cool fingers pressed into his cheeks, and she drew his face around until he was forced to look at her once more. "You *never* speak about yourself this way again, Max. And I mean *never*." Despite her words and her tone, her thumbs stroked his jawline. "It makes me angry, and I do not like to feel that emotion." She gave his head the same shake that he'd given her when he spoke moments ago. "I look at you and my entire *body* aches with wanting you. Did you know that?" She shifted in his lap, and he could feel the wetness between her thighs. "I grow drenched with needing you here." She shifted again, and Max gulped as his fingers dug into the fine muscles of her back. "I long to know how you feel inside of me more than I long for my next gulp of air." She leaned down until her words brushed against his lips as she spoke. "I want to taste you. Everywhere. To wind my fingers through your hair and pull your face between my breast. My thighs." Her lips parted, and she seemed lost as she gazed at his lips with her brow furrowed, her eyes desperate.

Max's arms began to shake. "On second thought," Max rasped in a hoarse voice, "you do the romance thing pretty damn well."

Her eyes rose to his. "I do?"

"God, yeah," he breathed. He wound one arm up between her wings until he could palm the back of her head, and then he pressed her down until he could claim her mouth with his. He slid his tongue into her mouth, and she moaned around it and kissed him back with all of the exuberance with which she approached everything in the bedroom. It took mere moments to get him back to the point of being breathless and desperate for her, and if the harried breathing he could hear and feel from her were any indication, she was right there with him.

He lowered his hands to the slight curve of her waist and lifted her up. When she followed his lead and propped herself up with her knees, he reached between them and positioned himself at her entrance. He parted from her mouth long enough to murmur, "Whenever you're ready," before diving right back in and tasting her.

And, of course, in typical Anahita fashion, she was moving as soon as his words left his mouth. He felt her thigh muscles flick against the outside of his as she lowered herself onto him. The moment her heat engulfed the head of his cock, he groaned deep in his chest and fought every instinct to thrust up into her with all of his might. *Slow.* She needed slow.

As she slid down, she broke away from the kiss to look in his eyes. Her breath kept catching on the release and then she would gasp a new set of air before releasing it with that little catch once more.

It was the most fucking erotic thing he'd ever heard, and already, only half inside of her, the tip of his cock felt like it was going to explode. Inch by inch, her body accepted his until he was seated all of the way. Her eyes were wide and luminous, and she was so tight around him that he feared to move, sure he must be hurting her.

She exhaled slowly, and he reached up to brush her cheek with his fingertips. "Does it hurt?" he asked.

Her eyes widened even more. "*This* is supposed to *hurt*?"

He felt his cheeks stretch with a grin as relief flooded him so quickly, he went lightheaded. "The first time does sometimes," he said. "I'm glad it doesn't for you."

"Did *your* first time hurt?"

His laugh was quick and loud. "Only my pride, pretty—"

She moved slightly—just a back and forward squirm in his lap—but it cut off his speech with a noise that sounded suspiciously like *arg*. She paused, looked at him with that tilted head again, smiled, and then repeated her movement, this time much more purposefully.

Max cursed long and low. He leaned forward and pressed his forehead against her shoulder, praying harder than he ever had in his life for the control to let her take the lead on this.

"You are very easy to read in this situation," she breathed, repeating the movement again, wrenching another groan from him and causing his body to shudder. "That makes me lucky, I think."

He nipped her shoulder, and she gasped. "Definitely feels like *I'm* lucky right now."

She set up a rhythm of rises and falls that was, actually, anything but a rhythm. Her untimed, inexperienced movements were about 90 percent enthusiasm and 10 percent acrobatic, and he'd never felt anything so amazing in his life.

After a few minutes, he placed his hands on her hips and began to guide her movements a little. He slowed her down and set up her timing, and watching realization dawn on her gorgeous face made his chest grow tight. He cupped her face and brushed his thumbs beneath her eyes. "You're so fucking beautiful, Ana."

She ran her hands across his shoulders, down his pecs, to his back—as though she couldn't touch enough of him. "Max," she moaned. "Max," she said again, this time, distress obvious in her tone.

"Shh." He trailed a hand over one breast and down her stomach to where they were joined. "We want to brush *this*"—he circled her clit with his thumb, and she gasped—"as we move."

He brushed her sensitive skin again, and her head fell back. "Yes, we want to do that," she moaned.

He chuckled and leaned forward to nip at her exposed neck. He moved his hand from between them—bit off another chuckle as she made a sound of protest—and sprawled it in the small of her back. Pressing down, he said, "Arch your back a little…"

She followed the pressure of his hand, and he used his other arm to wrap around her hips and reposition her just so—

She cried out as he thrust up into her, his cock dragging along her clit the entire way. Her core clenched tightly around him, and for a moment, Max was sure it was all over. She was just too much. The sounds she made, the softness of her skin, the unbelievably tight hold her body had on his, that lily smell that filled his lungs. "Ana," he groaned, biting down on her shoulder. A minimal amount of control surfaced—a gift from God, surely—and he used the arm around her hips to help her move against him again.

"I just ... we have to ... *faster, Max*," she babbled, her nails digging into his back.

"Fuck," he groaned, helpless to do anything but what she asked, even though the chances of this lasting longer than a minute through *faster* were close to zero.

Control slipped its leash. He began thrusting up into her hard enough to make her bounce, which had the most breathtaking effect on her breasts. Even as he acknowledged that he was being too rough for a virgin, he leaned forward and captured one of those bouncing nipples with his mouth, sucking it between his lips and biting down with his teeth.

She cried out his name and clenched her fingers in his hair, holding him to her breast as she continued to buck into his thrusts. "Max," she moaned, breaking off to cry out again. "I ... you cannot stop ... I ... *Max*."

He felt every muscle in her body clench, and she froze in his arms for a moment before crashing down on his lap and writhing back and forth on his dick. She made a high, keening sound, and Max released her breast to glance up at her. She sounded like she was coming…

"Oh, my *God*," he breathed, taking in her face, the wonder on her features. She bit into her bottom lip as her brows drew together and her eyes slid shut. "Oh, Ana," he groaned. One thing became very clear as he watched his angel come apart in his arms: this was anything but *just sex*. He had severely underestimated this, the power that this act would have.

And as her inner muscles clamped down on him and pulled him right over the edge with her, the unimaginable pleasure he felt as he came was tempered with the shame of betraying her. Of doing *anything* but bringing her the pleasure she felt right now in his arms.

She sucked in a ragged breath, and all of her muscles relaxed. She slowly straightened her head from where it had been thrown back and looked down at him. A sexy, satisfied smile stretched her lips, and she laid a palm over his thundering heart. "That felt…" Her smile turned a little self-conscious. "Oh, Max, I think I loved that," she whispered. She laughed. "I could Fall for that."

God, I loved that, too, warred in his brain with a horrified echo of *Fall* on repeat. The backs of his eyes burned, and he worried for a moment that he was going to start weeping. She was ready to Fall for him?

"Max?" He watched as all of the newfound wonder vanished from her face. "I was trying to make a joke." When he looked away, she fidgeted in his lap. "Was that not ... did I not do good for *you*?" Her eyes darted back and forth between his. "Just show me what to do for next time, and I will—"

"Stop that," he said gruffly. "Stop right now. That was the most amazing thing I've ever experienced, Anahita."

Her shoulders sagged. "Ana*hita*," she repeated. "Why do I not feel as though this is headed to a good place?"

He leaned down and pressed a quick kiss to her shoulder—the last time she would let him touch her?—and lifted her off of him to settle her on the bed. "I have to tell you something."

The light in her eyes dimmed, and she looked down and around, obviously searching for something, before plucking at the edge of the comforter and pulling it up to cover her breasts.

He'd finally managed to make her self-conscious of her body. *Great.* One more thing to add to his list of indictments. "Stay right here," he muttered. He pushed to his feet and stabbed his legs through his pants, snatching them up to his waist before treading into the living room area to retrieve her robe. The heavy feeling in his gut grew heavier as he walked back to her and handed her the robe, which she immediately pulled over her head and fretfully arranged to cover her whole body.

Was he really about to do this? Throw away the one thing in his life worth preserving? She didn't know they had been spying on her—at his request and urging. Who was to say she would *ever* find out?

That thought sobered him. She *might* never find out. And then she would have Fallen for someone who had shamelessly used her. He would never be able to enjoy her—her company or her body—knowing what was hidden between them.

"I just..." He swooped down and planted a brief but passionate kiss on her lips, which she, in apparent shock, allowed. When he broke the kiss and stared into her eyes, he already had a hard time catching his breath, and his body protested what he was about to do as it plowed straight into full arousal. "I had to do that one last time," he muttered.

She pulled away from him and crossed her arms over her stomach. "I do not care for the way that sounds."

Max straightened and shoved a hand through his hair. "You and me both." Not liking the way she eyed him, Max walked across the room and leaned against the wall, giving her plenty of space and shoving his hands in his pockets while simultaneously telling himself to stay here and not touch her, no matter what happened next. There was no easy way to do this, so Max just dived in. "I've been using you," he blurted.

Her head rocked back a bit, and she blinked. "Using me?" Her brows drew together. "*Using* me?" Her arms tightened around her stomach. "I take it you mean for more than just sating the Impulse."

And the fact that she seemed to think him using her for *that* was in any way acceptable nearly made him vomit on the spot. "What we just did…" He paused to point to the bed, and her eyes followed. A blush spread on her cheeks, and she looked away. "That was *not* using, Anahita, you hear me? That was … not using." His fucking voice *cracked*, and he closed his eyes. He obviously couldn't talk about *that* anymore. "We've been spying on you," he said, his voice firm once more. "Using you for intel against the armies of heaven."

She laughed, and her arms dropped from her waist. "Oh, really," she said, smiling. "And you are confessing now because you realize how ineffective such a thing turned out to be?"

"I told them," he blurted.

She froze. "Told them what?"

"What you told me in confidence. That you're half Guardian. That you are … *my* Guardian. That I can keep you from completing your mission."

Her expression didn't change, but she said, "Oh."

He was truly going to be sick. His eyes searched the walls for a thermostat, hoping he could maybe generate some more air. Nothing in this room, and he couldn't bear to walk out and look for it elsewhere. He sucked in a steady breath and willed it to help. "And, we were able to gather more information than you probably guessed." He was all-in now. "That this mission stands between you and becoming a Warrior. That Remiel is—"

"Enough," she cut him off. "Well." She cleared her throat. "It seems humans are more resourceful than we have given them credit for."

"Ana, I'm sorr—"

"Do not call me that." She pushed to her feet, and a hot blast shot from her body, making Max sweat even more. "Did you also find out that I have to complete my mission or I go to my death? That you die, or I do?"

Max felt the blood drain from his face. "What?"

"Hmm. Missed that part, did we?" Her hands clenched into fists at her sides. "I had hoped that we ... I thought to find another way..." She broke off. Her wings fluttered behind her. "My misguidedness does not bear discussion now, at any rate."

Max drew his hands from his pockets and held them out in front of him. "Okay, Ana ... hita," he finished when her eyes narrowed. "Let's just take a breath." In all of the scenarios that had played out in his mind, Max had never seen anything but her leaving him. Her *life* could be forfeited? And she looked as though she were preparing to attack. This was ... unexpected. As her stance changed, the Knowledge in his eye began screaming that she was *evil*.

"Perhaps you should not have been so cocky in your assumptions of your power over me." And then she reached beneath the edge of the bed and drew out a long sword that was flickering with black and red flames.

In the next instant, her eyes shot through to straight black. For the first time since encountering her in his dim cell, Max was sure of one thing: she could and would kill him.

• • •

The world simplified in an instant. Black and white. Wrong, right. This human had done wrong.

He seemed desperate for her to understand. Understand what? That he followed type? That he was as bad as all of the other deceptive, manipulating human beings? Even as these thoughts formulated, she could not figure out why they seemed accompanied by emotional pain. Angels did not feel such things. And what could *he* have done to her to merit such a visceral response?

Even in her black and white vision, she could see that he was pale. The finest indications of suffering played across his scarred face. His brows were drawn; his hands were supplicating.

A distant corner of her mind screamed at her to stop what she was getting ready to do before it was too late, and it was screaming loudly and desperately enough that Anahita paused as she stalked toward him. It sounded as though it were screaming the word *protect*.

Anahita shook her head in an attempt to dislodge that voice from her mind, but it would not budge. In her black and white mindset, she could not figure out *why* such a voice would even exist within a Warrior. She felt as though she were forgetting—or missing—something.

She narrowed her eyes at the target. He had a mark on his neck, and as she noticed it, an ache panged in her belly. She had the overwhelming feeling that *she* had given him that mark—and not in violence.

"Who ... are you?" she asked suddenly.

"You don't ... you don't know who I am?" he asked. "Ana," he said, straightening. "Pretty baby, focus."

She shook her head. "No." He took liberties. Shortening her name? *Pretty baby?*

"You're mad. I get it." His words came fast. "But Remiel was using you too, Ana. We had to figure out why."

Some of the chaos in her mind evaporated. "Remiel? What about Remiel?"

He dared to take a step forward, and she flicked her sword up, the point nestling in the vulnerable spot at the base of his throat. She should just finish this now. She tensed.

His Adam's apple bobbed, and he whispered hoarsely, "We think Remiel is leading a rebel army, angel, and you're his weapon of choice."

Blood ran cold through her already chilly heart. "More deception," she spat.

"Truth, angel," he said. He smiled softly. "Surely you can tell at this moment."

She narrowed her eyes. He was right. She sensed no untruth in him, and her black and white vision *would* be able to do so. Still. Her mission—

She pressed the sword forward slightly, stabilizing it before thrusting home. He sucked in a breath, and a single crimson droplet gathered in the dip of his throat beneath her sword, and then began to track down his bare chest.

Her lips parted around a whimper. She had hurt him.

She had hurt him!

"M-Max?"

His eyes grew glassy. He cleared his throat. "Yeah, pretty baby?"

Between one blink and the next, her black and white vision vanished to be replaced by a golden glow. She heard Max mutter, "Thank God," but she was almost too distracted to notice. That crimson trail down Max's chest glowed the brightest gold. Her eyes followed it up to the sword, and down the sword's blade to her double-handed grip. Her hands were glowing the brightest of all.

She was the biggest threat to his safety.

With a cry, she drew back the sword and dropped it. It clanged against the floor.

"Ana," Max said quickly, stepping forward with his hands outstretched.

"Stop!" she yelled, taking a step backward. "You're bleeding."

"I don't fucking care," he said, continuing forward.

"Don't let me touch you!" she pleaded, holding her hands out in front of her and hoping to ward him off. "Oh, holy God. You will *die* from that, Max."

That finally stopped him. With drawn brows, he raised one hand and dabbed at the almost negligible wound on his neck. He glanced down at his red-smeared fingers and then looked back up at her. "From *this*?" he asked.

"It will never heal," she said. "You need the Tree."

"Okay," he said slowly, drawing out the word. "We *have* the Tree, Ana. It's okay." He stepped toward her again but froze when she moaned. "I'm more worried about you at the moment."

"Oh, go," she said. "*Please* ... just go. Jayden knows how to help you fix the cut."

He stared at her for several long moments before sighing, and she relaxed, realizing he was finally listening to her. His eyes darted to the door and then back to her. "I'm coming right back, Ana. You stay right here."

Anahita did not bother to answer; she *could* not answer through the tumultuous rioting of her thoughts. He backed out of the room, keeping his eyes upon her at all times until he was out of sight. Anahita heard the apartment door open then close.

A flood of anger and rage—mostly self-directed—swept over her, and in a snap, she'd snatched up the sword. "Remiel!" she yelled to the ceiling. She waited only a moment before bellowing his name again.

That angel *was* going to show his face, or she was going to *him*, and he would not like it. Were the humans right? Was Remiel ... *using* her? She clenched the hilt of her sword even tighter and charged into the living room area, only to pull up short.

Remiel stood in the center. He crossed his arms and wore the closest thing to a scowl Anahita had ever seen on any angel's face. "So, you summon *me* now, is that it?"

He was here. He was here? Yes, she had been determined to see him, but she had been sure her attempts to summon him would not work.

Holy God, she could *summon*! She was one of the few angels who had more than one or two gifts. How many centuries had she wasted being at the beck and call of others when she could have been the one doing the calling? Perhaps she should have tried it earlier. Perhaps she should try more things.

She affected a modicum of calmness and shoved aside this startling discovery for consideration at a later time. More pressing matters awaited her. "Remiel, what were the Most High's orders concerning these humans?" she asked, giving each word its own, heavy weight. The insubordination in her tone shocked her.

Remiel didn't move or react in anyway. In fact, he seemed unnaturally still. "You know what they were. Those who eat of the Tree of Eternal Life must die, Warrior. Though," he paused and smiled unkindly, "those are not Warrior eyes I see now, Guardian."

Anahita clenched her teeth. "Beside the point, and you will not distract me from this. What were the Most High's orders concerning *these* humans?"

She saw the slightest flicker along Remiel's brow. "I do not understand, angel. Do you suggest that the Most High should repeat himself on a trial-by-trial basis? His orders were clear."

"Millennia ago, yes," Anahita said. "They were very clear. But then His anger cooled. He has changed many of His edicts since then. It would not be remiss to verify His orders every five thousand years or so." She was employing sarcasm now? Apparently, yes. She took a step toward him, the fire from the sword burning her hand with its overbearing heat. "So, I repeat: what is His will in this particular situation?"

The tips of Remiel's wings shifted. "The Most High has not expressly addressed the Tree of Eternal Life since delivering those orders. The Warriors have not been told directly that the orders have changed."

"That is enough," Anahita said. "How very political of you, Remiel." His word choices—*expressly, directly*—allowed him to skirt the edge of honesty. While no angel could lie, Remiel seemed to find a way to play with this line and blur it for his purposes. Her gut sank. If he were innocent of this grievous error, he would simply say so, as would any angel. The humans *were* right. Just how blind had she been? Had they *all* been?

Her Warrior side was protesting in broken mewls from the corner of her mind as her Guardian side grew stronger and stronger. She could allow her Warrior Compulsion to feed off her energy. To become stronger. And perhaps it could have the slightest chance of beating back her Guardian side. But to what effect? The death of humans that the Most High may very much want to live?

Anahita exhaled a shuddering breath and allowed herself a moment's sorrow as she prepared to forever strike her chances of becoming Warrior from her realm of possibilities. She closed her eyes and her Guardian Compulsion swept all remnants of her Warrior side away in a violence that made Anahita sway on her feet.

But in the aftermath of that violence, the push and pull she'd been feeling within her since her dueling Compulsions had set vanished. Utter peace lay in its wake.

She drew in the first easy breath she'd ever taken. What in God's name had she been fighting?

"So, you have chosen to forsake your calling?" Remiel asked, his tone of voice shifting.

Her eyes darted open to find him observing her with distaste. The change in her must be apparent to others. Oddly enough, that did not bother her. "Perhaps I've chosen to embrace something else," Anahita said, lifting her chin.

"I told you once, failing in this mission would mean your death."

Anahita narrowed her eyes. "You wish to take my life? Come and claim it."

For some reason, Remiel seemed disconcerted by this. He shifted his weight back and forth before straightening and staring at her with an odd gleam in his eye. "I tire of so many failures in this simple task. Give me the sword. *I* will finish what should have been done years ago."

Not while she was still breathing. She gripped the sword with both hands and brought it up in front of her, quickly assessing the location of all Remiel's physical vulnerabilities. No one would ever harm her Ward. *No one.* "I repeat: come and claim it."

Remiel's eyes flicked to a point over Anahita's shoulder, then back to her face, and then back over her shoulder. She knew he was not looking at anything; there was nothing behind her. Something was happening here that Anahita could not quite place her finger on. Remiel seemed ... *hesitant* to engage her in battle. It made no sense. He was the fiercest of all Warriors. Surely, a simple Guardian posed no real threat to him.

And, yet, Anahita had never felt more powerful than she did now, wielding her sword in the protection of her Ward. Maybe Remiel was *right* to be hesitant. Perhaps he would not fight her at all.

The attack came so quickly, she was caught off guard. With only the snap of his wings as a warning, Remiel was upon her, arm banded across her chest as he launched them both across the room.

Her wings crunched against the wall with the mass and power of two hurtling bodies, and Anahita cried out as she felt bones snap. Her grip upon the sword loosened slightly, and she gritted her teeth as she begged her hands to tighten and not lose their hold.

Remiel pulled back his fist and drove it into her stomach. Anahita gagged as all of the air in her lungs tried to leave her body at once. And then her lungs froze; for several panicked heartbeats, she could not draw another breath. It was a long enough paralysis to keep her from defending herself, and Remiel was able to lay another of his powerful punches into her.

Stars winked behind her vision. She needed air. She needed to *fight*! Centuries of training—of being taught to be subordinate to the angel now attacking her—were as paralyzing as her inability to draw breath.

But then Remiel made a grave error: he laid his hands upon the sword's hilt and tried to pry it from her loosened grip.

In her golden vision, Remiel's glow launched to a higher, more florescent degree. His intent was clear: he was going to take the sword from her, and he would not stop until Max was dead. He posed the highest threat possible to him.

Strength filled every vein, every muscle of Anahita's body. *You will not harm him!* her oxygen-starved brain screamed. With a jerk, she threw her elbow up and caught Remiel in the chin hard enough that the clack of his teeth striking each other echoed through the room. His head flew back, and some of the pressure across her chest eased beneath the bar of his arm. Finally, she was able to suck in life-giving air. The dots behind her eyes cleared. Her strength doubled again.

His body still crowded hers, so she pulled her knee up and plowed it into the place between his legs, shocked, as he bellowed and pulled away, that he had allowed her to get that move in on him. His desperation must have been intense indeed to have his guard down in such a way.

His own training kicked in enough to keep him from doubling over and giving her the opportunity to apply her knee to his nose, so she brought the sword hilt to his face instead, smashing his nose with a crack.

His head snapped back, and he stumbled a few feet away, and when he looked back at her with stinging tears swimming in his eyes and blood trickling down his face, she could swear that another wary expression was fixed upon his face. But as he blinked away the tears and swiped at the blood running along his upper lip, the expression vanished, and she had to wonder if it had ever been there at all.

He bared his teeth at her, and the rage pouring off of him was so strong that she could feel its heat roll over her. The implacable angel was gone; a wrathful creature was in its place. In that moment, still feeling the calm of a Guardian in protection mode, Anahita knew she would win.

Just as she suspected, Remiel grew sloppy. He charged at her with no finesse, a war cry bursting from him, and she easily dodged the attack and brought the hilt of the sword crashing down between his wings, sending him to the floor with a heavy thud.

Shifting the sword to her left hand, Anahita reached down with her right, hauled Remiel up by a fistful of robe, and tossed him toward the wall a few feet away. He landed against it chest first, hands sprawled out on the white paint in a too-late attempt to catch himself. By the time he'd turned around to face her, she was already upon him.

Her hand was a vise around his neck, and she increased the pressure, feeling the blood flow beneath her fingers slow. She raised the sword and placed the tip at his sternum. His eyes glazed, and Anahita loosened the vise only enough for him to retain consciousness for a few more moments. "You will never harm him," she gritted out from between clenched teeth. She prepared to slide the sword between Remiel's ribs.

"No," he gasped. "Anahita, no."

Something in his tone caused her to pause. His face grew fires-of-hell red with his lack of oxygen, but his eyes—the same blue as hers—had finally grown calm and rational. The angel was back.

She should still kill him.

A large part of her rebelled at the thought. This angel had been a brother and mentor to her for centuries. Had given her a chance when few would have.

"Anahita," Remiel rasped. His shaking hand rose beside them, and Anahita tensed for another attack, but Remiel simply wrapped his fingers gently around her wrist where she clutched his neck. "Sister. Mercy, please." Anahita's resolve wavered further. "I am doing my best," he continued. "Many gifts; many Temptations." He closed his eyes. "So hard. I am doing my best," he repeated, defeat and exhaustion dripping from each syllable.

Understanding dawned, and with it, empathy. Many Temptations? Her one Temptation was bad enough. As repugrant as his actions were, they were incredibly intelligent. Remiel was able to keep his *own* hands clean by having other angels act on his behalf. However, none would do so anymore.

"You will confess your misguided actions to the Warriers," Anahita said, the grip on his throat already loosening. "Avoid your Fall and eliminate the possibility of further abuse of power at the same time."

Remiel's eyes widened, but she saw the moment he realized his ruse was over anyway. Someone was always watching; his actions were no doubt already known. He nodded.

After a tense silence with her sword poised, she asked, "You will never harm him?" There was no doubt as to whom she referenced, and she almost couldn't believe the question was coming out of her mouth. It seemed she truly intended to let him go if he answered favorably.

She could feel him swallow beneath her now slack grip on his neck. "I give my vow," he rasped past the vocal cords she had no doubt damaged.

As she hesitated still, the bright golden glow of Remiel's threat faded. Her eyes widened as it reduced to nothing. She had no real reason to slay him now; he was no longer a problem. She released him and stepped back.

He collapsed to his hands and knees, sucking in great, wracking breaths. His wings heaved with the effort.

"Leave now," she said to his back, "and never again return."

He raised his head and looked up at her through eyes that appeared tortured by her words. Anahita frowned, but before she could contemplate his unlikely reaction further, Remiel vanished.

Anahita's shoulders relaxed, and the various aches and pains of battle rushed in as adrenaline seeped away. Her wings pained her the most, and she stretched them with a groan, suddenly more tired than she had ever been in her existence.

"Um ... wow."

The words came from behind her, and she whipped around, sword raised, only to find her Ward and Oliver standing in the doorway to the apartment.

"You kicked ass," Oliver said. "That was seriously hot."

He smiled the smile she had learned was typical for him, but she could see faint lines of pain around his eyes. As she looked at him, she had no desire—no Compulsion—to end him. Her Warrior side was beaten into submission.

Her eyes shifted to Max, and every fiber of her being screamed *Protect!*

His eyes were focused on her. "You're hurt?" he asked in his rumbling voice.

She quickly took in his form. No part of him gleamed brighter gold than any other. The spot on his neck had vanished. Jayden must have applied the fruit to heal it. She relaxed completely. "But you are not," she said.

He took a step toward her while saying, "Ana—"

She raised her hand to stop him, and his words cut off. He had been right: Remiel was leading a rebel band of angels. And because she had been so focused on her own dream of becoming a Warrior, she had almost allowed her Ward to be harmed.

It was unforgivable. Unacceptable.

Repeatable.

She had to focus. Her Ward needed to become her primary objective, his protection her life.

As Max continued to talk to her in urgent tones, she closed her eyes and her Guardian Compulsion surged to the forefront of everything. She felt the rest of the world fading away until all that was left was the driving need to protect.

When she opened her eyes again, she felt it taking hold while at the same time feeling everything that made her *her* slip away.

And she let it go.

Chapter Fourteen

Max was in mourning.

As he trudged down the hallway to the quarters he now shared with the angel who was always with him and at the same time wasn't, he rubbed his palm over the eternal ache in his chest. Before, if he'd ever dared to think about living with her, it had never been under these circumstances: with him sleeping in a cold bed and her standing even more coldly by, watching over him with an expressionless face.

It had been several weeks—Six? No, eight—since she had gone into her Guardian shell. He flopped face down on the bed and, out of habit, tried to discern some of the lily scent that had evaporated from the sheets after about three weeks. "Goddamn it, Ana," he muttered. Though she hadn't spoken to him since he'd witnessed her beating that uppity angel's ass, he could still feel her every moment of every day. For example, he knew that right now she was standing against the wall by the bedroom door—a location that allowed her to watch both him and the main door to the apartment for any threats to his safety. It was where she always stood, her eyes watching him indifferently while he burned away inside with the need to touch her. To fucking *talk* to her.

The hell of it was, the eight weeks that had passed in tense, ever-present silence had been just long enough for him to fully comprehend what he'd thrown away with both hands. Just long enough for him to fall flat on his face into the shithouse that was love.

He rolled over with a groan, and threw his forearm over his eyes. After a couple of seconds of ineffectual resistance, he cracked his eyelids a bit and peered at his angel from the shield of his arm.

The sight of her, like always, was an anvil to the gut. Each time he looked at her now, the Knowledge in his eye told him nothing. She was not good. She was not evil. She barely *was*.

One thing that she was, however, was beautiful. She was just as beautiful as she had been when he'd first seen her—with her blond waves tumbling about her shoulders and the body that he had briefly been granted the ultimate boon of enjoying. But she was not his Ana anymore. Her joy, her constant discoveries—hell, even her blue eyes—every defining characteristic that *was Ana* was gone. He missed her so much he was sick with it.

The first week had been easy. She was always with him, and he had been stupid enough to be optimistic, to think that this would be enough. Then Oliver had died for the first time since being stateside. Max had been more devastated than he could have guessed. To make matters worse, as soon as Oliver recovered, he and Luke left the compound. They'd headed for the Middle East to search out Oliver's mystery woman. It was the first time Max had been without his friends in a decade, and he had so desperately needed a friend to talk to and someone to hold him, that the full magnitude of what he had lost struck him all at once. Ana, *his* Ana, would have taken such good care of him, just as she had that afternoon in the medical wing after his nightmare.

That day, he'd tumbled a little bit into love with an angel that no longer existed, and he'd fallen farther and farther with each painful milestone. Like waking up thrusting into the sheets after dreaming of being inside her, and turning over to find Anahita watching him with a passive face—no reaction at all. Not the slightest hint of lust or desire. Hell, he'd even have taken anger. *Any* reaction. Or discovering after those first few days that the pleasure he'd had to sneak for himself in the shower because it was the only time she couldn't see him was now going to be the norm and the only way to keep the Impulse pain at bay. And the first time he'd accidentally turned to her and started a conversation without remembering she wouldn't be talking back until that first awkward stretch of silence after he'd stopped to hear her opinion.

As he watched her beneath his arm, she shifted her weight from her left foot to her right. Her robe pooled around her body and shimmered with her movement, and he caught a glimpse of the curves of her breasts against the fabric, which, of course, caused him to shoot hard as iron.

He flicked his eyes to the open door that led into the bathroom, both longing for and dreading one of his sad showers. He'd delayed his necessary orgasm for about as long as possible.

But a knock sounded at the door. Max craned his head back and looked at the alarm clock on the nightstand. Right on time, of course.

Bastard.

With a sigh, he pushed himself to his feet and walked into the living room, automaton angel dogging his steps all the way. He pulled the door open and stepped aside to admit Jayden, who pulled his wings in as he walked through the door frame. He nodded at Max in greeting but walked right past him to stand before Ana.

"Hello, Anahita," Jayden said softly.

Max didn't know why he always held his breath when someone else attempted to talk to Ana—she didn't answer *anyone*—but he did. And the disappointment Max felt when Anahita ignored Jayden and continued to stare at Max while breathing steadily in and out was sharp. Jayden moved to the sofa with obvious reluctance and sank into the leather with a frown, his eyes still upon Anahita.

Max walked to the armchair. "Where's Grace?" he asked while taking a seat.

Jayden's head swiveled to him. "She is still angry with you on Anahita's behalf."

Max looked at his hands clenched in his lap. "Fair enough." Max had never seen Jayden and Grace apart since Ana had gone silent, and so he had made a habit of avoiding them. Their happiness burnt like lemon juice in a cut, so Max couldn't say he was too upset that Grace had declined his company. Max's eyes found Anahita again, as they always seemed to do, and he lost himself in the curve where her neck met her shoulder. He loved that curve. Wished he could lick it while he—

"Why did you wish to see me?" Jayden asked.

Max jumped in his seat and jerked his eyes away from Anahita. Jayden raised an eyebrow at him, and Max shifted a little bit, crossing one leg over the other, ankle to knee, in an attempt to hide what his wayward thoughts had caused. He cleared his throat and gripped the arms of the chair with tense fingers. "Ana needs to become a Warrior."

Jayden narrowed his eyes. "Ana*hita*," he said, stressing her full name with a glare of disapproval, "cannot do so. You ensured that. She is a Guardian, and a Guardian she will always be."

Max squeezed the armchair tighter. "But I can't…" Max stopped and took a breath to dim his desperation as much as possible. He reminded himself this was not about *him*. When he was as calm as he could make himself, he continued. "She is not herself. She cannot be *this*," he paused to gesture her way, "for the rest of her existence. She would have hated that!" He broke off and shoved a hand through his hair. He had to know, even if it would kill him: "She'll be like this always?" His voice cracked.

"She is a Guardian under Compulsion with a Ward. She will be this until you die."

Max started and then leaned forward.

Jayden narrowed his eyes. "And you will not *die* by your own hand during her watch, human, or I will chase you down in the afterlife myself. You will not do that to her. It would not help, that failure to keep you safe."

Max slumped down in his chair. He had hoped for a second that … Who was he kidding? While she was living, he could not be apart from her, even in death. "I don't understand why she can't pull herself out of this." He looked at Jayden. "She's *strong*! She beat Remiel for God's sake. Why can't she beat the Compulsion?"

Jayden frowned at him, but did admit, albeit grudgingly, "She can if she Falls."

"No," Max said quickly. "She will not Fall for me. I don't deserve it."

"Agreed." He raised his eyebrows when Max glared at him. "I *did* warn you of this probable outcome," Jayden said.

Max straightened. "You did no such thing!"

"I did."

"You said to me, 'Max, your plan will turn Anahita into a Goddamn robot angel. Perhaps reconsider'?"

"It was implied in the subtext."

"Fuck your subtext."

Jayden rose to his full height. "I think we are done here."

Max rose to his feet as well. "You have to do something!"

"What can I do?" Jayden roared. "You think I don't want to? I'm not an angel anymore, Max." He took a quick step in Max's direction. "I'm as useless as you!"

Before either of them could react, Anahita was between them, Max staring at her back, Jayden facing down the point of Anahita's sword.

Jayden muttered something that sounded awfully curse-like. His shoulders drooped, and he took a step back and held up his hands. "I will not harm him, Anahita," he said. When Anahita still did not lower her sword, Jayden heaved a beleaguered sigh and looked over her shoulder into Max's eyes. "I am sorry I raised my voice," he said with actual sincerity, effectively taking the wind out of the sails of Max's anger.

As though they were magic words, Anahita sheathed her sword and moved back to where she had been standing by the door, her eyes fixed and unblinking once more.

An awkward silence descended, and Max knew they were both trying to ignore the fact that Max's guardian angel had made Jayden apologize to him as though they were both toddlers fighting over Legos. When the silence grew too oppressive, Max decided to break it. In a whisper, he said, "I know you are still connected to heaven, Jayden. Eli told me."

Though he seemed relieved to move on, Jayden frowned. "I would not say *connected*. That implies a two-way path. I know what is going on there: that the heavens are in chaos. The Warriors all but disbanded in the wake of their scandal and without their leader."

"Without their leader? Look at her," Max said desperately, flinging a hand in her direction. "*She* could be their leader! She beat Remiel. She exposed his rebellion. She's *earned* his place as head of the Warriors."

"Yes, she has." Jayden froze. "Wait, how—?" He frowned. "That is right. But ... I am more intelligent than you," he said, almost as though he were talking to himself.

Max clenched his teeth. "And more handsome." Jayden cocked an eyebrow at him, and Max said, "You know, if we're going to start a list. Asshole."

"No." Jayden shook his head. "*I* should have thought of that. She's the rightful leader of the Warriors! It is ingrained in her as much as being your Guardian is. It just might be enough to get her back to herself."

"You mean"—Max tried to squelch the warmth flooding his chest before it bloomed into hope—"it's a possibility? She could snap out of this?"

Jayden looked at Anahita before turning back to Max. "A remote one," he said finally. "She is hardly cognizant and able to lead. The Warriors will not accept a catatonic leader. And a Guardian at that."

"It appears to me that the Guardians are stronger than the Warriors. They need to nut up and admit it."

The corner of Jayden's lips tipped up, and if Max was not mistaken, he chuckled. "Well, I cannot tell them *that*, but I can tell them something. I am not completely without allies in the Warrior ranks. Perhaps one of them will meet with me…" Jayden straightened. "I must go."

"Go, man," Max said quickly. "Get it done."

Jayden turned toward the door, but paused and looked at Max over his shoulder. "This was a good idea, Max. Grace may actually talk to you some day." Jayden strode to the place where Anahita stood guard. "Balance, Anahita," he said to her. "It is the essence of life. There is no reason you cannot live with both parts of yourself."

Max swallowed around the lump in his throat. This had to work. He'd broken Anahita—broken her heart. He owed it to her to give her her dream.

He was so focused on Jayden's departure and his own thoughts that he missed it when Anahita blinked and looked at the door after Jayden closed it behind him.

Chapter Fifteen

She had been underwater once—she thought, at least. It was hard to remember the past in specific detail. The world around her passed by in the muffled tones she sometimes had a vague recollection of experiencing with her ears submerged in water. The world was blurry as well. All except for her Ward, who was in vivid, golden focus, as was anything that became a threat to him.

It was, oddly, a fulfilling existence, this life lived in the protection of another. And, yet, she felt as though something were missing. Something she had very much enjoyed. Over the passing days, that enjoyment had morphed—the missing of it accentuating and augmenting it—until she was sure that she loved something. Maybe someone.

But she couldn't remember who, no matter how hard she tried to focus.

She knew most Guardians were invisible to their Wards, but for some reason, she did not feel the need to be invisible around hers or those he interacted with on a daily basis. Sometimes, when she watched over him as he slept, she wondered at this comfortability she felt around him. Around them all. As though she had once belonged with them—or to them. Or to *him*. It was an unsettling thought in that it made her think of something outside of her duties with fondness. It was dangerous, and therefore, something to be avoided. Yet it kept creeping in.

In the recent handful of days, her Ward's activities had suddenly increased. He went from wandering the halls aimlessly, lying in his bed, and taking long showers, to rushing to and fro and meeting with the same winged man over and over, another being she felt a connection to.

And something changed. She began to hear every word of their conversations when before she had just heard noise. But she was only able to pluck a few words from them, such as *meeting soon* and *Anahita must be there*. Though she heard these words and suspected she knew what they meant, she was unable to glean any understanding from them. She watched the winged man closely, however, remembering the time she had thought him a threat to her Ward. He consistently behaved, but she refused to let her guard down.

Her Ward was hurrying along now, and she was a foot or so behind him. Urgency poured from him, and he kept looking over his shoulder at her. Those looks became so frequent that for the first time, she seriously pondered rendering herself invisible. He was liable to run into a wall or hurt himself in some other way if he did not focus on where he was going.

Just as she was about to disappear, however, he walked them both into a room outfitted with a long mahogany table and several leather chairs, all of which were vacant, though the room was filled.

Four angels and the winged man she watched constantly lined the walls, their arms crossed over their considerable chests, and when she and her Ward entered, they all straightened their already impeccable postures. The winged man stepped forward. Had he once been an angel? It was the first complex thought she'd had since ... well, since she could remember. The four angels stepped forward as well.

She put herself in front of her Ward, her sword in her hand so fast they would never have been able to see her reach for it.

The perhaps-former-angel spoke to her in calming tones, but she couldn't place any of the words, only that he and the rest meant her Ward no harm.

She relaxed her battle stance, sheathed her sword. The four angels behind their spokesperson were staring intently at her.

Taking her measure. Anahita tucked her chin and returned them each stare for stare. *They should not be challenging me this way,* she thought. They were her subordinates, and they should show her respect.

Anahita felt her eyes widen and immediately schooled the reaction. Subordinates? Respect? Where were these thoughts coming from?

The not-angel was speaking again, and Anahita's throat went dry as she understood each and every word he said. "—your Warriors, Anahita. They are ready for you to take your place as leader. There is much to be done."

Some dim, closeted part of her came bursting forth, shoving the golden glimmer of her vision aside and casting the world in a different type of clarity. She blinked several times—the lights too bright—as thoughts bombarded her one after the other.

She was Warrior. She was Guardian. She was both and neither.

"Yes." The word left Anahita's mouth before she knew it was forming. She jolted. Clenched her fists. This was *right*. "Much to be done."

She saw the almost imperceptible straightening of each of the backs of the four Warrior angels. She also noticed that each of them respectfully lowered their eyes. Not one of them challenged her any longer.

She was their leader.

She stepped forward and quickly took their measure. Four strapping Warriors. They would do well for her. She must call together her men. "Where are the rest of the Warriors?" she asked. They had a rebellion to quash.

"My ... l-liege," one of them began, stumbling on the form of address.

Some of the tension within her unknotted. "Anahita," she said gently. Remiel had not stood on ceremony, and she *certainly* was not going to. She expected her words to relax the Warriors. Instead, if possible, they were *tenser*.

"Anahita," the same angel said. "There are none but us left on the side of good." The four Warriors looked at each other, eyes shifting uncomfortably, and then back at her. "The rest were on the side of the rebellion and are in revolt."

It was the greatest effort of Anahita's existence to keep from outwardly reacting. She felt a sick stirring in her stomach. She may just go down in history as a worse leader than Remiel. Five Warriors against an entire battalion of rebels?

"Six," Jayden whispered to her. He startled her, until she remembered that her riotous thoughts would be easy for him to glean. "You have my sword as well, Anahita," he continued. "Well, *our* sword, I suppose." He smiled. "Though you may not wish a Fallen to fight with you."

"I wish it," she said quickly. "We will find another weapon." She gulped and tried to calm her galloping heart. "Thank you for your help," she whispered to him. She turned her attention back to her men and gestured to the vacant chairs before them. "We have much to discuss and plan. Won't you please take a seat?"

Each Warrior—and Jayden—moved to stand behind a chair, but they waited to take their seats until Anahita had placed herself at the head of the table. Amid the cacophonous sounds of chair rollers on the floor, Anahita heard the clearing of a throat. Her head snapped up. Max stood in the doorway, an expression halfway between lost puppy and elated devotee on his face. As she looked upon him, she felt no pull to either protect or kill him. Her two angel sides seemed to be in balance. The pull behind her heart, however, nearly bowled her over.

Max smiled at her, but it did not quite reach his eyes. "I'll just be going," he said, placing one of his large hands upon the doorknob.

An awkward silence descended on the room. The heads of her Warriors swung from looking at Max to looking at her in unison. Their eyes were flooded with query, and she felt the back of her neck heat.

Anahita nodded curtly at him, and with a slight hesitation, he turned and left the room. A pang shot through Anahita's heart as the door *snicked* closed behind him. It was with both relief and sorrow that she realized her Guardian side was not commanding her to follow him and keep him in her sight for always. She swallowed hard. Yes, that pang must be merely Temptation-centered. And she could handle it.

Her four Warriors still watched her with wide eyes, but Jayden leaned toward her and whispered, "He arranged for this."

Anahita brought her eyes to Jayden's.

Jayden lowered his voice even more as Anahita felt the attention of her men focus in on their conversation. "He demanded I put you in charge of the Warriors," he whispered.

She frowned. "You have no authority over the Warriors."

"That is what I told him." He smiled. "And yet, here we are. Here *you* are. I did not know if the pull on you to be leader would be strong enough to break the Guardian Compulsion." He paused and flicked a quick glance at the angels around them. "Is your Warrior Compulsion back? Do I need to move the humans?" he asked quietly.

The question shocked her, but only because she had not thought of it first. It was a grave concern that should have been pressing on her mind already. Anahita quickly took stock. "No," she breathed. "*Neither* Compulsion is there."

Jayden relaxed back into his seat. "I was hoping it would work that way. There have not been too many dual angels, but I had heard a rumor that they were the only ones able to defeat Compulsions, and they did it by denying neither part of themselves."

Anahita clamped her lips closed, afraid that she would do something foolish and weak, like whimper. Or even cry. All this time, fighting who she truly was had kept her in a direct place of conflict. If she had embraced who she was earlier...

One of the other Warriors cleared his throat, and Anahita snapped to attention, brushing as inconspicuously as possible the skin beneath her eyes and exhaling a slow, relieved breath when her fingertips came away dry. She gave a small shake of her head to focus. She had a job to do. A very *important* job to do. She leaned forward and began to address her small, ineffectual band of Warriors.

She was relieved when the Warriors agreed with the need to accept the immortal humans as part of their forces. They were not as strong as angels, but they were trained soldiers and had much heart. Jayden quickly informed her that Oliver and Luke had left in search of Oliver's mate. Finding her for him would take little time and was priority number one so that the men could return and focus on the task at hand.

Though she was focused as she made battle plans with her men, her thoughts kept drifting to the man she could sense was waiting right outside the door.

• • •

He would not fucking cry. He would *not* fucking cry.

A traitorous tear cascaded down his cheek anyway, riding over the raised edge of his scar and dripping off his chin to land on his shirt with a splat. "Great," he muttered, wiping his entire face with one massive sweep of his palm and then looking down the hall to see if anyone had witnessed him crack in two.

She was back. Holy God, she was back, and he could not be happier. The feeling choked him as it made his throat and chest too tight to draw in much air.

And at the same time, the joy was tempered with a fear so intense that he was not sure his legs would hold him upright for much longer. He was leaned precariously against the wall just outside the door of the meeting room, knowing he *definitely* didn't have the strength to walk away from her.

That curt nod of hers had felt like a dismissal. She was back, and she had dismissed him. Which, he reminded himself, he more than deserved. And yet, this sick fear would not abate. The fear that she was still just as lost to him as she had been under the influence of her Guardian Compulsion.

Another damn tear spilled over and jetted down his cheek. He tipped his head back, pressed the top of it to the wall, and hoped that gravity would keep the other bastards in check.

The door next to him burst open, and Max nearly fell over as he straightened too quickly for his body to support him. He cleared his throat and blinked while Anahita's four massive angels filed out of the room, glanced his way with open curiosity upon their faces, and walked down the hall and out into the main room.

Jayden was next out of the room. He paused next to Max, looked over his shoulder back into the room, and sighed before meeting Max's eyes. "She said she will see you," Jayden said. Then, leaning in with something that looked like a smile, he whispered, "Be sure to lock the door." He winked—the oddest fucking sight Max had ever seen—and then followed the angels out.

A blast of hope shot through Max, and he stumbled over his feet as every limb of his body fought to get to his angel. He swung into the room, and Anahita, who had been facing the back wall, turned and locked eyes with him.

What he had barely had time to notice before rocked him back on his heels. Her eyes—those blue eyes that he had fallen in love with—were back. He took a step toward her, fingers reaching out and spread with the need to pull her to him.

"Max," she said, her voice unsure.

He froze. That waver in her voice had nearly slain him. He reminded himself to prepare to be as angel-dumped as he deserved to be. He turned and pulled the door closed behind him, clicking the lock into place. The sound of the lock engaging shot through the room, and when Max faced her once more, Anahita's brows were drawn together. Before she could say anything, however, Max was walking toward her. He did not stop until they were toe to toe.

Max reached up and cradled her face between his hands. Leaning down and covering her lips with his own was like the first breath of air after being underwater too long—life-giving and healing. He groaned as he tilted his head to the side and locked their mouths together more firmly, schooling himself not to deepen the kiss—not yet.

Every fiber of his being wanted to dive into her, but he forced himself to end the kiss. He pulled back but stayed close enough that he could brush his nose against hers.

Wide, blue eyes stared at his. She looked so adorably shell-shocked that he nearly laughed and ruined the moment. Instead, he set out to do the thing he had been waiting to do for weeks. His fingers flexed on her jaw. "I love you," he said firmly, trying to beg her with his eyes to believe him. To hear him.

He had not thought her eyes could get any wider, but they did. "What?" she asked. Her voice was breathless and raspy, he noted with some satisfaction. His kiss had not left her unaffected.

"I love you," he repeated. He tilted his head to the side and watched in fascination as his finger traveled over the delicate skin of her cheek and down to her neck, the fact that he was touching her again—and she wasn't pushing him away—so heady that he was dizzy with it.

"You cannot love me," she said, frowning. "We barely know each other!"

"You forget," he said, his voice rumbling with the effort to hold back a smile. "I've had a good long time to sit and consider my behavior and what I've lost. I know enough of you to know that I already love you. The more I find out in the years to come, the more that will grow."

Her forehead scrunched. "How long is *a good long time*?"

"Ten weeks," he breathed, unable to believe he had gone that long without touching her as he was touching her now.

"That is not—" She batted his hand away. "That is an *incredibly* short amount of time, Max!"

"It was interminable."

She began to move away. "Max—"

He placed his hands on her shoulders and gave a gentle squeeze, cutting off whatever she was about to say. "I'm sorry," Max said.

Anahita froze.

"You don't have to forgive me, but you more than deserve an apology, and this is it," Max said, the words flowing quickly in an effort to get all of them out before she stopped him. "I was every kind of ass. I put others before you. I went with a plan that, had I bothered to tell you about it, you would have endorsed, and I chose instead to use you. And worse…"

He broke off and pulled in a shaky breath, hoping against hope that he wouldn't break down and bawl again—this time in front of her. "I betrayed your trust. I took something you had told me in confidence and in a moment that I treasure, and I told others so that I could expose your weakness." He shook his head. "You know what? *Don't* forgive me for that one. I don't deserve it. But, Ana—" He couldn't stop himself from ducking in and stealing a quick kiss again. He lifted his lips and breathed, "I will never, *never* betray you again. And you don't have to believe me. I'll just spend the rest of my life proving it."

Anahita licked her lips, and he felt her shoulders tremble beneath his hands. "That was … a very good speech," she said

He smiled. "I had *a good long time* to think it up." He groaned and gave up a small portion of the tight leash he had on himself, pulling Anahita into his arms and wrapping himself around her. "And, pretty baby, you don't have to love me back. I'll earn that, too. I know ten weeks doesn't feel like enough to you, especially if your Compulsion didn't allow you to think of me—"

"You were there," she said, her words muffled against his neck. "I did not know exactly what it was that was always present in my thoughts—that I was inexorably drawn to—but ... it was *you*."

He closed his eyes and buried his face in her hair. "That's the best thing I've ever heard," he said. Damn. His eyes were stinging something fierce. "Ana, give me a chance," he said, not even trying to hide the fact that he was begging. "No one will ever be as devoted to someone as I will be to you. I love you. *God*, I love you."

He felt her wings droop, and a stone landed in his belly. She pulled away and looked up at him. "I cannot Fall, Max. There is so much to do."

Max stiffened and told himself to take it easy—keep his anger at *himself* out of his voice lest she think it was directed at her. "You will *not* Fall for me. Now or ever," he said firmly. "That's not how this is going to work between us. You don't give up who you are for me"—he paused to grip her chin—"or anybody."

She frowned, and he plowed headlong into the silence that was weighted with the implied *including yourself*. "You Fall when you create life with your Temptation or when you choose to Fall for your Temptation, yes?" he asked.

She hesitated, but finally nodded. "More or less."

Max shrugged in a way that he hoped was casual and put her at ease. "Then don't choose to. I'm here; I'm not going anywhere. I'm not going to die like a normal human Temptation, so there's no reason to join your life span with mine. And we will be very careful. Always. We can make sure there are no children."

Anahita's face blanched. "But ... I *like* children," she muttered.

The lump in Max's throat expanded. And she thought ten weeks was too short to fall in love with her. He'd just fallen a bit more in the last handful of heartbeats. "Then we will adopt. Or wait until a better time. We will have forever, after all."

• • •

Anahita gazed up into Max's face and felt her world shift. She could do this. He asked little. In fact, it seemed he asked nothing but that she be with him. She wouldn't have to Fall. She wouldn't have to sacrifice.

Was she truly getting everything that she wanted? Leading the Warriors but not having to deny her Guardian side? Living with and loving her Temptation but not having to Fall?

Before the universe could right itself and snatch back these boons, she decided to act. "I think," she began, "that a chance sounds good."

If she had any remaining doubts about taking this step, the look upon Max's face at her words would have cleared them. The widest smile she'd ever seen on him graced his face, causing his scar to nearly disappear, and before she could catch her next breath, she was swept into his arms and twirling around the room so quickly, she was dizzy.

As often as she had felt the emotions she was forbidden to feel as a Warrior, she had never felt the one that currently flowed through her. It was so powerful and so pure that in an instant, she was able to name it though she'd never before known it in this particular way.

She loved him.

She gasped and clutched him tighter as he continued to spin her. She loved him—she did—but it was only a start, and maybe that was what made love so exciting. Love did not work the way she had always thought it did. It was not an all-at-once endeavor, but something that grew and grew. Already she loved him more now than she did five minutes ago, and tomorrow she would love him more. Next week even more. How wonderful to discover that love is a masterpiece in progress with two artists.

Max stopped twirling her about and settled her on her feet. He stared straight into her eyes without even the slightest flinch to cover his scar with his hair, and Anahita took the opportunity to look upon his face to her heart's content. His wide, nearly silly grin sobered before her eyes, and his gaze dipped to her mouth. The mere touch of his eyes on her lips made her belly ache, and she stepped toward him, bringing their bodies together. His pupils blew, gobbling up the mismatched gold and brown, and he began to lower his head. Though she wanted his mouth on hers more than she wanted anything, she could not let him continue before giving him the same joy he had given her. "I love you too, Max," she whispered.

He jerked into a frozen state, his lips hovering above hers, and he looked into her eyes with wide ones of his own. "I could have sworn you said…" he muttered in a raspy voice that trailed off.

"It's true," she said. "For a good long time, I have loved you."

The corner of his mouth twitched. "Is that so?" he asked. "Define *good long time*."

"Well," she said, feeling her own lips turn upward. "I knew for sure about thirty seconds ago."

Max gasped, and it took her a few hectic heartbeats to determine that he had done so dramatically. He placed his open palm over his chest. "And it took you thirty seconds to tell me? Damn, woman, why would you make me wait so long?"

"I had to be sure," she said. "Let time tell and all of that."

"So wise," he whispered, his eyes crinkling around the corners in a way she had never seen before. He was happy, and she had made him so. The realization was more fulfilling than she could have ever guessed.

"You are certainly waiting a good long time to kiss me, Temptation," she said.

His gaze sharpened on her mouth. "Apologies," he muttered. Though they were already close enough that they were touching, he wrapped an arm around her back and pulled her in even more. Her hips came into contact with his, and she could feel that she'd already made him hard. Her skin flushed hot.

He ran his fingers over the edges of her feathers, and with his other hand, he reached up and cupped her cheek with his palm. He ran the rough pad of his thumb across her bottom lip, and Anahita felt herself shiver. He leaned down and followed the same path his thumb had taken with the velvety trace of the tip of his tongue, and Anahita was undone.

She opened her lips and breathed him in, pulling his tongue into her mouth and wrapping her own around it.

A harsh groan ripped from his chest, and the gentle hold he had on her body turned fierce. His arm around her waist snaked up between her wings; his fingers dug into her shoulder as he fastened her to him and plundered her mouth. His chest was hard and unforgiving against hers, and she could feel his quickened breathing in the billowing of his stomach. She palmed his pecs and smoothed her hands up and over his shoulders until she could wind her fingers through his hair. She found herself pressing into him more, discontent with their closeness not being close enough. A mewling sound slipped past her lips and into his mouth, and her knee began to travel up the outside of his thigh, seeking to bring her center into closer contact with his erection.

He grunted and suddenly, his hot hand was wrapped around the back of her knee, and he hiked her up, grabbing her other knee as well. She followed his lead and climbed him until her knees were straddling his hips. His head was canted far back as he refused to break their kiss, and she doubted they could hold this position for long without one of them crashing to the ground and pulling the other along. No sooner had the thought floated through her head than he turned and sat her bottom down on the table with only the slightest stumble in his step.

He deepened the kiss; she wrapped her legs around his waist fully now, crossing her ankles over the exquisite firmness of his behind. She was confused when he began leaning forward, forcing her to lean back as well, but when she discovered that he was laying them down, she was wholeheartedly on board. Her wings spread out on the table, and she wrapped her arms around him.

But he placed his palms on the table and pushed himself up. With a noise of protest, Anahita loosened her hold and allowed him to rise. His eyes flashed, and she got the feeling he had better plans in mind than even this, so Anahita relaxed into the refreshing coolness of the wood beneath her back.

He placed his pointer finger between her breasts and then slowly dragged it down her ribs and belly. She arched her back into his touch. Reaching to his right, he snagged one of the rolling office chairs from around the table. He pulled it over and sank down into it, pressing a kiss to her left knee as soon as he was settled and directing her feet to plant firmly on the chair's armrests.

She felt a breeze caress her thighs as he grabbed great handfuls of her robe and pulled it up to drape over her waist. He then grasped an ankle with each of his hands to keep her put and rolled the chair right up to the edge of the table.

His shoulders brushed the insides of her thighs, and he stared intently at the place between her legs before casting his eyes to hers. "This is going to be the best thing I've ever eaten at a table."

Anahita felt her brows draw together as she tried to puzzle out the meaning behind his words, but then he was pressing open-mouthed kisses to the inside of her left thigh. "Oh," she breathed, sudden understanding rushing in. She repeated the single syllable, drawing it out until it turned into a moan, when his hot tongue traveled even farther up her thigh. His beard tickled the sensitive skin at the bend of her leg, and her knees fell open.

"Good girl," he mumbled, his breath stirring the curls covering her center. She felt one of his fingers run down the middle of her sex. "I like this no-panties rule heaven seems to have. Who knew it was so naughty up there?" he teased, kissing the skin just below her navel.

"Please," she breathed. This had to be some kind of torture. Her skin felt too tight for her body, and she arched her hips trying to find the elusive mouth he seemed intent on denying her.

He looked up and smiled wickedly before leaning in. She felt his breath first, but at the first scalding lick of his tongue, she thought she would perish of pleasure. "Max!" she exclaimed. Her back bowed, and her hands shot down and buried themselves in his hair, pulling him in until his face was pressed against her so hard that she could feel the ridge of his nose. He groaned loudly and deeply, and she snatched her hands back. "Sorry," she said, heat filling her cheeks as she resisted the urge to cover her face.

He reached out and snagged her hands, directing them back to his hair. "You never apologize for that." He kissed the inside of her thigh gently. "Grab on, pretty baby."

She hesitantly wove her fingers through his hair, but when he kissed her clitoris and then opened his mouth over it to suck—*hard*—inhibitions vanished. She fisted that hair and pulled him in, grinding against his face.

He groaned anew and set in to licking her in earnest. He set a pace that reminded her very much of the way his body had rubbed hers to bring her to climax, but this was both softer and more intense in some way, and she found herself at the edge of orgasm almost immediately. "Max," she said uneasily, her back arching. "It is too fast. I am going to—"

"Oh, God yes," he mumbled into her flesh before licking her with the flat of his tongue and pushing her over the edge.

The oddest sound filled the air, and she realized with a start that it was her wailing. He set in with a vengeance then. "Eating her" turned out to be an apt description, and as her pleasure kept climbing and climbing, she wondered if it would never end.

As she started coming down, she was dimly aware of him pushing to his feet and kicking the chair back until it hit the wall with a crash. She heard the crinkle of one of those foil squares, and then he was there, his hips between her thighs.

The hot brush of his erection against her was perfection itself. She reached out and grabbed at his shirt, fingers desperate for his skin. She fumbled for the buttons, and his hands joined hers in the quest. In moments, her fingers were encountering the hot and smooth skin covering his abs. She bit into her bottom lip and smoothed her hands upward.

He grunted as her fingers brushed over his tight little nipples, and in the next instant, he was surging into her, his erection filling her to the depths. She sucked in a breath.

He paused. "Oh, God. Did I hurt you?" His face twisted, and he began to back out and pull away.

She tightened her legs around his waist to keep him from leaving. "Absolutely not," she said firmly, more a command that he not pull out of her than an answer to his question.

The corner of his mouth tilted up slowly. "Yes, ma'am," he said, knowing instinctively that she'd commanded him.

She canted her hips, pressing down on him and squeezing him at the same time. They groaned simultaneously, and his hands shot up and cradled her breasts. She arched into the touch, raking her nails down the ridges of his abdomen.

"I love you," he said, surging into her and grinding against her clit.

"Yes," she breathed, moving her hips in time with him.

"Say it," he grated, his teeth clenched.

Immediate understanding. Her hands shot up and grabbed his shirt, dragging him down until she could crush his lips with her own. She kissed him thoroughly but quickly before she pulled back from the kiss. "I love you," she whispered to him.

His eyes flashed, and he dove back down to kiss her once more, his thrusts picking up speed and intensity so that all she could do was hold on and kiss him back.

That same climb to completion began anew within her, and she could tell he was nearing the end as well. His breathing grew hectic and uneven and the muscles beneath her fingers bunched and quivered. "Ana," he groaned. "I'm going to—"

At that moment, the tension within her snapped. She arched her head back and cried out.

"Oh, thank God," he said, thrusting into her quickly three—four times before stiffening completely. He roared into her neck as his body jerked atop her.

When he finally stilled, he slowly raised his head and looked down at her. His smile was wide and showed all of his perfect teeth. He brushed her nose with the tip of his and drew his fingers down her cheek in the softest of caresses. "I think we should find our bed," he muttered, his eyes focused on the waves spread around her head. "We need to do that again, and then I want to hold you while I sleep."

A knock sounded at the door three times before someone tried the doorknob. At the jingle of metal tumblers, Anahita stiffened and prepared to jerk her robe down, but Max refused to move—rather stubbornly if Anahita said so.

"Door's locked," he said, continuing to stroke her cheek. "And I'm not done touching you yet so they can just go the fuck away."

"Anahita," a male voice said—one of her Warriors. "We have news that cannot wait."

"It's going to have to," Max called. His muscles had stiffened, and the slightest hint of resignation flitted across his scarred face.

"My love, it may not truly be able to wait," Anahita said, smoothing her hands over his shoulders, already regretting the inevitable end to this intimate moment.

"Hell," Max said. He dropped a quick kiss to her lips. "You call me *love* one more time, and you can get me to do pretty much any damn thing you want." He straightened and pulled slowly out of her. They both moaned at the loss of connection. With a sigh, he began doing up the buttons of his shirt.

Anahita sat up, wincing slightly at a twinge between her legs that told her she'd been well loved, and straightened her robe over her knees.

Max reached out and pinched her chin between his thumb and finger. "Okay?" he asked softly. "I wasn't too rough?"

She leaned in and kissed the hollow of his throat before saying, "Next time it is my turn to make *you* sore."

He swallowed hard. "That is most definitely a date," he said, voice husky. The knock sounded again, and Max growled. "Your men are going to drive me crazy."

"You are my only man," she said absently.

"Damn straight, and they better recognize that." He stalked over to the door, clicked the lock, and pulled it open so quickly, the angel on the other side nearly stumbled into the room. The three angels behind him looked in with wide eyes, and Anahita tried to slide off the table as nonchalantly as possible. "You get five minutes with her," Max said, wagging a finger in the face of her stunned Warrior. "Then, if she's not in our apartment, I'm coming back here and throwing her over my shoulder to take her there."

Something wicked and delicious rolled over in Anahita's stomach, and she stared hungrily at Max's tight behind as he stalked from the room. Her Warriors filed in as sheepishly as Warriors could, and she gestured for them to take their seats. Biting back a smile, she said, "You have six minutes, Warriors."

About the Author

When she's not writing or teaching, Micah Persell spends time with her husband, brand new daughter, and menagerie of pets in her Southern California home. *Of Alliance and Rebellion* is her sixth novel; she has also published *Of Eternal Life* (Operation: Middle of the Garden #1), *Of the Knowledge of Good and Evil* (Operation: Middle of the Garden #2), *Of Consuming Fire* (Operation: Middle of the Garden #3), *Persuasion: The Wild and Wanton Edition*, and *Emma: The Wild and Wanton Edition*. Learn more about her at *www.micahpersell.com*, or visit her on *Facebook*, *Twitter*, and *Pinterest*.

More from This Author
(From *Of Consuming Fire* by Micah Persell)

Dr. Grace Tucker pulled herself deeper into the corner and tucked her arms tighter around her unshapely belly. As her hands and arms touched her large middle, it repulsed her nearly as much as it seemed to repulse the opposite sex. No, there was no disappearing a plus-sized woman, but her sloppy appearance got most people to look away quickly, which was as close as Grace was ever going to get to being blessedly invisible.

And, not for the first time, she desperately wished to be invisible.

Grace huddled in the main room of the top-secret government facility where the Trees stood. As always, she ignored them. She was never awed by the ancient trees. She'd taken one cursory glance at their branches that most described as majestic. Their fruit — covered in glittering diamonds for the Tree of Eternal Life, swirling black and white for the Tree of the Knowledge of Good and Evil — was interesting only in that it loosely related to her work. She didn't stand there and stare at them for hours as she was told was the expected behavior for new employees.

And yet right now, Grace wasn't the only one ignoring the Trees. The somber mood in the facility was nearly suffocating. Not one of the dozens of employees had spoken in hours. They moped from room to room, desk to desk, casting great, wide-eyed glances upon everyone they crossed. But that wasn't the reason Grace retreated to the corner.

They were *touching* one another.

Any person they came into reaching distance with. A hand on the shoulder. A hug. A squeeze of the arm or lingering pat on the back.

It was only a matter of time before one of them tried to touch *her*. And that simply was not going to work. End of story.

And, so, she was in the closest thing to a corner the domed room provided.

A young soldier in army fatigues walked by, and Grace went rigid, holding her breath until he passed.

He didn't once glance in her direction. Grace's breath flew from her frozen lungs even as her heart seized at the casual snub. She hugged herself tighter as she cursed her weak emotions. Without fail, every time her carefully cultivated armor of acerbic wit and slovenly appearance actually worked as she'd meant it to by keeping others away, her irrational side would come up bruised, as though it didn't know perfectly well the reasons human contact was not in Grace's cards.

She sighed almost silently, and forced herself to look cheerfully upon the fact that standing in the corner was working. She would make it through this. She *would*. It wouldn't be like all of the other times. There would be no scene. No gut-wrenching screams shooting from her body without her control. No hysterical sobs. No sedation. No awkward return to work. No inevitable summons to the boss. No starting over with the knowledge that this was her life — on repeat.

She closed her eyes. The sad truth was, this *was* her life. And right now, she was huddled in the corner, praying to be invisible, worrying with all of her strength that someone would touch her.

But her friend's impending death? Not even a blip on her emotional radar. Jericho Edwards was dying, and Grace was worried about herself.

Jericho was everyone's favorite, but for a reason Grace couldn't explain, he was *her* favorite as well. It had been thirteen long years since Grace considered a man as anything other than something to be avoided at all costs. Thirteen years since Grace had carefully erected a wall around her heart. And yet, somehow, Jericho found his way around that wall the tiniest bit.

It might have been the very obvious fact that Jericho would never, ever pose a threat to her. She'd known two seconds after being introduced to him that he was head over heels in love with someone: his Impulse mate, Dahlia. Jericho was nice to *everyone*, men and women alike. In fact, Grace had never met anyone so good.

And he'd taken one look at her — her frumpy clothes, excess body weight, bird's nest of red hair, black-rimmed glasses, and man-hating glare — and deemed her a friend, working tirelessly at cultivating a relationship with her when everyone else just avoided her.

And now, he was dying. Worse, his survival depended upon *Grace* and Grace's work.

Three months and a week or so ago, Jericho cut his finger on the sword — the artifact that Grace was commissioned to work on. It was a flesh wound that should have healed in seconds given that Jericho, Dahlia, Eli, and Abilene were all immortal after eating the fruit from the Tree of Eternal Life. But the simple wound hadn't healed. And things came to a head a few days ago when Jericho returned to the facility with his brand new wife, Dahlia. In the process of moving, Jericho managed to rip the tiny, unhealed wound wide open from the tip of his finger into his palm. It had been bleeding profusely ever since, and his body couldn't keep up.

And suddenly, Dr. Grace Tucker was very much in demand. She couldn't count the number of times she had to remind them "I'm not that kind of doctor." Their situation was so unique that her PhD in dead languages made her much more qualified to help Jericho than an MD would on its best day, but her work took more time than medication or surgery ever would.

She'd made her breakthrough this morning.

The ancient, dead language on the sword said *What the Tree gives, the Sword takes. What the Sword takes, the Tree gives.*

At least, she was ninety-nine percent sure that's what it said.

Grace gritted her teeth, closed her eyes, and reassured herself that she was never wrong when it came to her work. Never. She was wrong when it came to everything else, but her work was infallible.

That's why she was here. She was the single most prestigious language expert in the world. And it was going to change her life. That was the plan. She'd worked hard to make sure no one noticed her. The weight she'd gained, the fashion-backward wardrobe, the overt hostility — when she couldn't disappear into her surroundings, she kept people away with every weapon her extensive intelligence and vast vocabulary could come up with.

But Grace's secret dream *was* recognition. She just wanted it on her terms. She was going to make *the* discovery of all time with this sword. It was the work she'd been waiting for her entire career. And now it was here. And, as long as her translation was right, it was about to save one of only four immortal human beings on the planet.

Career. Made.

Everyone would know her name; everyone would know she was something. And the best part? She'd be absolutely untouchable in a way she could not dream of cultivating on her own. No one walked up to the winner of the Nobel Prize and gave them a hug. They got the recognition without all the messy social baggage associated with being members of the human race. They were members of a class considered above such things. And Grace couldn't wait to be admitted into their ranks.

Grace's eyes snapped open when she heard the sharp clack of men's shoes on the hard floor of the facility. Sergeant Collins was approaching.

Grace shrank back further into her corner, her shoulders bending in on themselves, but it was too late: he was looking right at her, and double damn, he'd noticed she was trying to turn into wallpaper if the arch of one of his salt and pepper eyebrows was any indication.

He stopped before her, and Grace couldn't prevent the hitch in her breathing. Reaching distance. The man was within reaching distance. She bit her bottom lip to avoid a whimper.

"Dr. Tucker?" Sergeant Collins asked in his smooth, Southern whisky drawl. He then looked her over once more. His eyes softened. He took a step back and crossed his arms behind him, effecting "at ease" posture.

Relief flooded through her so strongly it momentarily overshadowed the embarrassment she felt at having someone else recognize her reticence at human contact. But only momentarily. Damn it, why couldn't she be normal?

She straightened to her full height — a whole five feet five inches — and worked her hardest to look as un-crazy as possible. "What can I do for you, sir?" A lock of her frizzy, red hair fell over her glasses, blocking Sergeant Collins from sight. She shoved it out of the way, tucking it behind one of the pencils stuffed into her "style" of the day.

"Nothing more than you've done, ma'am," he said with polite distance. "I've come to report that your findings seem to be accurate."

Grace wanted to sag in relief, but was so wary of causing Sergeant Collins to think any less of her that she clenched her jaw and forced iron into her spine. No one would know how worried she'd been about her translation. She'd emit cool confidence all day long. Her "findings" included the recommendation that whatever damage the sword caused could be un-done by administering the fruit of the Tree of Eternal Life topically. They'd been forcing the fruit down Jericho's throat for days to no effect. It was a nuance of the language that had given Grace the idea to apply the fruit to the site of Jericho's wound.

"So, Jericho's recovering?" Grace forced herself to ask, alarmed a little at the obvious worry in her voice. She didn't care about him that much, did she?

A new voice sounded as it approached. "His skin is knitting together before our eyes." Dahlia Edward's brown eyes peeked around Collins's shoulder, warm for the first time ever that Grace witnessed.

Grace actually liked Dahlia a lot, and not just because Jericho did. Grace hadn't met many people who seemed to hate all others as much as Dahlia did. She was even more socially hostile than Grace. It was … refreshing.

"They think he'll wake up any moment now, and I want to be there when he does, but I had to come thank you first," Dahlia continued.

Grace felt her eyes widen. "Thanks" often involved touch of some kind. "That's not necessary," Grace muttered, crowding the corner again.

Dahlia rolled her eyes. "Relax, Red," she said with a laugh. "God, it's not like we're going to attack you with hugs or anything."

Grace didn't laugh. She didn't even notice when the two before her exchanged a worried look as her eyes glazed, and her mind turned over one of Dahlia's words.

Attack. Attack. Attack.

A loud snap erupted in front of her face.

Grace refocused to see Dahlia's fingers before her eyes as the woman snapped again, this time accompanied by a sharp, "Grace!"

Grace sucked in a breath.

"Is she … " Sergeant Collins trailed off as both women's heads snapped around to glare at him.

Grace opened her mouth to speak, but was cut off with Dahlia's curt, "She's fine, Collins, God." She then stood directly in front of Grace, blocking her from Collins's sight, giving her a chance to compose herself. "Nothing some lunch and a good night's sleep won't fix. We've run her ragged. Give her some *grace*." Dahlia snorted.

Collins threw Dahlia a wobbly smile. "I'll just … um … call Miss Esperanza then. Tell her Jericho's fine." His mouth moved like a caress over the name of Dahlia's former mother-in-law, his accent adding at least two syllables, and his eyes twinkling like a kid.

Dahlia looked at Grace and winked. "You do that, Collins."

He cast one more concerned look toward Grace's corner, not quite meeting her eyes, and backed off, hurrying away to his office.

As Dahlia watched him go, her hand fell to the small bump beneath her shirt. Grace was pretty sure she was the only person in the facility who had guessed that Jericho and Dahlia were expecting. There had been no announcement; there hadn't been time before Jericho fell gravely ill. But Dahlia made that little movement often when she thought no one was looking.

She turned to Grace now and arched a perfect eyebrow.

"I really am fine," Grace offered weakly.

Dahlia scoffed and muttered something in Spanish that Grace perfectly understood — dead languages weren't her only specialty. Grace bristled. "Look, I'll just get back to work." The news of Jericho's recovery was already spreading if the increased chatter in the room was any indication. She could re-join life now. She needed to get started on writing this up, though she knew publishing any of her top-secret findings was going to be an uphill battle. Possibly an impossible one.

Dahlia nodded once and began to turn away.

"Hey," Grace blurted. Dahlia turned back to her. "Um … when he wakes up. Tell Jericho … I'm glad he's okay." Grace was shocked to find out she meant it.

Dahlia's eyes roved Grace's face for a moment, but then she smiled. "You've got it, Red." She took two steps toward the medical wing, then stopped.

Grace watched the black waves cascading down Dahlia's back rustle as the stunning Latina tilted her head to the side.

"Do you hear that?" Dahlia asked.

Grace frowned. "Hear what?"

Just then, the lights flickered. A distant rumbling seemed to seep in through the walls of the facility.

All of the hopeful chatter in the room faded and then fizzled out as people began to look around curiously.

A huge clap of thunder rent through the building with such force that loose items throughout the main room clattered where they sat.

The lights went out completely.

Emergency lights along the walls illuminated, casting Dahlia's caramel skin in an unearthly glow as Grace stared at her in barely subdued panic. The others in the room began to mumble to each other, their voices rising in pitch. She felt her nails digging into the skin of her arms and realized she was hugging herself again.

A man in a lab coat raced into the main room, skidding around the door and barreling toward Dahlia as soon as he spotted her. "He's waking!" he yelled at Jericho's wife. "Come quickly."

Dahlia took a quick step toward him, but then stumbled. She threw out an arm to catch herself against the wall. "*Shit*," Grace heard her mutter.

Dahlia spun around and pinned Grace with a wide-eyed look. "Earthquake," she told Grace in an odd, disbelieving tone. "Big one."

Dahlia lunged forward and grabbed Grace by the arm, hauling her quickly to a nearby desk and shoving herself and Grace in the small area beneath it.

Shooting pains emanated from the skin Dahlia's fingers touched. Grace hissed and tried to wrench her arm from Dahlia's grip as she spluttered, "What — how do you — "

"I can hear it coming," she said impatiently. "Take cover!" she bellowed to all the gawkers.

No sooner had the words left her mouth than the first wave hit the building. A sound, louder than the eardrum-cracking clap of thunder, ricocheted through the room like a freight train, and Grace watched with wide eyes as the floor began to ripple at the edge of the room and move toward them like oncoming ocean waves.

And, even though paralyzed with fear, all Grace could think of was the scorching pain of Dahlia's fingers where they still clutched her arm.

Screams began to echo as the men and women who worked at the facility realized what was happening. Feet thundered as everyone sought shelter.

But Grace scrambled away from Dahlia and out into the open as soon as the woman's grip on Grace's arm slackened.

Dahlia's arm snaked out and captured the back of Grace's jacket. "What the *hell*?"

"Don't *touch me*!" Grace shrieked so loudly that Dahlia drew back in shock.

A huge chunk of plaster fell from the ceiling to land right beside Grace. A cloud of white exploded from its impact and dusted both of them. Desks began to skitter across the floor.

"Do you want to die?" Dahlia yelled, blinking the white powder from her lashes.

Die or be touched? No contest. Grace didn't move.

The earthquake gained in intensity. The glass that made up the ceiling of the dome tinkled and Grace looked up as a crack spider-webbed from one end of the dome to the other.

"Okay," Dahlia said fast and low. "I won't touch you. Just get your ass under here right now!"

Grace dragged her eyes from the ceiling to look into the dim space beneath the desk. Dahlia pressed herself against the side, leaving more than enough room for Grace to fit without having to be against the other woman. And still she hesitated.

Across the dome, bookshelves began to fall like dominoes, each one hitting the ground with a resounding boom. The tinkling of the glass ceiling increased and one or two shards escaped and plummeted toward the ground.

With a deep breath for courage, Grace dove into the area beside Dahlia just as the ceiling gave way.

The glass chimed like clock-tower bells as it fell. It tinkled off of every surface and bounced from the floor in glittering arcs. Grace watched in horror as a huge shard caught one of the soldiers as he tried to dive under a desk a few feet away. His scream cut off as the glass sliced through his chest and pinned him to the floor right where Grace had been kneeling seconds before.

Grace huddled into the corner and buried her face against the wood of the desk so hard she thought her nose might break.

The waves of the ground moved as though alive beneath Grace, hitting her in the shins and knees again and again as she knelt and causing her stomach to lurch as though seasick. Beside her, she heard Dahlia begin to recite the rosary in Spanish in a low, breathless voice. As a backdrop, the glass on the floor clacked and pinged as the entire building shimmied with the rage of the earth.

And in the next heartbeat, everything stopped.

Grace's frantic breaths in the sudden absence of sound were excruciatingly loud, but the silence didn't last for long. Moans from the wounded began to fill the air.

She heard her boss, Eli Johnson, bellowing his past-due pregnant wife's name as he barreled through the dome from his office and toward the medical wing.

"Jericho," Dahlia breathed next to her. Then she scrambled from her hiding spot, sliding in the blood that slicked across the floor from the impaled man before gaining purchase and sprinting in Eli's wake.

Grace stared dumbfounded at the glassy eyes of the dead man in front of her before forcing herself to emerge from the desk.

Utter destruction waited for her. Her eyes skimmed over the demolished main room of the facility. Everything was … gone. Desks were smashed. Books were flung to every wall of the room. The glass on the floor glittered like diamonds among the pools of blood. It looked like after-pictures of a tornado.

But the trees stood resolute in the center of the room. Not one fruit had fallen from their branches. And on the desk beneath them, where Grace did her work, the sword glowed. The sword, usually covered with flickering green and gold flames, was now … *angry*. It was the only word she could use to describe what she was seeing. The green and gold flames had morphed into red and black. The metal, engraved with the words she had translated to say *what the tree gives, the sword takes; what the sword takes, the tree gives* was now pulsing with emotion. And coming off of the sword in waves was an otherworldly *heat*. The sword had always emitted a cool indifference. Now it was raging.

"Oh, God," Grace gasped. Her breathing sped up even more, and black began to edge in on her vision.

Something had angered this inanimate object. Fear, so familiar and yet, in this case, so different, choked Grace's throat. She had a gut feeling that in completing her job she betrayed a secret. The sword's secret.

Someone was coming. Coming for them. Coming for her.

She had one thought before losing consciousness: *What have I done?*

Also by Micah Persell:

Of Eternal Life

Praise for *Of Eternal Life*:

Winner of the 2013 Virginia HOLT Award of Merit in the paranormal category.

Second place in Lyrical Press's first annual "How Lyrical Is Your Romance" contest.

"If you enjoy military suspense and a strong romance try this book. *Of Eternal Life* is a good page turner to the end."—Night Owl Reviews

Of the Knowledge of Good and Evil

Praise for *Of the Knowledge of Good and Evil*:

"I give this action-packed, sexually-charged story a definite thumbs up and rate it with four stars. The author has a good series going, and I was left gasping for breath and searching for more pages. It's a great story . . . I'm glad I took the read. I can't wait to hear more."—The Romance Reviews

Persuasion: The Wild and Wanton Edition

Praise for Persuasion:

"Micah Persell has near perfectly captured Austen's voice and explored some of the subtle nuances of *Persuasion* that Austen hinted at but never ventured to pursue ... As a fan of Austen retellings, I appreciated how seamlessly the additional text was worked into the classic storyline."—The Romance Reviews

"Micah Persell exceeded [expectations] by deftly and for the most part seamlessly working in backstory, dreams, and interior monologue in very Austenesque language . . . it's just ideal for a reader such as me—one who loves *Persuasion* but also can take pleasure in a talented wordsmith having a bit of fun with it."—Romantic Historical Lovers

Emma: The Wild and Wanton Edition

Praise for *Emma*:

"This 'wild and wanton' rewrite of Jane Austen's Emma did not disappoint...The transitions are seamless, the writing styles matched extremely well. I like to think that Austen (after getting over a bit of shock) would have welcomed these spicy, but tasteful, additions to her story. I know that I certainly did."—4 stars, Tatooed Book Review

"...the wild and wanton version of *Emma* made it more accessible to a modern audience in the sense that it was similar to modern ideals of courtship. Jane's characters find relationships in the meeting of compatible minds, but the modern romance reader expects zing. The zing made me think of Emma and Harriet more as the very young women they are, and also added an extra level of complication to the story."—4 stars, Plot Driven

"Keeping true to the voice of Jane Austen, Micah has improved upon a classic. She has made it even more romantic, if possible." 4 stars, Unwrapping Romance

In the mood for more Crimson Romance?
Check out *An Angel Fallen* by Holley Trent
at *CrimsonRomance.com*.